Harlem Mosaics

Whit Frazier

With an Introduction By

Marc Primus

For Deborah Wilchek, a book full of butterflies.

Contents

ACKNOWLEDGMENTS

I have met so many fascinating people in search of the historical literary luminaries featured in this novel, I'm sure to miss some in these brief acknowledgements. I want to express sincere gratitude and admiration for Dr. Jon Woodson, who added such great depth to my way of approaching the work, and my way of thinking about research in general. I also owe sincere thanks to Marc Primus, who has written the introduction to the novel, and who offered so much support, advice and encouragement along the way. I want to thank Aubrey LaBrie, who read the manuscript, and offered invaluable feedback. I also want to thank Arnold Rampersad who reviewed part of the manuscript, was very encouraging and also offered a lot of helpful feedback. Finally I want to thank Tom Wirth, who helped me understand and appreciate the amazing Bruce Nugent. And of course, much love and thanks to my mother and father.

Introduction

By Marc Primus

This book is the novelized story of two of America's greatest writers, Zora Neale Hurston and Langston Hughes. My first introduction to Zora Neale Hurston was via a book that I happened on called Negro Caravan,[1] an anthology of plays, folklore, poetry, essays, songs, etc., first published in 1941. I discovered the book in 1957 while I was volunteering at The Negro Historical And Cultural Society Of San Francisco.[2] I couldn't put the book down. But it was when I came upon the work of Zora Neale Hurston that I was pierced with excitement. Her stories had the sound of truth; strange in a time of massive white distortions. The persons that she imitated had the sound of intelligence, always missing from white depictions. The essence of minstrelsy, (the denigration of black culture for the entertainment of whites), seemed to be missing from her work. Her representations of the "folk" were not filtered through white eyes, but directly from her own proud experience. A black reader could simply relax and enjoy her stories, without the humiliation of the white filter. The same was true with the works of Langston Hughes. His incorporation of a blues and jazz ethic into his poetry and prose was innovative in the twenties. It was an exploration of the essence of black urban life, proud and unapologetic. Hughes' explanation of his point of view is delivered in his famous manifesto, "The

---

[1] The Negro Caravan Writings by American Negroes, Selected and Edited by Sterling A. Brown, Howard University; Arthur P. Davis, Virginia Union
[2] The San Francisco Negro Historical And Cultural Society, (Now called The San Francisco African American Historical And Cultural Society,) founded 1955

Negro Artist and the Racial Mountain,"[3] He begins his essay by saying, "
One of the most promising of the young Negro poets said to me once, 'I
want to be a poet---not a Negro poet,' meaning, I believe, 'I want to write
like a white poet'; meaning subconsciously, 'I would like to be a white poet';
meaning behind that, 'I would like to be white.' And I was sorry the young
man said that, for no great poet has ever been afraid of being himself, and I
doubted then that, with his desire to run away spiritually from his race, this
boy would ever be a great poet....." He finishes his great peroration by
saying: "Let the blare of Negro jazz bands and the bellowing voice of Bessie
Smith singing the Blues penetrate the closed ears of the colored near-
intellectuals until they listen and perhaps understand. Let Paul Robeson
singing Water Boy, and Rudolf Fisher writing about the streets of Harlem,
and Jean Toomer holding the heart of Georgia in his hands, and Aaron
Douglas drawing strange black fantasies cause the smug Negro middle class
to catch a glimmer of their own beauty. We younger Negro artists who
create now intend to express our individual dark-skinned selves without
fear or shame. If white people are pleased, we are glad, if they are not, it
doesn't matter. We know we are beautiful. And ugly too. The tom-tom
cries, and the tom-tom laughs. If colored people are pleased, we are glad. If
they are not, their displeasure doesn't matter either. We build our temples
for tomorrow, strong as we know how, and we stand on top of the
mountain, free within ourselves."

His take on Zora Neale Hurston was telling too. In his autobiography,
The Big Sea,[4] he describes his first impression of her: ...." Of this
'niggerati,' Zora Neale Hurston was certainly the most amusing. Only to
reach a wider audience , need she ever write books---because she is a
perfect book of entertainment in herself. In her youth she was always
getting scholarships and things from wealthy white people, some of whom
simply paid her just to sit around and represent the Negro race for them,
she did it in such a racy fashion. She was full of side-splitting anecdotes,
humorous tales, and tragicomic stories, remembered out of her in the South
as a daughter of a traveling minister of God. She could make you laugh one
minute and cry the next. To many of her white friends, no doubt, she was a
perfect 'darkie,' in the nice meaning they give the term---that is a naïve,
childlike, sweet, humorous , and highly colored Negro.

But Miss Hurston was clever, too---a student who didn't let college
give her a broad a and who had great scorn for all pretensions, academic or

---

[3] "The Negro Artist And The Racial Mountain" a manifesto by Langston Hughes,
The Nation, June 23rd, 1926 in The Collected Works Of Langston Hughes, vol. 9,
p.31
[4] The Big Sea, An Autobiography by Langston Hughes, Hill And Wang, New York,
1940, P.238-9.

otherwise. That is why she was such a fine folklore collector, able to go among the people and never act as if she had been to school at all…"

Langston Hughes and Zora became fast friends and collaborators. Hughes introduced Hurston to his patron, Charlotte van der Veer Quick Osgood Mason and the subject of this novel, the disintegration of the relationship between Hurston and Hughes is presented here.

I was privileged as a young man to be mentored by five passionate advocates of black culture at the Negro Historical And Cultural Society Of San Francisco: Mrs. Ethel Ray Nance, Mrs. Elena Irving Albert, Mrs. Sue Bailey Thurman, Mrs. Frances Roston Miller, and Mr. James Herndon, Esq., all of whom knew Langston Hughes and were acquainted with Zora Neale Hurston and her works. Ethel Ray Nance was the "Harlem Renaissance Hostess," who with her roommate Regina Andrews Anderson had received the almost penniless Zora Neale Hurston when she first arrived in New York City, and who first bunked on the roommates sofa. Mrs. Nance had many stories to tell of her association with Hurston and Langston Hughes. As a student at San Francisco State College I began my studies in anthropology and became interested in folklore, which led to my examination of Hurston's works. In 1962 I created a company called The Afro-American Folkloric Troupe[5] who performed the works of Hurston and Hughes,(among others), throughout the United States, chiefly for black audiences until 1971. The Folkloric Troupe was sponsored by SNCC in its voter registration drive of 1966-1967 in Georgia, Alabama and Mississippi. The reception of the troupe's performances was, to say the least, enthusiastic. Langston Hughes, hearing of the Troupe began sending unpublished materials to the company as early as 1962. At the time of the Folkloric Troupe's formation I did not know of the dream of Hurston/Hughes to create a folkloric company who would use the authentic materials of black culture, unfiltered by white interpretation. In 1978, The Folkloric Troupe's presentation of Zora Neale Hurston's High John De Conquer[6] was produced by Vinnette Carroll's Urban Arts Corps and received several AUDELCO awards. We had not truly realized that we had contributed to the vision of Hughes and Hurston.

---

[5] The Afro-American Folkloric Troupe, 1962-1971, founded and directed by Marc Primus, was originally comprised by Norman Jacob, Stella Beck, Charles Columbus Thomas and Primus, made its New York debut in 1965 at the Town Hall.

[6] High John De Conquer (He Top Superior To The Whole Mess Of Sorrow) Folktales with music, arranged and directed by Marc Primus, based on the folktales collected by Zora Neale Hurston

As Rampersad reports[7], by mid-summer of 1926, the two were planning a Black jazz and blues opera. Hemenway[8] calls it 'an opera that would be the first authentic rendering of Black folklife, presenting folk songs, dances, and tales that Hurston would collect." .....and by April, 1928, she shared with Hughes her plans for a culturally authentic African-American theatre, one constructed upon a foundation of the Black vernacular : 'Did I tell you before I left about the new, the real Negro theatre I plan? Well, I shall, or rather we shall act out the folk tales, however short, with the abrupt angularity and naivete of the primitive 'Bama Nigger. Quote that with native settings. What do you think?....Of course you know I didn't dream of that theatre as a one man stunt. I had you helping 50—50 from the start.....but I know it's going to be glorious! A really new departure in the drama.'[9]

In its own way, Whit Frazier's lyrical novel is a praisesong and cautionary tale of our literary black ancestors who imagined the creation of a black theatre reflecting the irony and sophistication of the true folk heritage.

Marc Primus
Atlanta, 2012

[7] Rampersad, Arnold, *The Life Of Langston Hughes. Volume I: 1902-1941: I, Too, Sing America*. New York: Oxford University Press, 1986.
[8] Hemenway, Robert. *Zora Neale Hurston: A Literary Biography* .Urbana, Ill., University Of Illinois, 1977
[9] Langston Hughes and Zora Neale Hurston, *Mule Bone, A Comedy of Negro Life*. Harper Perennial 1991

HARLEM
MOSAICS

Chapter One

A parachute balloon of a dandelion moon dispersed diaphanous evening clouds. Langston Hughes lounged passenger side *Sassy Susie*, leaning in and out of the window, leaning in and out of sleep, listening to the music of Zora's voice as she told stories from Eatonville; but now the sun had gone down, and the moon had come up, and some time had gone by since Zora had said anything. Langston was only distantly aware of this, a whirr where *Sass* slipped through the shadows of sycamores.

"Say, Lang, I keeping you up?"

His eyes bleary, blinking open. "No. No, I was listening; listening and thinking."

"About what?"

"About what you were talking about."

"And what was that about?"

"Hm? Well? Howsabout a drink?" Langston sat up, leaned the tin of gin reclining in his hand easy and lazy toward Zora.

Zora shrugged it away. "I like you Langston," she decided after a while. "For what little anyone knows about you."

"Aw, what's that mean?"

"Well, you've heard me go on and on about myself. My work. My husband. You never do that. Everything's guarded with you."

"I don't know about all that." He smiled at her, winked. "You must have me confused with someone else."

Langston dozed awhile again, and waking, felt like waking and dozing and waking again were all a thread of the same dreaming, so he said: "Well, I'll tell you something, Zora. I'll tell you something about myself that's a little bit of a secret."

They were headed north to the plantation where Jean Toomer wrote *Cane* to lie in the wheat fields beneath the full moon moonlight night and discuss the future of black blues opera. "I shouldn't tell you, but I love you, Zora, so I'm gonna tell you."

"What's that?"

Langston lolled in his seat, took a drink of gin. "I'm being patronized."

Zora glanced over at Langston, frowned. "You're drunk, Langston. Just go back to sleep."

"That's true, I'm drunk. What's true too, I'm being patronized. Rather I have a patron. I call her Godmother. She's going to finance my being a poet."

"What are you going on about?"

"And I think she should patronize you too. I'm going to make sure the two of you get to be good friends."

"That's nice," Zora, patronizing.

Langston sat up straight. "I know; I know how I'm being. But really it's true. There's a white lady back in New York, and she wants to act as my patron. She gives me money, and I write poetry. I'm not supposed to talk about her with anyone, so it really is a secret, but it's true too. I'm not making it up."

"Oh. And what do you give this white lady in return for her money?"

August outside Atlanta, fresh from the bootlegger, Georgia roads reaching east, the southern spirit. The clouds haunting the lonely narrow roads. The moon lighting marigolds and the moon lighting fields planted full of peanuts; the southern soil spells the story of a culture. Some spells take root in your soul. They swell and grow until you ain't yourself no more. This is a story everyone buried in the ground already knows.

"It's not what you think," said Langston. "It's not like that at all. Makes me want to crawl outta my skin just to ponder upon it. Jeez, Zora. She must've been born sometime during the Jefferson Administration, she's that ancient. She's from this old New York money, lives on Park Avenue and everything. She just happens to be fascinated with everything Negro; especially art."

"Another New York Negrotarian?"

"Anyway you should meet her, is all. I'll introduce you two when we get back."

Zora didn't say anything.

"How far out are we from Sempter?"

Zora smiled, and sat up so the moonlight lit her like *Ethiopia Awakening*. "Sparta? Here we are."

Sparta spread your majesty in moonlight all across roads now granite, now grass. The sky was wide and dark, driving east on West Broadway.

Langston leaned into the wind off the lake; Georgia swept swift through the open window, rolling a low hill of trees.

"Let's stop here."

Out of *Sassy Susie* into a perfect Georgia summer night. Langston and Zora in the light of the moon, faces floating like two copper pennies. They walked for a while down a sloping street, surrounded by trees. They walked past tall green oaks and for a while, neither said a word. Langston was thinking about Georgia, and the songs he would write about Georgia when he was back at Lincoln; was he too happy now for poetry? *Fine Clothes* was a fine book, but could he do it again? And did he even want to? He'd come to the south to deepen his understanding of folk poetry, but what if his folk poetry phase was finished?   A blur of ripples of light on the surface of the lake, the moon, a crafty fickle frail, Zora.

Zora winked right back at that liquid moon. You'll stick by me, that's what you'll do, because I outran my husband, and I'll outrun you, too. She laughed and Langston gave her a look.

"What you thinking about?"

"Nothing much. Jean Toomer."

"Say, you want some gin?"

"Sure. I'll take a nip."

Zora took the flask, drank and whooped and wiped her mouth. "Powerful stuff there, partner." She sucked in air, considered and continued. "But really I was thinking how I'm like Moses when he crossed over."

"How so?"

"I didn't – couldn't write my research out right. Went there thinking I'd just take all these stories in, and spit them right back out beautifully, right? What could be easier? Just show the world what I see plain as day. But it's not quite through with me yet, the work, I mean, and I didn't expect that. I don't know that I'm ready to write the book I want to yet."

"What's it mean when Moses crossed over?" Langston took the gin from Zora and took a drink.

"When Moses crossed over. You know. Well, here. I'll tell you a lie about it."

"I'd prefer the truth."

"A lie's a story, silly. Of course my lie'll be true. Listen. It needs a little litery first:

Looked down the road,
Saw a golden hen.
It laid no golden eggs, so I
Looked down the road again.

Moses was born of the Jews, but raised by the Pharaoh's daughter, so one day the devil comes to Moses and he says, "Say, Moses. You go round here longfaced and blue all day, and Ah know why: You know you not like the Pharaoh and all the others round here, but you won't admit it. Well, Ah'm here to tell you, you not like dem. Youse a Jew, you is, and two-headed to boot, which means you got the hoodoo in you. Here's what you do: you g'wan to God and tell Him you knows your birthright, and you gointer free your people, because that's what's in your heart."

Now Moses wasn't no devil's fool, so he says, "How Ah know what you say is true? What if God just laughs me off, says you lying and Ah ain't nothing but the fool son of a Pharaoh's daughter?"

"Ah ain't lying. Even if Ah was, what's that to you? What you care if God laughs at you? You need God to validate you to be a man? Ah thought you had the hoodoo in you, but now Ah see Ah was wrong. You ain't no conjureman."

"Yes Ah am too. Ah'm gointer go up to say my piece to God."

"G'wan then."

So Moses went on up to God, and when he got there, God just grinned and said, "So what you after then, Brother Moses?"

Moses got right to it. "Ah know Ah ain't no blood nor kin of the Pharaoh's daughter. Ah been chosen for something higher."

Which is how come we call the people of Moses the Chosen People, but that's all by the bye.

Well God asked Moses, "What you been chosen for then, Brother Moses?" and Moses just looked around, remembered the devil's words, and said the first thing that came to his heart.

"Ah'm gointer free my people."

"Well g'wan then."

"Ah need you to tell me how."

"How am Ah gointer do that?" God asked him. "Ah ain't chosen. You is. If you chosen, you gointer do it, and if you ain't chosen you ain't. Dat's all Ah know."

So Moses left there no better off than he gone in. Some might say worse. He went on back to the devil, and he says, "Say devil, God won't tell me what Ah need to do to free my people. Ah need you to clue me on in."

The devil shook his head and sighed. "What Ah tell you, but you wasn't no conjureman. Still, Ah'll tell you what you ought to do, even tho' Ah know you won't do't. You say you gointer free your people, right?"

"Ah ain't just beating up my gums."

"Ok then," says the devil. "Here's what you do: You see Ol' Massa over there whipping on the Jew John?"

"Ah see him."

"You gwine hafta kill Ol' Massa if you gointer free your people. But you ain't got it in you."

"Yes Ah do too."

"G'wan and do it then."

So Moses went on up apace where Ol' Massa was whipping on the Jew John. He took that whip from Ol' Massa, wrapped it round Massa's neck and swung 'im up on a tree for all to see.

When the Pharaoh got keen to that, he went to speculatin' how Moses jes showed up all uninvited and such as a baby in the first place, and now here he go making trouble, and what should he do about it? He decided best thing was to get rid of Moses right away and set his weary mind at ease, seeing as how him and Moses wasn't nor skinfolks nor kinfolks nohow, so what could it matter? Once he got that worked out, he percolated the word down Broadway, a price was ready to be paid for Moses' head.

Well it wasn't long before Moses learned of *that*, so he went to the devil, and he told him his troubles. "Ah did what you said, and now Pharaoh wants me dead. What should Ah do next?"

The devil just smiled a devilish old smile, and said, "Looks to me Moses like you gointer die next, is what it looks like to me."

That wasn't no help, so Moses went on up to God.

"God," says Moses, "Ah'm in trouble deep. Pharaoh put money on my head because Ah tried to free my people. What am Ah gointer do?"

"What you telling me for?" asked God.

"Ah figured you might know, being God. But where should Ah go then, an tell my story, if not to you? Ah need help, Lawd."

"Go tell it on the mountain, for all Ah care," God said, and he wouldn't say no more.

So Moses crossed over. He crossed over the Red Sea and disappeared. He took to thinkin', took to marriage and then took off again. He crossed over. He didn't trust no damn devil and sure as hell didn't trust no God, neither. He crossed over. Moses was all alone, an aired out stormbuzzard bumbling around, a two-headed hoodoo genius, and jes dumb to the fact. So that's what folks mean when they say they crossed over like Moses. They mean they feel like that."

"That's a complicated feeling," said Langston.

"You're telling me."

"So you crossed over like Moses and what? Nothing to show for it?"

"I thought I'd have a book."

"No book?"

"I sent some essays back to Boas, but I don't have a book. I got a head full of unfinished ideas, and a notebook full of stories, but they don't have structure or form enough for a book yet. No book, not even close."

Neither one of them spoke for a while. Sweet maple scents sweated the summer night. They walked up the road a spell, and Langston thought about Moses crossing over while Zora debated with herself how anyone could fit all the fullness of life on a page. Better off living it on a living stage.

The whirling whorl of a loon looped suddenly off the lake. Langston listened, wondering why he wasn't afraid. He contemplated his lack of fear, detached, like a poet. Would a Langston Hughes be afraid? Would the Deep South woods at night frighten a New Negro Talented Tenth; a Lincoln man? Langston laughed at the thought. Maybe, he figured, it was the liquor that made him easily at ease; maybe it was Zora. Maybe both.

"What do you think a Negro opera would look like anyway," Zora was saying. "I mean what does an American opera even look like? Something between *Shuffle Along* and *The Emperor Jones*? I don't know, Langston. There's also the music. What do we do about music? I can always write and use old folksongs, but how do we write a score? I'm against us bringing anybody else into this. It has to be just us two."

Zora looked over at Langston. He was looking away over the hill, likely startled by the loon, so she went on: "Negro art doesn't seem like it should be scored, the way European operas are anyway, you ask me. In the same way that Negro literature almost feels like it shouldn't be written down, but recited aloud. There has to be another approach. I wonder if we could get away with the music just being the interplay of rhythm, dialogue, beat and song. It would make for a busy production, but maybe we can get away with it. It's worth experimenting with at least."

Langston nodded his head up, with a tilt to the gin, and then down again, like he might be agreeing, when the sound of the loon came whooping in loud as an angry old owl, and they saw a silhouette sway between the shadows and greenery of the trees.

"It's Moses, and he done crossed over!"

"Quiet, Langston."

Langston wondered why he wasn't afraid.

Zora sought his hand and squeezed it. "Go along with what I say.'"

The outline of a black Walt Whitman lumbered against the clearing. He walked from out of the woods, and the moon caught him in a slant through a thread of sweet-gum trees. He was tall and lean, leaning to the left in a pair of trousers pulled up too high. His shirt was dirty, dark, sleeveless. The neck was low, and hair sprouted up his chest and neck and became a head, a wooly froth of hair to shock. He looked right at Zora; his eyes seemed swollen like pustules, and he smelled like bourbon. For a moment he looked unblinking from Zora, then to Langston, and back again. The whole time he shuffled slowly along, never minding his step.

A moment later and the seraph had slumbered past. As he crumbled into the trees, his straw hat floated from his head and drifted onto a patchwork of leaves and grass.

"Hey, your hat!"

"Will you be quiet, Langston. Let it pass."

Langston picked up the hat and sized it up. "Say, it's not a bad old sky piece."

Zora shuddered. "Spare a gal a drink, will you?"

Langston shoved the hat into his shoulder bag, turned up the tin and frowned. "It's fresh out."

"Well, hell."

"Hold on, don't get bluesy on me yet. I have just the thing for the occasion." He reached into his shoulder bag again and produced a jar of Chinese whisky. "This jar's blessed. I came by it by way of a conjure-man in New Orleans." He passed the jar to Zora.

"Oh yeah?"

"That's right. I bought some wishing powder off him, and the very next day I found myself sailing for Havana where happily, they have no 18th Amendment. I was saving it to give to Carlo when we got back to New York, but I think our occasion now calls for it more."

"Agreed," said Zora, twisting the cap.

They meandered their way through the woods to a path somewhere on the other side. They talked and passed the Chinese back and forth, slipping sips between small talk played out clever like they'd play a play. Zora, tipsy, tipping past the threshold of the trees where the moon met a dale, sang folk songs:

"I got one, two guys at the Chucklebutt,
I got two guys waitin' on me!
I laugh all the time, they don't chuckle much,
I got two guys waitin' on me!"

"I'm thinking," said Langston as they stumbled downhill, the moonlight lighting the river below like a marquee, "our blues opera can be one of the old folk tales. And we'll pepper it with songs and dance, just like you were saying. We don't need a whole score. We'll make something really new out of it. Change opera forever. Invent American opera even."

"An opera from our people, for our people!" Zora drank to the idea, passed the jar to Langston. "If the white critics like it, let them like it."

"If they don't they don't."

"Let them not. The Negrotarians will love it of course."

"And the Countee Cullen critics?"

Zora guffawed. "The Countee Cullen critics will feel crucified!"

"Oh, they'll hate it."

"All the more reason to write it."

"I'll drink to that."

Which they did. They drank walking down to the river, and drank talking along it. They decided their blues opera would star Paul Robeson, and would be written straight from the south, with the language and litery of the south, and it would have to have religion in it – but not hoodoo, Zora decided. No hoodoo, or at least no more than is part of everyday life, which it would surprise you how much of that there is. They clowned a bit at it, playing the parts of different odd characters, singing, talking, making up blues lyrics on the spot. They laughed themselves sleepy, and snuggling like a couple of tired children by the bank of the river, they lay down with the jar of Chinese whisky nestled between them, and fell into the stars.

When the night got cool with morning dew, they made their way up to town where relatives of Jean Toomer's father lived. Sparta was a sparse, spread out southern farming town. It was all black, and small, so everyone knew each other, and everyone but everyone knew the Toomer family; they lived just on the other side of the hill.

Right on arrival a whole township of folks was inviting them in to breakfast. There were mothers and children and young men, too. There were cousins, aunts, fiancées and even a couple of elders. The whole lot of them went all across the color scale.

"I can see where Jean got *Cane*'s spookiness," Langston said at one point, happily reminiscing as they enjoyed a southern banquet of coffee, fried bacon and apples, eggs and grits. "Last night an old man came across us like an apparition. From out of the trees. Right from out of nowhere; and he disappeared the same way. Ain't it so, Zora?"

Zora looked up to speak, but the whole table had gone quiet.

"That's Uncle Monday," said one of the elders.

"Who's Uncle Monday?"

"Well, young man. Uncle Monday is a conjure doctor and a versifier. Some say he's something more than that. Doesn't come around anymore unless someone calls him up, and he usually means trouble. Jean and Waldo saw him out there." He peered at them curiously. "What were you all talking about anyway?"

Zora and Langston exchanged a glance.

"Well, nothing," Zora said after a while.

"Y'all know, I suppose. Don't blame you for not wanting to say."

"Well, I don't know if it's serious as all that," said Langston. "Uncle Monday's gone now, and I don't expect we'll be seeing him again."

By afternoon they were back on the road, headed southeast on Route 22.

"Where we going?" asked Langston.

"We're running away to the south."

"Don't it usually work the other way around?"

"Folks always did say Negroes were backwards."

Langston laughed. His breath caught the sour summer wind. Nothing felt better, better than driving through the south with Zora. Every moment down here was pregnant with life, and watching it fly by the window felt like living life over and again. The south's spooky beauty evoked memories: Africa, the Congo, Matadi with its white buildings, colonialism, the dusty roads and dying mango trees in the impoverished towns; Mexico City, and the long dreadful summers there with his father; Paris, cold and wet, the stately old museum-like city streets, mazed in the shape of a shell; Italy, Venice, the regal air of the Piazza San Marco, the nights there with Alain; all that he'd seen, all the places he'd been, and he'd never really seen the south. Had he been afraid of it?

"Bessie Smith is singing in Macon tonight," said Zora "That's where we're going. Don't tell me you've forgotten already."

"Good God, no! Let's go."

Zora smiled, stuck her tongue between her teeth. "Too bad Carlo and Dottie couldn't make it."

Langston shrugged, lit a cigarette. "I met her before, you know. Bessie."

"Yeah? What's she like? She's great, ain't she?"

Langston smoked, rubbed his jaw. "Aw, I don't know that she was all that taken with me."

Zora gave Langston a glance. She looked back at the road and shrugged herself. "Oh."

They arrived in Macon with the day still waylaid in daylight. Georgia responds to Jim Crow, the colored Douglas Hotel was right next door to the Douglas Theater where Bessie would be singing. They spent the rest of the afternoon walking around downtown and caught a proper supper of fried chicken and watermelon, all without irony of course.

Zora nibbled at her fingers after. "Say Langston, you dance?"

"Sure, I dance. Given half the chance."

"I don't believe you."

"What's not to believe?"

"Well now, I don't think I ever did see you dance in Harlem. What can you do?"

"Baby I can dance the Black Bottom, I can Ball the Jack; I can dance like an African. Hell, I can even dance to Gershwin."

"We'll see about that."

"Is that a challenge?"

"Can you dance to Bessie?"

"Can I dance to Bessie Smith!"

"Will you dance with me when we go?"

"Sure."

"Sure you can keep up?"

"Sure I can. Can you?"

By the time they left the restaurant the sky was already dark. They walked, skipped and danced the short distance back to the hotel. They dressed up, had a couple drinks from Van Vechten's swiftly diminishing Chinese, and went on down to the theater. The Douglas made Zora think about Florida jooks, the energy of everything, what with the people congregated outside, talking loud and smoking, so she loved it right away. It had a wide triangular marquee overhang out front that lit up the block. Inside the whole building hushed in red and gold, and the seats semi-circled forward toward the stage. There was an orchestra area open in front for dancing. Zora took Langston's hand. They took a seat.

"We need the bootlegger's what we need," she said.

"No need," Langston replied. "I brought Van Vechten's libations."

"Let's get a couple Cokes and pour some in."

"Zora, I believe you can read my mind."

When the lights dimmed and Bessie came swinging her great big hips around, the whole room roared like a Bessie groan. The trumpet dipped in a muddy slide, muddy waters, gypsy moonlight.

Langston leaned into Zora. "This," he said. "This is what I've been trying to get at in my verse."

"Don't I know it."

Bessie's tenor wavered between alternating octaves, while the piano clipped a slow blues. The whole room wandered into silence, and the horns wailed like weepers in a Baptist church. When Bessie howled, *"Muddy water, in the street!"* a few folks even returned *Amen!* A couple couples caught the feeling up to the orchestra in a lazy muddy sway. Bessie's music mattered the world to everyone in the world that mattered. To Zora she was a kindred spirit. Zora fished out her Pall Malls, lit one and reclined in a huff of smoke, titters and the double takes of folks not used to seeing a woman smoke. She looked at Langston, he winked at her. Bessie intimidated Langston, sure. Spiritually, intellectually, artistically and sexually.

"Say, Langston, howsabout that dance?"

"What – now?"

"I knew I never did once see you dance a step in Harlem. I mean maybe I seen you trip over your big old feets a couple times, but damned if I seen you dance."

"Come on. What are you going on about? Let's go, then."

They went right up front and danced the Black Bottom to *Trombone Cholly* in great big chomping steps. They slapped their black bottoms, stepped in and stepped out, swinging and swaying suggestive. Langston thought back to that cold night in Baltimore when he first heard Bessie sing, and how he met her backstage that night, and he thought about how he'd changed since then, how young and naïve and afraid of life he'd been. He wanted to catch Bessie after the show again. He wanted her to see how much he'd changed, how much more he understood her now. He hadn't, he decided, grinning into a step, bumping his thigh into Zora's, put his best foot forward.

After the show Langston bustled against the crowd, trying to get a good layout of the stage, and see where Bessie went, while Zora hummed *Young Woman Blues* and looked at him with a bewildering smile.

"Say, let's go find Bessie, Zora."

"They won't let us back there, Langston. Don't worry. We'll meet her."

"How's that gonna happen, unless we go back there?"

Zora shrugged. Langston pushed out against the crush of exiting patrons and collapsed back into the seat next to her.

"Fine. Let's just go. I'm tired anyhow."

"I could use a nightcap."

"I know. That's what I meant."

II

Somehow they must've left a victrola running somewhere, a sleepy voice in the sleepy air, familiar as Bessie Smith singing about the man that wrecked her life.

Zora stirred and sat up, blinking. It was morning. A warm Georgia summer sun rose as a plum. The walls flickered orange and red. She looked down at Langston. Still sleeping; slumbering even. She got out of bed, went to the bathroom and dashed water on her face. She looked up in the mirror and made a face at herself.

"Love, oh love, oh careless love…"

Bessie Smith's voice, unmistakable now, coming through the walls, and no victrola neither. Zora jumped in and out of the shower, got dressed and hurried out into the hall. Bessie's boom could be heard from the back corner, loud and sure, a grand piano of a voice belting out the blues. Zora tripped down the hallway, right up to the door.

When Langston woke up Zora was gone. He got out of bed and checked the bathroom. Still steamy, Sherlock Hughes. She's showered and hasn't been gone long. Maybe she went for coffee? Zora's Pall Malls were slumming on the nightstand, so Langston lit one. He threw on a shirt and pants, and wandered out into the hall, listening. It was a beautiful morning. The sun came in through the hallway windows and all through the corridor came the smell of fresh coffee and tobacco, the clink of silverware, the sound of Zora's voice down the hall? She talked loud enough, you could hear her all the way from Atlanta. Langston followed her voice to a door in the corner, knocked quick like a speak.

"Langston?" Zora.

"Hey."

"Come in."

Langston walked into a warm, smoky room. The sun cut through the open windows and the smoke conjured periwinkle ghosts; Bessie sitting big as an empress in a midnight blue dress, Zora turning to face him, smiling, smoking.

"Ladies."

"Take a seat," said Zora. "We're having a chat."

"I met you once before haven't I?" Langston took Bessie's hand, kissed her cheek. "A couple years ago in Baltimore," He sat down, fidgeted. "I'm afraid I may have come across a little starstruck."

"You were a sweetheart," said Bessie. "Didn't you ask me about my artistic intent?"

All three of them laughed.

"You asked her that?" Zora gave Langston a disapproving smile.

Langston shrugged. "I was young, what can I say?" He turned to Bessie. "It's grand to see you again, though. What's the chances we're staying at the same hotel, eh?"

"Where you think I'd be staying, other than the only colored hotel downtown?"

"Got a point there."

"And right next to the theater," added Zora.

"The Douglas hotel and theater," Bessie explained. "Black entrepreneur Charles Douglas built all this. I've even seen him here a couple of times. A man who studied his Booker T."

"Charles Douglas? Never heard of him," said Langston.

"He's local. We need more like him. Folks who do things. There's artistic intent for you."

"Amen," said Zora.

Langston looked at his fingers. "Yeah, yeah. You know what I meant, though, right? Just where it all comes from. I mean are all your songs about you, how you feel, or are you inhabiting other people, other voices? It all comes across as so real, like it's all really been felt and lived."

Bessie didn't say anything. She smoked and looked at Langston.

"And who you write for too, you know?"

"I write for black folk, that's easy," Bessie said right away. She puffed on her cigarette, continued, "It's funny when white people buy the records. I don't mind it, mind you, it's money after all, but it's funny, too. What's blues got to do with white folks? Some of 'em even singing the blues nowadays. How they gonna sing the blues when they ain't got its history built in their souls, that *lowdown* you need for the blues." She took a royal puff of her cigarette. "But how about you, Langston Hughes? Howsabout your poems- they all you, or you just inhabiting voices?"

Langston opened his mouth; closed it. "Touché."

"I told Bessie about our opera," said Zora.

"Sounds great, that," said Bessie. "A real blues opera. I always loved the theater. My brother ran off with a troupe – course I was too young to have the sense to run on off with him. Picture me in the Pictures. Now that would be something."

"You probably will be one of these days. If you can put up with movie business folk," said Zora.

"No different than any other business folk. No different than this music thing. A lot of politics in this music business, that only the money makes the business side of the business worth worrying with."

"But love makes the music worth it for its own sake, wouldn't you say?" offered Langston.

Bessie brightened. "We were just talking about love, Langston Hughes. You're a poet. Wax poetic for us about love."

"Aw well," Langston scratched the back of his head. "I don't know what to say. What – uh… love is: the heart's bright flower. Howsabout that?"

"That was alright," said Bessie. "I would've expected something more original from a poet, but okay."

"More original!"

"Baby, that was pure naïveté and cliché."

"Naïveté and cliché, oh yeah?" but Langston was smiling. "Well you g'wan then. What's love to you?"

"Love is a fire without insurance."

Zora smiled. Langston paused, impressed. "Well, I don't know. Haven't I heard that somewhere before?"

"You heard that in your heart before, that's where," said Bessie. "Blues ain't as simple as you think it is, Langston Hughes. But how about you, Zora? What's love to you?"

"Aw Bessie, I just up and fled my newlywed husband. How you gonna ask me that?"

They laughed.

"So you got no answer then?" Langston asked after a while. "All that anthropology and not even a clue what love is?"

"What's anthropology got to do with love? One's a science, the other's a calling." Zora smiled devilishly. "You're probably one of them that thinks you can love a whole people, and all that kind of abstract non-fact."

"What, like black people? Like love black people as a people kind of thing?"

"Yeah, like that."

"Of course you can."

"Why do you say of course?"

"Because black folk are beautiful."

"Oh really? Why's that?"

"Well hell, Zora. There's all sorts of answers for that. Because we –"

"Howabout this – can you love white people?"

"Oh, *hell* no!" sang Bessie.

They laughed for a good couple minutes.

"Now seriously," said Bessie after a bit. "I know how this is gonna sound, but I've been around, and you can't trust white folk, that simple. It's not entirely all their fault, neither, but even the good liberal whites grew up thinking about us different, and that never goes away, no matter how much they decide they don't wannabe racist no more. And don't get me wrong, we are different in a whole lotta ways, ways black folk can love and embrace, but not white folks, cuz they ain't got the history in 'em. And that's why I say you can't trust a white person, and ever if you do, you'll either live to regret it or die a fool."

"You don't really believe that do you, Bessie?" asked Langston.

"You bet I do. You'll see. You're young yet. You'll see. Think back over your whole life, and how many white people can you say you trust and never did you dirty not the once?"

"What about Carl Van Vechten?"

Bessie belted a laugh, and said, "Mister *Nigger Heaven* himself!"

"Hey, he's got to sell books, right?"

Well, they kept at it a good long while, and they got along together like old pals. Zora and Bessie bonded like the best of them. Langston was a little more quiet, distracted by what Bessie said about white folks, trying to storm them all up from his past: Van Vechten, Vachel Lindsay, friends from his youth, and it seemed either they were straight up racist or Negro fetishists. It bothered him. It bothered him a lot because here he had just taken old Mrs. Mason, Godmother, as his patron. He'd taken her money. She was an ancient reliquary of Negro primitive fetish cliché, sure – and yet, he had decided to trust her. And why not? Artistically he had his freedom; financially he was as secure as he'd ever been, and supposing he played his cards right, one day he might even be wealthy. Imagine that! A wealthy black poet! The world's first!

But what if Bessie was right?

Langston and Zora got back on the road late in the afternoon. They took 22 off Broadway and headed north. Langston decided Bessie was just messing with him about white folks, sure she was, but then Zora made him rethink himself once they hit the highway.

"You know that patron of yours back in New York you told me about a couple days ago?"

"You mean Godmother?"

"Right, her. What's her real name?"

"Oh. Mrs. Mason. She likes people to call her Godmother."

"Why's that?"

"She's just a little eccentric like that."

"A rich old white woman who loves Negroes, right?"

"I guess. I mean she's even building an African History Museum in Harlem," Langston said, more to the window than to Zora.

"You think you can trust her?"

The Georgia sun rolled late into the afternoon; spells of waves of heat sweated from the highway. All by the sides of the road acres and acres of farms surrounded small boxed brick and wood houses full of history and secrets, puzzle pieces of the jigsaw landscape of the south. Verdant rows of trees with ugly broken branches jagging outwards brought thoughts of ghosts of swinging black bodies.

"I don't know. Maybe not. Maybe Bessie's right," Langston said after a while. "But you don't really believe it do you though? There's not one white person you can trust? What about Carlo?"

"Carlo's an honorary New Negro," laughed Zora. "He doesn't count."

Langston forced a laugh. "Maybe the best an ofay can aspire to is a Negrotarian."

"Now there's a depressing thought."

"But it's not like you can trust all black folk, either."

"Ain't that the truth." Zora lit a Pall Mall. "Speaking of – who'd you say introduced you to this Godmother lady again? Black? White?"

"Um…" Langston hesitated a bit. "Alain."

"Alain? Alain Locke?"

"The one and only."

"Oh Christ, Langston. You let Alain find you a white godmother? She must be a slave driver!"

Langston smiled a genuine smile, and then he bit his lip. He looked over at Zora. He loved her. He opened his mouth; closed it.

Touché.

CHAPTER TWO

Slave driver or not, Zora figured she could slip the lash and quip some cash from this old white woman one way or the next; so a month later she found her fanny parked in the parlor of Mrs. Mason's Park Avenue penthouse of a brisk September afternoon. Those warm somnolent summer days in the south with Langston felt a lifetime away. Zora missed them and Langston already. Why hadn't he introduced her to Mrs. Mason himself? Instead he arranged for Alain to set up the arrangements, and went on back to Lincoln. Now here she was alone, left to fend for herself.

The apartment was more Astorperious than a palace in Paris; a penthouse, it overlooked Manhattan with wide, tall windows for walls. Even in the gray September light, the apartment seemed aglow. The furniture was regal, European, perfectly placed, like the whole place was a museum. When a prim, pretty young white woman – a woman you might see shopping on Fifth Avenue – came out with a freshly watered vase of flowers, Zora stared at her longer than properly proper.

"This is Cornelia, Zora. You'll get to know each other in time."

Cornelia bowed. "A pleasure to meet you, Miss Hurston."

A cool and unsettling shuffle of light brushed the room. Zora blinked, and looked over at Mrs. Mason. The old lady's eyes were gray, folded deep in fleshy crow's feet. She was looking right at Zora. Their eyes met, and Zora expected Mrs. Mason to smile, but she didn't smile.

"You're trying to remember something."

"Well, yes," said Zora. She glanced at the flowers in the vase; they had fluted trumpets for petals, white calla lilies. For a while neither of them said a word. Frail gusts of rain pelted the windows, and Zora looked at the calla lilies thinking about the déjà vu feeling she was having, and remembering the calla lilies from Bruce's story, and feeling like the woman across from her could not only read her thoughts, but was influencing them through communicating with them at the same time.

"I prefer to be referred to as Godmother," removing a pair of pince-nez eyeglasses.

"Of course."

"Langston speaks the world of you."

"As much of you."

"You must think me highly eccentric. At best. A wealthy older white woman who asks to be referred to as Godmother."

"Not much out there to shock me, Mrs. Mason."

Which produced a frown. "Please do not ever refer to me by my real name. Especially to anyone outside our circle." Mrs. Mason sipped cautiously at her tea. "Can I tell you a story, Zora?"

"Please do."

"It has something of the myth to it. It begins where my life begins: with the death of my husband. Have you ever been married, Zora?"

"I –,"

"A comedy ends with a marriage, a tragedy begins with one. My story begins as a tragedy. I met my husband Rufus when I was very young, perhaps around your age, even. He was much older than I, but he was brilliant, charming, more handsome than men my own age. I met him at a lecture on metaphysics, and it was love at first sight. For both of us. We understood this right away. There was a connection between us that I've never felt with anyone else.

"You see, Rufus was a parapsychologist, Zora, and this may sound fanciful to some more positivist minds out there, but he could read other people's thoughts. It's a skill that he taught me over time as well, and it's a skill that I have developed on my own to a considerable degree since his death. It's a gift; not everyone has it. Rufus had it. I have it. You have it as well, Zora. But not everyone has our gift."

"I do believe you're right," said Zora.

Mrs. Mason blinked, paused to sip her tea. "So when he started reaching the end, he knew it because his body told him so. And since he knew it, I knew it, because I could read his thoughts. And since he could read my thoughts, he knew I knew he knew it."

"Like two characters in a play, suddenly conscious of the farce of the whole thing, but stuck saying the lines."

"I see we understand each other better then I'd hoped." The old lady gazed at Zora, her eyes oddly liquid without the spectacles. "Well, it changed the way I thought about his death as it approached. I came to anticipate it. I *hoped* for it. I wanted him to die. It sounds awful. These kinds of thoughts surprise us, and we have trouble accepting them ourselves. But there was only so much one dedicated to the truth could deny. His protracted dying was a nightmare. I wanted it over with. It would be my only relief. He knew I felt this way, of course. He could read these thoughts.

"So I tried to run away from him; but we could read each other's thoughts at great distances, we were that well connected. Uncanny… It was awful to watch him die by not watching him, by hearing his thoughts echo in my guilty head, alone in a hotel room halfway across the world.

"After he was gone I fell apart. Guilt is a powerful demon. I had too much money, and so there was nothing to do but philanthropy. We are on this planet, after all, to help others more in need than ourselves. But you see, at first it was just something to lose myself in. Then, as I learned more about ideas and worlds I'd never thought much about, I began to wonder about my own sincerity as a philanthropist. It was easy for me to write checks and do nothing else. I knew nothing of the world.

"There comes a time in our lives when we have to decide, are we on this planet to be passive automatons, or active conscious beings? New York was turning me into a cog in its machinery. I had to get out. So I left New York to live with the Plains Indians in the Southwest. Rufus had been studying Indian parapsychology in his later years, and I thought I might add to his work in some way by going out there, getting away from society."

Zora, genuinely impressed, "You traveled out to the Southwest to live with the Plains Indians by yourself?

"No, Zora." Mrs. Mason offered a thin smile. "I wouldn't have known where to begin back then. I went there with the brilliant Natalie Curtis, an anthropologist I met through my philanthropy. Natalie wanted to write a book about the Plains Indians, but didn't have the funds. So with my money, and her expertise, we went out there together. She went on to publish *The Indians Book*, which is a masterpiece of anthropology, and will have to be the touchstone resource for any future study of the subject. It is a tremendous gain for science. But I gained from the experience in more profound ways. Those years with the Plains Indians changed everything for me. I had to unlearn an entire lifetime of assumptions and beliefs while I was out there. They were my most alive years, ironically, at a time when I thought my life had come to an end."

"I'd like to trade you Negro folk stories for Indian folk stories some time."

"I believe we are already doing just that, Zora. And you'll be able to read the folk stories yourself in Natalie's book. What's important is what I learned there, after I had unlearned everything I knew before. I learned about the essence of spirituality, Zora. Not a specific religion; religions are crude and clumsy constructions that obfuscate our understanding of spiritual ontology; no, I learned about the very essence of human spirituality itself. I came to understand it, and how it guides us, and how we can learn to use and channel it to our advantage, instead of being carried along by it, like most people are."

Zora moved to jump in, but the old lady just went on:

"Naturally, I wanted to stay with the Indians, but I had to come back to New York. I began having visions again. You see, I'd had visions all my life, one by one, they would come true, until I met my husband. Then they stopped. But they started again when I was living with the Indians. I saw myself sitting in a chair surrounded by the greatest Negro artists of the age, and I knew this vision was my destiny, even though I didn't understand it. I also knew that if I stayed with the Indians, the darker forces would eventually work to destroy me, and others. That would be my punishment for ignoring my fate.

"So I came back to New York, and for a long time I wondered when and how I would resume my work. Natalie's book came out, and that was wonderful, but my path lay with the Negro: I had yet to discover that my purpose on this earth is to save America and the white man worldwide, by first saving the Negro before he becomes too civilized."

"Oh."

"Well, when I heard Dr. Locke speak on Cultural Pluralism, it was a revelation; revelations are few in our lives, and we must learn to recognize them when they come. For me, I knew at that moment that my calling in life was to become the greatest patron for Negro arts in American history. It's what everything beforehand had been leading up to.

"Which is why I insist on Godmother. It is who I am: the Godmother of Negro art and literature, and what's more, it gives code and symbol to our agreement. You are an artist, and I am your patron. I am particularly interested in you, Zora Hurston, because I hear you are also an anthropologist."

"Yes, that's right. I studied under Franz Boas."

"Boas has his few virtues. I am an anthropologist as well, obviously. You'll find I am nothing like Boas. But I would like to hear about your work. Langston says you've just finished doing research on Negro folklore in the south."

"Langston speaks the truth."

"You're not satisfied with what you accomplished."

"He told you all that?"

"It's no surprise. You were supervised by Dr. Boas." Mrs. Mason sighed, took another sip of her tea. "You'll find I'm not like other whites, Zora. Most of these new white liberals are nothing more than pretentious faddists. I'm not interested in what's vogue. Negro culture still retains much of the simple wisdom of Africa, and I am interested in harnessing that wisdom in the context of the modern. Europe is lost already. I believe Indian and African wisdom can still save this country."

Zora didn't say anything.

"I'd like to send you back south," Mrs. Mason said. "If you're up for another try, under my guidance, and sufficiently funded."

"Of course," Zora responded too quickly. "Of course, you know, I'm also working on another project with Langston."

"Oh? No. I do not. Why don't you tell me about it?"

"Well, it's a blues opera. The idea is to take folk songs and poetry from the south, work it into the framework of an old folk tale, and make an authentic American opera out of it. It seems to me lots of white folks have been trying to capitalize on our culture lately, but none of them can get it right."

"I think you and Langston are the only people on earth who can," said Mrs. Mason.

Back in her apartment on West 66th Street, Zora considered her conversation with Godmother. Her own apartment, a small but cozy efficiency near Central Park felt suddenly humble and sad; it had always felt just the opposite – its grandiosity gone in a moment compared to Godmother's palace. She heard Godmother's voice again, *You are an artist, and I am your patron*, and she walked over to the window to watch an autumn sun set into evening in her little Negro enclave on the Upper West Side. *You are an artist, and I am your patron*. Well, not yet I'm not old lady, so don't throw me in your young suit if my ambition's already outgrown it. Shit, a Nigra artist ain't nothing but a mule or a pickaninny, pick your pick. Godmother was different from other white folks, though, sure, she said so herself, just like every other Negrotarian in New York: they all love Negroes and hate Negrotarians. Zora smoked and watched a little black boy run out into the rain. His mother came thumping right after, and dragged him back inside.

She hadn't agreed to anything, after all. Still, she felt like she was there – Godmother was there – communing with her thoughts as she was having them, and through communing with them, influencing them. The thought was highly disturbing, until she let her vision blur the rain outside with New York's damp city streets, and tried to concentrate on communicating back to Godmother. Time passed, and she didn't notice it. The sun went down and the apartment went dark, and Zora stared out the window, communicating with Godmother, or the city. She went to bed thinking about Godmother, and going south and really getting to learn the folk songs and stories and hoodoo religion right, and then wondered if this was her own thought, or Godmother's – like they were still up in Godmother's penthouse passing words.

The next morning Zora woke up early with a call from her husband.

"Hey baby, how you been?"

"Good, Herb. How about you?" Zora grimaced, sat up in bed, and scratched her head.

"I'm good." He paused. "I was thinking of moving on out to New York."

Zora made a face. "I'd like that."

"Good."

"When you thinking of coming in?"

"Next weekend, if that's okay." Another pause. "I mean, if we want to see things work, I mean."

Zora wondered who he thought she was. She wondered who she thought she was herself. She sat up in bed and swung her legs from under the covers. "Of course, Herbert. I'll be overjoyed to see you." She bit her lip. "I've missed you."

"I've missed you too, baby."

There was a long silence between them.

"So, I'll talk to you when I get there."

"Yeah."

"Okay."

"Okay. Bye-bye." Zora hung up. The rain had passed, but it was another cloudy morning. How depressing. She thought about Langston and felt wistfully winsome. She would write him a letter.

We write letters to frame a reference for ourselves in the perspectives of other people. Zora wrote all about her meeting with Mrs. Mason, about the blues opera and all that talk of travel, and how she might travel south again for more folklore, this time with money! About how they discussed spirituality and parapsychology, and marriage and tragedy; why, Zora had been so caught up in the quippery she even promised to take Mrs. Mason to their favorite church in Harlem. Now what did he think of that!

She folded the letter into an envelope with some stories and then went out to post it. It was chilly and cloudy, but it was nice to be out of the house, so coming home, she decided to take a detour through the park. The trees were changing, leaving the leaves earthy autumn colors that whirled with the wind like incantations. Inviting Godmother to church up in Harlem had been something of a test: would the old anthropologist agree to get out of her comfort zone and come on up to Harlem on a Sunday night? Folks would stare, Zora warned her.

"Let them stare!" Godmother declared. "I'd love to see and hear the real spirituals. I'm sick and tired of all these George Gershwin white frauds!"

Zora laughed to remember it. Suddenly she was in a good mood. Hadn't her own life proceeded like a series of symbolic visions – just like Mrs. Mason talked about? Like recreations of ancient myths, relived through personal allegory? Sometimes, back at Howard, she could even conjure up perfect allegorical visions, like the poems and paintings of Blake, but that was frightening. She would take naps midday in the Howard Library, and when she awoke, invariably she experienced a sleepy paralysis. The visions would begin to flicker through her head, while Zora, fully conscious but unable to move for waking dreaming, observed them. They were images from her past, images from her future, images from folklore, the twelve chambers of Tubber Tintye, one by one, she had passed challenge after challenge, each more seductive than the last, from Home to Johnnie to Howard to Bernard to Herb to Boas, trials and distractions all. Might Mrs. Mason be the key to her well of fire?

The sun started to break out from behind the clouds, a well of fire, as Zora circled around the red and gold and blue reservoir in the park. Heading home she considered what a wonderful afternoon it was turning into for a long mid-day nap.

Autumn awoke with brisk visionary weather. The cool sunny days washed a palette of leaves over the city in ghostly floating gusts for the rest of the week. On Saturday morning Herbert arrived at Pennsylvania Station looking awkwardly charming as he stood gazing around the vast halls with all his bags dangling down from his oversized coat sleeves like pendulums. Godmother had given Zora some money, so they splurged: they took a taxi back to Zora's pad, and they giggled and kissed and made small and sweet talk the whole way home. Back at the apartment, Herbert slumped into a chair and looked Zora up and down.

"Baby, you look beautiful."

"Thanks, Herb."

"And this place you got here," looking around. "It's not bad for New York, huh?"

"Aw, it's alright."

Herb looked good too. Still that boyish seal brown face, the sloppy slapdash smile, those bright eyes, and his cleft chin.

"How was getting here?"

"Trip wasn't bad." He shifted in his seat, lit a cigarette and cast those wide bright eyes out at her like magnets. "Say, I brought some records. You got a victrola? You ought to hear some of the blues they got going out in Chicago."

It was early yet, but they popped open some Windy City moonshine, and they danced through highballs until early in the evening. When they got hungry, they nibbled and kissed, and kissing a breath, Zora, "We'll go grab something up in Harlem. You're gonna adore Harlem, Herb. It's like Negro Mecca."

They were a little slurry drunk and the lights were blurry and bright coming outside, night time in Manhattan. Zora didn't usually like to drink much, she drank whenever Langston was around it seemed, he had that effect on her, but mostly she didn't drink, so blame it on the likker, she was really liking Herb, and Herb here in New York, here with her. They rode up to Harlem, to a little speakeasy on 129th and Lenox, and they had a couple stands of gin. Zora got to feeling fine, let me introduce this here man of mine, and since the band was between sets, Herb went on up to the stage and played *Weatherbird* in a wet, lingering way that set the whole speakeasy in a sentimental sway. Herb pulled the notes out of the piano in a cool crescendo so it was like the lull of a storm passed through, and left all the women in the room with wet cheeks.

They'd forgotten they were hungry, they'd been so busy bailin' in the jook, but once they were back outside, warm kisses in the chilly night, they remembered again. Herb took hold of Zora's hand, and they promenaded Lenox Avenue smoking Pall Malls.

"Let's just go to your place, Zora. We'll whip something up."

"Say, that's not such a bad idea, husband. I know a grocer right up round the way should still be open at this hour."

They were drunk, so they were silly in the grocers: they grabbed everything: chicken, cornmeal, rice, thousand on a plate (black-eyes only of course), sharp and stinky cheddar cheese, collard greens, watermelon, milk, eggs, fresh parsley, fresh oregano, garlic sprigs and onions; they grabbed beefsteak tomatoes and cherry tomatoes too, they got some squash and they got macaroni; they hopped a taxi back home to West 66th Street, so they ended up spending more money than either of them could afford, two children in love, competing madly in the candy store.

Back at Zora's apartment, breathless with clanging up the five flight walk-up, they collapsed side by side against the wall, dropping the bags. A tomato rolled across the floor, casting an eerie amber shadow in the warm orange lamplight, up to where Zora's fingers grasped a maroon pack of Pall Malls from one of the grocery bags. She opened it, lit a cigarette and passed it to her husband. Then she lit one for herself.

"It's good to be here," said Herb after a while, exhaling little gasped rings of smoke. "Home," he added, trying the word out for size.

Zora winked at him and blew a luxurious large round smoke ring. "I'm glad you're here too." She took a couple thoughtful drags on her cigarette. "So how is Chicago anyway? What's going on there? Is it like here?"

"South Side is where it's all at. Like those records I played you. There's a movement starting over there too. I bet it's next, after Harlem, and I think the things they're doing with music are already more daring than the New York stuff I hear." Herb smoked. "You really think the New Negro movement gonna's change things for us?"

"Aw, a lot of this talk about a New Negro Renaissance is just a whole lot of big talk anyway." Zora flicked the ash from her cigarette to the floor. "Charles Johnson orchestrated the whole thing, mostly. Dragged all sorts of Negroes from park apes to dicties from all over the country just to say we got an arts movement brewing." She exhaled, frowned, then looking up at Herbert smiled again. "I shouldn't dozens it down, though. As is, I'm betting everything I got on it."

"Naw, I think it's real enough from what I see happening in Chicago. It ain't just Charles Johnson. We got our writers and poets, too. Musicians to spare; philosophers and all that. I think something's happening. It was bound to."

"How's the medicine going?"

Herb's face slackened, and he smiled, so his cleft chin winked at Zora. "Harlem got poverty, Zora, but damn, not like the South Side. I'd like to see more Negro schools and businesses. Education and business-savvy, Du Bois and Booker T. both got it right. But for the medicine, well, I know you won't like this Zora, but I really can't abide the way our people are so quick to turn to witch doctors and superstitions and such for healing. Home remedies and all that. You know why I think our people do that? Because if you see the way they treat Negroes in real hospitals, you wouldn't think much of traditional medicine either."

They were quiet for a while. Outside a group of people strolled by, slurring, singing. Zora considered Herbert's Hoodoo medicine theory. He was right. She didn't like it.

"Let's make dinner," Zora decided.

So on with some quiet Ellington blues, and going about dinner. They made a butternut squash, small enough for two, boiled chicken, and baked macaroni and cheese. Dinner took them almost three hours juiced to prepare, and by the time they were ready to eat it, 'twas more breaking fast than dining. The bootleg made them animations. They drank through the lot of it, and talked off the last few months of their lives. Zora admitted to Herb she'd been nervous – nervous and unsure on their wedding day – waylaid by doubts, as it were. Herb looked a little crestfallen to hear it. You gotta treat a man's ego gentle, after all.

"Well gee, Zora," a little pathetically. "And I always thought if I ever got married I'd be the one with cold feet."

"Men do tend toward self-mythology."

By the time they got to bed, they were getting on like old times. They laughed and tickled each other and undressed between kisses, and oh my, and ooh ain't love some sexy function blues, and mmm, in the morning, rolling over into the early September sunlight, Zora kissed Herb awake.

"I've got to get up love," she said. "I have to spend today with Godmother. I'm supposed to take her to church tonight up in Harlem."

Herb blinked, looked at her smiling the while. "You're crazy, Zora.

You know that? Why you call that old white woman Godmother all the time? What's her real name?"

Zora sat up, got out of bed and lit a cigarette. "I guess you just wouldn't get it."

Herb propped himself up on one elbow. "Come on now, Zora. I didn't mean nothin'. What's with the tone?"

"I can tell what you're getting at."

"And what's that?"

Zora didn't deign to answer. She gathered up a robe and dragged it into the bathroom.

"Listen," she called. "I'm going to be all day, up until tonight." She paused. "Just so you know. Make yourself at home. Leave a note or something if you're gonna be out."

"Thanks," he called back. "I'll do that."

In the car crosstown to Godmother's Zora wondered why Herb irked her so much that morning, and so suddenly. The sun was finally coming out from behind its week-long blanket of clouds, and morning drafts of sunshine swept through the colorfully changing trees in warm slanted patterns over her face and shoulders. What did Herb know about any of this? Anything really Negro, and to Herb it was just Tomming for an older white woman. Like Herb had never Tommed. She'd seen him pull off Tomming with such tomfoolery even Locke'd be like to blush. She lit a cigarette. She was angry with herself more than Herb, she decided; angry because she didn't have the right words with which to respond that morning, and she made a point of pride in always having the right words at just the right time; she was angry with herself for still dwelling on the thing at all, like it still bothered her or something, when she was self-confident enough to know she did what she did out of empowered will, not just to Tom to whites for money and favor. Godmother wasn't your typical Negrotarian anyway; some of them were different after all. Consider Carlo. Consider the Spingarns. Some of them were different. No, she decided, she wasn't angry at herself, she was angry at Herb. She was angry with him because here was this man, her husband, insinuating that she was compromising herself for Mrs. Mason, when really her marriage to him had been more of a compromise than any other decision in her entire life.

At 399 Park Avenue, Zora was greeted with a reassuring smile by Cornelia, who led her through the parlor where she'd met with Mrs. Mason before.

Then into a long series of passages which apparently connected to an entirely new section of the apartment. As they moved through the hallways, Zora snatched glimpses of Indian and African art on the walls, placed here and there on pedestals and sitting on tall oak shelves. Each hallway was bright with wide windows, and smelt of burnt cedar. At the end of the passage there was a heavy wooden door with African engravings carved into it, studded with rubies.

"You've been admiring some of the art?"

"Oh, it's -,"

"Some of it is my own."

"You mean you made some of it?"

"Yes, that's right. Godmother insists on only associating with artists and philosophers."

Zora turned to look back at some of the work, maybe ask Cornelia which works were hers, but the jeweled door swung open, and before she got fully turned about, the sight in front of her – speechless, spellbound.

The room was decorated in red, brown, purple, black and gold, adorned with African paintings, parchments, statues, tapestries, rugs. In the back center of the room there was a high golden throne thronged with jewels, and sitting on the throne in regal African robes, was Mrs. Mason. All around the throne were shorter silver stools.

"Zora," said the old lady brightly. "Come in. All I've been able to think about these last few days has been our meeting on Tuesday. How have you been?"

Zora wandered into the room, a gush of sleepy opium incense. She looked around sheepishly, tried not to look at the shocking sight of Mrs. Mason on a throne surrounded by silver stools. Certainly she didn't expect –

"Please take a seat," said Mason, gesturing to a stool at her center left. "I know this is somewhat idiosyncratic, but you will find I am an idiosyncratic lady. Better to establish our formalities right away, than to run into a misunderstanding later."

Zora, slightly dazed, took a seat on the stool. "Of course."

Now she was Tomming for sure.

"All my artists congregate with me here," Godmother explained. "When I have business with Alain or Langston or Aaron or Miguel, this is where I prefer we have our discussions. There are delicate spiritual forces at work in this room Zora, and I have seen things and understood things here I could not see or understand anywhere else."

"Of course."

"You'll come to see what I mean in time," said Godmother. "For now it's enough that you understand that whenever possible, this is where and how we shall meet."

"The atmosphere here reminds me of places down south," said Zora, and maybe it wasn't all Tomming, even if sure it was; because being in this room with the thick sweet scent of opium burning in holders attached to walls draped in the deep bright colors of African tapestries, really did seem to swell a religious and spiritual sleepiness Zora had only felt before in the temples of Florida and Georgia Hoodoo Priests.

"I have designed it after certain West African temples," said Godmother. "Speaking of which, where will we be going this evening?"

"Macedonia Baptist Church. It's way up in North Harlem, almost up by the Heights."

"Wonderful. I can't wait to see it. Tell me something about Harlem. I'd like to hear your own stories in your own words."

Religion is violence: it's sexy and passionate and truly unholy. Pastor Aaron Banks, a deep black brother, skinny and small, could belt out the Bible in blues that'd shout down the walls of Jericho. He wore midnight blue robes, two sizes too big for his body, and his hair was wild and woolly, like the lightning of the Lord woke him up come Sunday.

Service began with the choir swooning into slow rolling spirituals, latecomers shuffling through the double doors, shifting into pews. The building was old and smelled musty like stale cigarettes and mildew. It was large, the benches ran all the way to the back, and they were all full. Sunday evening's twilight came in through opaque windows, lighting the whole church an eerie yellowy blue.

Dem bones, dem bones, dem dry bones,
Can you hear the voice of the Lord?
Dem bones, dem bones, dem dry bones,
O hear the voice of the Lord!

The choir acquired a slow soft hum with the rhythm of the spirituals tiding the chords. For a minute or more the piano rolled on alone, softer now but steady still.

"I'd like to begin today's service with a story. It comes from the book of Ezekiel; Chapter 37. Folks know it as the Valley of the Bones:

Dem bones, dem bones, dem dry bones,
Can you hear the voice of the Lord?

For a vision came to me as I passed through Babylon,
The sky grew bright, and the earth leveled
Descending into a valley, and the valley surrounded me
Even to where my eye could see the vanishing meridian

O hear the voice of the Lord!

Zora (as so often happened in church) drifted with the rhythm of

Pastor Banks' voice; the cadences had their own music, after all, easy enough to miss through purely focusing on the message and the meaning of the thing. A woman goes to church to worship, and worship for Zora had become something much different than the parables of the pastor, compelling as they may be. And you're telling me? She even figured she'd write her own sermon one of these days, set it in a book proper, really these stories were just the outgrowth of the stories folks told all the time down south, only without the good parts, like a jook without no gin.

Hoodoo, blues, gospel, spirituals, Sunday shoes to move with the spirit of the music, the truth of the sermon. The theater of church was like the theater of the jook; what was it but the birth and death of art moment to moment? A story's only as good as the music that tells it; if jazz seems like to bust at the seams, especially that Chicago jazz Herb was going on about, it's because the black arts, like the Black Arts, ain't meant for books and libraries and museums, but for the fullness of life reacting with life, and when you try to contain them, they scream!

Tell 'em Uncle Monday!

Pastor Banks seized and whirled:

O heed the voice of the Lord!

Release yourselves, Babylon,
From the undead wickedness we are well rehearsed in,
Bones drying in the valley, flesh without breath."

Zora blinked in surprise to hear her name – to hear herself singled out, and just as her mind caught hold of the homophony, it occurred to her that legally she was no Hurston no more, no, not at all, she was Sheen; cleaned of her name and made nothing but the spit polish of a man. Bone`s drying in the valley; flesh without breath.

Outside on Lenox and 145th, Zora hugged Godmother hard and said no car for her, she'd walk back home, it wasn't so late yet that it wouldn't be safe.

"I want to thank you for that Zora," Godmother took Zora's hand in her own, soft, warm with age and smooth like wrinkled velvet. "I have important matters I want to discuss with you when I get back in town."

"Until then Godmother," kissing the pale bluish white hand, the pale bluish white streetlights of Harlem flickered like itches walking down Lenox, Harlem, the swarms of colorful Negroes, colorfully dressed, out for a Sunday evening on the town, scratch a daydream, and she was thinking of the blues opera. She swung on over to Broadway right before the park, and lit a Pall Mall. Not so keen on going straight home this afternoon, not so much. Why not get a little lost in Times Square on the way home? Passing West 66th Street, she kept right on going, south on Broadway, passing on by like a runaway mulatto.

The rhythm of Pastor Banks' sermon moved her; made her shiver in the chilly autumn afternoon, someone walking over her grave; she couldn't recall his words, hadn't paid attention. The cars looked like beetles, flat topped and fragile, the trolleys like caterpillars slinking down the Broadway tracks, insects in the soil, someone walking over her grave. The stores and shoplights were lit bright like daylight, and thinking over the music of Pastor Banks' words again, it suddenly seemed to Zora that she saw him – or someone familiar, if not him, disappear around the corner. Pastor Banks wouldn't be here. Who else? Zora quickened her pace, thinking it over. Uncle Monday conjured anew? She turned where he turned, 52nd and Broadway, in pursuit.

Turning the corner, a brisk wind scattered a few leaves beneath the arch of the Guild Theater. The man was nowhere in sight. Zora walked up to the door of the building. There was an ad for a play based off the novel *Porgy*. She blinked. She'd heard something about this from Wallie. More white folk writing for black folk, and where were Zora and Langston? Still with nothing done. She turned back around the corner, lit another Pall Mall, and finally headed back north, homebound.

II

Zora was just starting to settle into the humdrum hum of everyday married life when Langston Hughes made a cameo. It was late October, and the city had yawned cozily into autumnal fall. His arrival felt like a holiday; suddenly everyone was scrambling to make arrangements. Bruce and Wallie wanted him to come speakhop uptown near Niggerati Manor; Carlo was calling all over town; finally they agreed on dinner at Eddie Wasserman's, an ofay jazz cat Carl knew. Nella would be there, and Carl said he'd see if he could get Ethel to stop by too.

Langston got in spinning happily on that perpetual grin of his. Zora met up with him in midtown, on the steps of the New York Public Library.

"How's married life?" he asked her right away, first things first.

Zora shrugged. "It's life." She lit a cigarette. "I'm not writing. New York's got me battle-hammed. I'm looking forward to getting back down in Bam."

"It's that good, eh?"

"What?"

"Married life." Langston winked, and Zora laughed. They got up and walked uptown, towards Harlem. They wandered westward onto Broadway, and beyond. They walked all the way west, with the afternoon sun just a dim shivering thing rippling the Hudson. They talked about the last couple months, Langston about Lincoln and Zora about New York, and New York folk and the happenings and such, jes gossip, so that her thoughts kept going forward, back to being in the south, collecting folk songs and stories; being out of Manhattan's inhuman machinery.

"You gotta get out there then," Langston told her. "Godmother will send you. I guarantee it."

For a while Zora didn't say anything. Then: "Why do we trust her, Lank?"

"There's something about her…"

"There's her money."

"That's cynical, Zora."

"Sometimes, it's smart to be cynical, you know." Zora said this with more barb than intended. She looked at Langston. He frowned, arched his eyebrows.

"It's just you remember what Bessie told us, is all," Zora added.

Langston didn't say anything. They walked along the Hudson without speaking, with the sun settling into a smoky periwinkle New York night. Coming up on Harlem the sounds of drums and pianos and horns came whistling across the avenue. Zora took Langston's hand. She squeezed it.

"We're both already married to our work, Bambino. Listen: about our opera. We need to do it now, Lank. It's hot, it's time; did you know they're making *Porgy* into a play, and it's going on Broadway."

"I did," said Langston. "Bruce tried out for it. I think Wallie did too."

Zora laughed. "We should go see it while you're here, if we get a chance. I've got a bunch of ideas I want to toss off you anyway, before you head back to Lincoln and I go back south. Then, once I'm back here, we can write our opera based off the old folk tales and songs I collect."

Langston squeezed Zora's hand back. "Deal."

Eddie Wasserman, son of a wealthy banker, lived in a large brownstone in the Flower District. Langston took a cab with Zora and Herbert, and boy was he ever glad when they finally got there, what with the two newlyweds had been making the necessary appearances around town the last month, and had settled into the banal banter married people make.

"It's been too long since I've seen Ethel… how do I look?" Zora gushed on the way up the stairs.

"You look lovely, honey."

"You always say that. No surprise, maybe I always do look lovely."

"Go on, now. Always talking yourself up. Only person you talk up more than Zora *is* Ethel."

"Ethel's a Goddess as far I'm concerned."

"There's a lady in Chicago who sings a little like her."

"Oh you and your Chicago."

"Well, now, you heard the records, Zora. You gotta admit-,"

"Yeah, I heard them records."

"Now what's that mean?"

"What's what mean?"

"That tone again. You know what I mean. Like -,"

"Say, I'll have to hear some of those records sometime," Langston cut in. "Anyway, here we are." He knocked on a blue and gray door at the top of the flight.

"Come in," Carlo!

Langston walked into a room that smelled like roast chicken, gin and tobacco, and there he was, old Carl Van Vechthen, dressed in a pinstripe suit, gesticulating to someone around the corner. Carlo turned as the door opened, and right on seeing him Langston felt a deep affection for the fellow.

"Langston Hughes!" a huge hug. "Look at you! How are you, man?"

"I'm good, Carlo. Good to see you in your usual spirits. Where's Fania?"

"Fania is awaiting the proper moment to make an appearance. Speaking of spirits, my spirit," Carl glanced back around the corner towards the kitchen. "You'll find we're fully supplied here."

"Gin?"

"How could there be no gin? Zora, Herbert, it's good to see the two of you again. So, let's go have ourselves a drink, yeah? Oh, and Zora – I believe there's someone here you'll want to see."

Zora already knew Ethel Waters was there, of course. She heard her mellifluous, sinewy voice winding out from the other room in a soft whisperthin melody. A piano accompanied her, a gloomy, groovy blues.

The piano was conjuring aroma and atmosphere, and perception was translated by Ethel's singing into sensation: the living room like an English drawing room, curtains and frills and divans, real high society, Eddie sitting at the piano, Ethel beside him, half humming, half singing. She looked up when Zora turned the corner, their eyes met and she went silent. Eddie kept on with his slow bluesy swing.

"Zora!" Ethel swept from the piano bench into Zora's arms. "How have you been, honey? It's been too long. I hear you been down south."

Eddie looked over at the group, smiled and winked, but kept right on playing. Eddie was a clean-cut kind of guy, good looking for an ofay, Langston supposed. He played jazz with Negroes up in Harlem and hung out with whites down in the Village, and Langston never figured he could figure all that much out about the fellow. For however well you can understand your average white folk anyhow, Negrotarian or not. Langston

31

smiled a sideways smile; Negrotarians were often harder to figure than your average peckerwood racist. Eddie nodded to Langston's smile, then turned back to the blues.

"This is my husband, Herbert," Zora was saying to Ethel.

"Oh honey, we gonna hafta lose him for a while. We got us some girl talk to do."

Herbert scratched his head self-consciouslike and chuckled. Langston looked at him and figured he looked out of his element. He wondered about them – Herbert and Zora – what their marriage was like. Figured he might as well go on and get to know the brother, but just as he was lighting a Lucky, moving to do so, Nella Larsen walked into the room with her funny, skittish gait, wearing a blue and black polka-dot dress and a black bowler hat cocked at an angle on her head.

Nella, nutty Nella Larsen, half Danish, half black, cream tea complexioned, she sometimes passed without trying; sometimes she flirted with passing, like a lover she was never so sure about, then came back black as the night is long in December, militant and talking about the New Negro; though she really felt most comfortable in pleasant mixed company like Van Vechten kept.

"Nellie! How's the novel?"

"Oh, the novel's finished all reet," said Nella, giving Langston a shrugging hug. "How's my Lincoln man?"

"They're inducting a new president this week. I took the opportunity to opt my way back to New York for a few days."

"You working on anything?"

"Not right yet. It's good to just take some time to relax now that *Fine Clothes* is out."

"I like that *Fine Clothes*, I do. I don't care what the critics say."

"Here she goes…"

"Well the irony, you know Langston, is how much the white critics loved it."

"What's not to love? It already is – I just put it on paper's all I did. But how about you? Let's hear about your novel."

"It's called *Quicksand*. Oh, Langston, I can't talk about it now. I'm too excited. Say, where's the gin? I could use a stand of gin. Come accompany me, Zora. I haven't seen you in forever."

The women worked their way to the kitchen, past the piano where Herbert was now standing next to Eddie Wasserman, half watching, half just appreciating the playing.

"That's my husband," said Zora. "Can you believe I'm all married off? Speaking of, where's Elmer?"

"Oh, he's at home working. Married life has its ups and downs. But I would've pegged you for the last of us. How'd it all happen? Last I heard

Boas had you down south collecting folklore."

"That's what it was, all right, and I picked Herb up along the way." Zora flashed Nella a confident smile.

"I heard you picked up Langston, too. Oh Zora, you're scandalous."

Zora's smile turned sly. "I've been known to leave a few men in my wake. But running into Langston was pure synchronicity. We ran into each other out of nowhere, like we were meant to meet up. So naturally, we went right away and visited Sparta."

"Oh, I'm jealous to death. You visited Sparta? What was it like?"

"I could feel the living spirits of the dead in every engagement with the soil and the air. Between the trees there were echoes of ancient conversations. Langston and I even saw an apparition."

"Zora, you're too much. Have you kept up with the Work at all?"

"In my fashion. That still going on here?"

"You could say. We've kept on having meetings."

"Wheresabout?"

"Here. At Carlo's sometimes, too. Sometimes even up in Harlem. Dorothy's in Paris right now. She went to the Gurdjieff Institute out there."

"Where Katherine Mansfield died?"

"The very one. Well, you know how she feels about Jean, and Jean was just out there. So she followed him out there, but then it turned out he was juggling three or four different women. The whole thing was a terrible scandal."

Nella laughed and Zora laughed too.

"So she's still out there?"

"She's still out there. Jean chased some other frail back to Chicago, and there you have it."

"I wonder what he's up to," Zora mused. "Who else is going to meetings here?"

"Aaron and Alta go. They never miss a meeting. Bruce comes by sometimes with Wallie. Even Charles Johnson has been holding meetings."

Zora lit a Pall Mall. "I've thought about that stuff. The Work's there in Hoodoo too after all, and it's there in all the old Baptist and Methodist bickerings. So I've thought about it. But I haven't had a group, you know. I've been on my own, so I've had to work things out in my own way."

"Well now that you're back you should stop by one of our meetings. I'll get Carlo to put you in the loop."

Herbert had joined Eddie on the bench, and now the two men were banging out a baroque galloping blues, riffing back and forth off each other, switching melody and rhythm roles mid-music, propelling the conversations like musical chairs, a conversation going on now between Carl, Nella and Langston, and a little ways down the hall between Zora and Ethel, who were engaged in animated theatricality, punctuated by laughter and gestures and slapstick. Zora and Ethel were trading stories about what they'd been doing and who they'd been doing, and what the people they knew had been doing and who those people had been doing. They were telling the stories in a folklore kind of way, because even real people can be fictionalized nicely in a folk talc, wid dc litery and all dat, just to give everyday life a little music. Zora told Ethel about how she met Bessie Smith down in Georgia, and Ethel sighed and said, "Bessie's – I love her, now, don't get me wrong, don't tell me nuthin' about Bessie – but, Bessie's a mean ol' bull who'll run you right on down if you ain't got it in you to spar her a few rounds." She told Zora about this time she opened for Bessie, and Bessie wouldn't let her sing no blues, because Bessie didn't care for no one competin', and all Bessie sang *was* the blues.

Zora laughed and said she could see that, Bessie came across real hard sometimes, had told her you can't trust white folks far as you can see 'em in a snowstorm, and Ethel nodded, and giggled an agreement.

"Bessie'll tell it like it is," Ethel said. "But you know what, Zora, I really find the whole thing curious. You know what I think? It seems to me the white folks in this country must be as mixed up as the niggers cuz they love us more than they love anything on God's Green Earth, themselves included, and they hate us more than we can git to hating ourselves at the same time, and the fact that they can be so mixed up about us just makes them love and hate us all the more."

Down the hall Langston found himself in a curiously similar conversation with himself. He kept looking over at Carlo – he wanted to tell Carlo about Godmother, but didn't know if he should – hell, if he could. Could? Couldn't he do anything he damn well pleased? He wasn't sure anymore. Godmother told him she wanted to discuss an arrangement while he was in town. What would that be? Kneeling down on a silver stool and kissing her great white old ass up there in that throne of hers? Yeah, he had to tell Carlo, but didn't know how.

"Years of the weirdest kind of alienation, black and white – a shadow," Nella shuddered like she had a sudden fit of sneezing. "That's what the book is Carlo; I'm shaking it all out like a fine rug that needs to regain its shine."

Langston tipped his glass to excuse himself, and headed through the hallway toward the kitchen. He poured himself a gin on the rocks, leaned against the counter, and lit a Lucky. It would be better to wait to tell Carlo. After he'd already made whatever arrangement with Godmother they might make. After all, Carl was white and had money. He didn't have to struggle day to day for his survival like Langston, a black poet, had to do. These Negrotarians, man. Langston puffed hard on his cigarette. Name one Negro, one American Negro in the history of the world, who ever had made his living by writing alone? None, Carlo, and you can only help me so much. No; no false moves until he met with Godmother first. He'd see how that went, and then he would decide his next move.

As it turned out, the whole thing was briefly conducted, a brief – well – seven hours – time's trickery in Godmother's penthouse apartment, eating venison in the parlor (not the throne room, thank God!), and discussing art, blues, life, love, God, opera, Zora, Alain, the New Negro, the future, Voodoo, the north and the south, the Native Americans and ritual. Godmother was in grand spirits. She couldn't stop talking about Zora. Langston knew the two would hit it off like threes and fours and fives and sixes, and Zora had gushed about Godmother, sure, but Zora tended toward the hyperbolic at times, who could tell when the curtain came down with her? – and here Godmother just went on and on about Zora, and Zora's native charm, and the blues opera Zora and Langston were writing. Some of the ideas Godmother told him were new to Langston himself.

"I love the idea of pitting Baptists against Methodists," said Godmother. "Zora took me to a Baptist church up in Harlem. The preacher delivered a sermon about the city of the bones. Do you know it Langston?

"I – I don't believe that I do."

"Well, you ought to. It's a powerful parable. Zora can tell it to you. She has such a fine African sense of storytelling."

"Well, wow… African…"

"I sometimes wonder, Langston, if we so called civilized people were wrong to ever write our stories down to begin with. A story, I find, isn't so much a bunch of words set in stone, but something passed down over generations, re-interpreted by each new generation in the retelling in a contemporary mode."

"Yeah, I guess." Langston frowned. "I guess. But writing books is my business."

"Well, we will always have the classics," Godmother sighed. "Of course Homer's genius was undone the instant someone wrote down his fluid epic, set it in their own words like law; it lost the spirit of the entire idea of passing on an epic, of keeping an epic Epic in its changeability. But yes, Langston, we are modern Westerners, and so we must write our books. Speaking of which, how is the novel coming?"

"Oh, the novel, well -," Langston grinned sheepishly, scratched the back of his head and said, "I'm still marinating on that."

"It's no surprise. The American system is built to frustrate the artist; it hates the artist. That goes triple if the artist is a Negro. Everything in our system conspires to frustrate your efforts."

Langston smiled a little too broadly in spite of himself.

"Zora's affected my thought lately, Langston. We have a connection, a spiritual connection, one I haven't felt so strongly with anyone since my time in the southwest. Her intelligent, unpretentious wit and southern spirit have made me rethink my plans for an African Museum of Art up in Harlem. Alain had me convinced African art was the answer for the Negro, and I still think it is important for the Negro to study that history. But I think it's more important to support living, working Negro artists. Which is why I'd like to extend an offer of support to you. A contract. You will receive a hundred and fifty dollars every month. This will give you your leisure time to write."

Langston scratched the back of his head again, this time more deliberately. "What's the catch?"

"Excuse me?"

"I mean – what do I give you in return?" A little meeker, his voice betrayed him.

"Langston, like my investment in the museum was to be, this is an investment in Negro arts. I ask nothing of you except that you remain an artist. I plan to extend similar offers to other members of your group, Zora included."

Langston blinked. A hundred fifty a month? To do what he'd do anyway? Was she for real?

"Don't decide now. Think it over. Alain will give you a formal contract. I look forward to your answer. You know, Langston, with this money you could even leave Lincoln, and that whole yapping crowd of talentless Negroes."

Langston winced. "Aw, Godmother. I couldn't leave Lincoln for love or money. I need to be around that yapping crowd, as you uh... hilariously call them. I love them like I love my own brother. I need to yap with the crowd myself sometimes. My poetry wouldn't be the same without it."

"Well, however you wish. Just make sure they don't distract you too much from your real work. I am especially interested in seeing a novel from you."

Langston had been avoiding thinking about that damn novel. He didn't feel particularly moved to write poetry right yet, let alone some long sustained work of prose. What would a novel by Langston Hughes look like? Well, that was a question in and of itself! If he took the offer, he'd have to write every last word of that experiment. He would owe Godmother and himself even, that much. It would be a short novel, Lord save him. Negroes don't write long ponderous novels like some half-mad Russian peasant. And what about Zora? Would Godmother want a novel from Zora too? Well! What would that be like? If they played their cards right, they could really do something with Negro literature, theater, hell, even music. Where was it all headed? He decided to give Zora a call the moment he got back to the Y.

"Slow down, Bambino, slow down," Zora laughed when he got her on the phone. "You're gonna talk yourself battle-hammed."

"Come see me off tomorrow at Penn Station," Langston insisted. "I'll tell you all about it."

It was a gray blustery morning when Langston left. Lank, in a long gray overcoat looked about as happy as Zora had ever seen him. They had coffee and chain smoked outside Penn Station, and Langston went on and on about Godmother.

"She's going to make you an offer soon too," he said. "She said so herself."

"So you're definitely gonna take her up on it?"

"I think so, yeah."

"And she really doesn't have a whole list of things she wants you to do?"

"Just be an artist. Well, I have to itemize my expenses back to her. That's a drag."

"Yeah." Zora frowned. "Small drag considering. Something doesn't seem right about it. When have white folks ever been okay with a Negro free to do whatever she pleases? Even when I worked for Fannie Hurst, even *she* wasn't that liberal."

"It's rare, I'll admit. But you said yourself, there's something just – spiritually different about Godmother."

"There is something about her. I dream about her sometimes."

"You what?"

"I dream about her sometimes. And then sometimes I dream with her. I mean we have the exact same dream the exact same night. It's spooky stuff. There's something about her, though. I'm investigating it."

"You're an odd one, Zora, but I'm sure gonna miss you when you're down south."

"Well you need to come join me. Will you?"

"That's the plan."

For the next several weeks all Zora could think about was the offer Mrs. Mason would make to her. Autumn aged elegantly into winter. December came in sweeping bursts of snow, sometimes light, sometimes heavy, but never lasting more than a couple hours at a time, and not collecting more than an inch or two. Being slightly snowed in made Zora and Herbert feel like an unhappy old couple. Zora had already bored poor Herb to death going on and on about Langston and Mrs. Mason and the south, and Herbert had bored her half to death with his medical talk. He wasn't happy in New York, she could tell. He didn't have anything here yet, and he didn't know where to start. A man without a plan. He didn't even know if he'd be staying, since all his wife did was talk about running away from home. They'd run out of meaningful things to say to each other, she supposed, and she felt guilty, like she'd somehow emasculated him. They sat in the living room day after day while the snow bleated against the windows, Zora reading literature and Herbert reading textbooks, and even when it got real cold, so the windows rattled in their little wooden frames, the old married couple never once snuggled together to keep each other warm.

Sex was an occasional requirement for them both. After all, a woman's got her needs.

Still, it was enough to make you wanna scream.

Days ticked by with the monotony of a metronome.

Then, in the second week of December, she got a call from Mrs. Mason.

"I've been anticipating your call," Zora told her right away.

"I know you have. I will see you Thursday morning."

"Of course. Thursday morning it is then." Zora hung up and turned to Herb. She shrugged, but awful awkwardlike; it was impossible not to scream farce. "That was Godmother. She wants to meet up on Thursday."

Like a metronome; flakes of snow flecked the window in the flickering winter afternoon.

"Figured."

"What are you gonna do, Herb?" Zora lit a Pall Mall. "If she asks to me to go south again, I mean? I don't know if I'll be able to turn down an opportunity like that."

Herb lit a cigarette himself. "I figure I'll go on back to Chicago, Zora."

Zora knocked the ash onto the table and started to pace. "We'll meet up again in due time."

"In due time."

Zora knew at that instant she couldn't stand Herb. She loved him, but she couldn't stand him, because suddenly the idea of getting away from him overjoyed her. She could barely keep her happiness contained inside her body. She almost couldn't even bear to be with him another day now that it was so close to decided.

"Herb," she said – best to end things now, then. Now that she knew she was getting away for good this time. Why drag a dead mule with you wherever you go just cuz you too scared to tell it it's dead?

"Yeah, Zora?"

"I- if I do go down south again, it will only be for a little bit, you know. We'll get back together again after that just like we always do."

"Sure, Zora. Sure." Herb smoked thoughtfully. Then added, "It's almost better this way, I suppose."

"See!" Zora stopped pacing and beamed at him. "That's just what I was thinking."

Thursday came and went in a haze. It was all Zora had been night and day dreaming about, and her thinking on it made her so fully in and out of it all the time, when it finally came, it kind of felt like a continuation of the same. Cornelia led Zora to Godmother's throne room, and for hours and hours, Zora and Godmother talked about work, love and travel. Zora felt like a spell was being cast on her in that room. All she could do was blink and nod as Godmother told stories of her time with the Indians.

"I'll tell you something I only tell those I feel closest to, Zora." Godmother said when Zora mentioned her disillusionment with married life. "I had to leave the Indians because I fell in love with one of them. I've never loved a man more completely than my husband, but I never loved more passionately than with Kachada. I had to leave him because I'd taken leave of my senses. I loved him, but there couldn't be anything lasting between us, and he'd been realistic about that from the outset. I had only tried to be.

"I never thought I would fall in love again after my husband died. It was painful and wonderful when it happened. I'm glad it happened, because it was meant to happen. But if I hadn't left I would have let myself be overwhelmed with negative, black forces. I would have destroyed myself and him."

The two women were silent for a very long time, Zora on her stool and Godmother throned. The incense gathered up strings of ghosts, chamber music.

They say you don't choose who you love; but you really do choose who you love. You either let yourself love or you don't. Zora let herself love Mrs. Mason. She realized it right away, right at that moment, that she loved the old lady. She loved her for her sadly quiet and troubled wisdom; she loved Mrs. Mason because Mrs. Mason needed her, and Zora needed Mrs. Mason, and they would learn how to trust each other. She also knew that there was about to be an offer.

"I've had a contract drawn up," Mrs. Mason said after a while. "I'd like you to look it over and let me know if it is acceptable. I've given the contract all of my thought. It is non-negotiable as it stands."

"I understand."

"Alain will deliver the contract to you directly, tomorrow. The stipulations are as follows: I will provide you with two hundred dollars a month. I will also provide you with a vehicle. What I would like you to do is resume your studies in the Deep South collecting Negro folklore and songs. This time it will be under my guidance. There will be no interference from Dr. Boas."

"Godmother, you're too generous!"

"There's more, Zora," Mason waved her hand to slight Zora's enthusiasm. "As you know, we are both anthropologists. While under contract, I will need to have the rights to any and all information you collect. In your role as active anthropologist, all your creative material will be under my estate. You will publish your book under your own name, of course. But just so you understand. I will own the rights to everything you write during this time, and you can only publish with my express permission. You have a unique gift, Zora, it really is one of a kind. Boas is shrewd, and he will try to manipulate you in ways Negroes wouldn't understand. It's a liability I can't afford to overlook. You must take it or leave it as is."

"I don't like it Godmother."

Mason glowered. "Of course you don't like it. Don't you think I know that already, Zora? I explained my reasons to you, and I have neither the time nor the patience to repeat myself to those unable to understand me from the start."

"No Godmother. Of course I understand."

Tomming for sure.

What Zora really understood was that everything suddenly seemed a lot more muddled to her. As if she had no interest in writing material that was her own; why write anything if the moment you wrote it, it was no longer yours?

"How long is the contract for?"

"We will start with a year. Depending on how things go from there, I might agree to extend it."

That evening, leaving Mrs. Mason's Park Avenue apartment, the ride down the crankshaft felt like the plummet in her stomach. Outside, Park Avenue's busy streets crawled with motorcars and trolleys, automatons. She walked north, not thinking about where she was going. She was conflicted, elated; two hundred bucks a month was more money than she'd ever made doing anything, let alone for being a professional anthropologist. But her writing had always been her one proud fortress of independence, and it was intimately connected to her anthropology. Be she Negro, be she woman, be she black man's mule in a white man's world, she always owned her thoughts – and she owned them in her own words when she wrote them down; they gave her grace and strength. What was it Langston always said? He only wrote poetry when he was blue? Well, he could write seven hundred volumes of poetry if he ever felt the way she felt now, only she couldn't write anything, because anything she wrote vanished from under her the moment she wrote it, like Countee Cullen liked to quote Keats, Here Lies One Whose Name Was Writ On Water.

Her name wasn't to be writ on water, however, she told herself, turning west on East 66th, passing a large gray building that blotted out the last red smear of the sun. Things were just different than she'd expected. She'd have to write this book for Mrs. Mason, and then she'd see what was what. She considered Natalie Curtis, the author of *The Indians Book,* the lady who had traveled to the plains. Where was she now? What had become of her dreams? Was she still writing? What had her accomplishments been since? Did she have any more accomplishments – or did she just vanish, exploited, like the Indian?

Zora would accept Mrs. Mason's offer of course, whatever it was. She knew it walking up West 66th Street, where her apartment building slumped against the props of other brokedown Negro urban dwellings; Herbert in there, listening to his funky Chicago jazz and blues. Drinking gin. Zora sighed, pushing up the outside stairs, then into the building, looking up the worn old black stairwell. She longed for the south. A soul could just wither on up and die here in New York.

Back outside then, into the crisp twilight, to light a Pall Mall. Light flakes of snow danced up and down in the night wind. She puffed nine proud circles of smoke, tears on her cheeks now, and considered the south, and her soul, like Dante, descending deep down into it.

CHAPTER THREE

Gentlemen Jiggers swing low on the spree, damned from here to Diddy-Wah-Diddy; Lawd, have mercy on folks like these!

Langston Hughes and Charles S. Johnson went out on the town to see *Porgy* of a chilly evening in February. DuBose Heyward's hit book was now a hit Broadway play, and a wonder of a production to witness. As such, too much of a wonder of a production if you were to put a problem to it, but well, it worked anyway. The whole stage a pageant of life, the colorful energy of Porgy's passion set against the social drama of the town, which of course lay mired in the larger racial tragedy of the country. If it wasn't as good as the novel, well, it was close. This, Langston decided, was what had to happen with his and Zora's opera: it had to unpeel those social assumptions Americans, black and white, had absorbed so completely they no longer even challenged them – all within the framework of a simple folk story. And their play would have what *Porgy* lacked: music.

"It was amazing how good it was without music," Langston observed after the show. They were passing through the doors of the theater where New York hummed electric.

"I know. It works." Charles sounded just as surprised. He added quickly. "The novel's still better."

It was late now, and the sky was dark. It was a clear night, bitter cold. Broadway blared around each corner, another orchestra and another theater. Charles lit a cigarette. "Besides, I heard Gershwin's already set to go ahead with a musical version next year."

"Gershwin?"

"Gershwin."

"No kidding."

"Yeah, no kidding. What do you think of Gershwin?"

"Oh." Considering the question. "I like him. I think. Howsabout you?"

"I like him." Charles smiled like a wink. "For an ofay, anyway. There's him and Seldes and Van Vechten and a few others who get it. How much American culture is Aframerican. *Porgy* is good. Real good. I can't wait to see what happens when Gershwin gets his hands on it."

"Yeah." Langston was tempted to mention his and Zora's opera, but they'd made a pact to keep it secret. "Seems to me a Negro would do a play like that best, though; something like *Porgy* I mean."

"Well, that's what we're all hoping."

"Sometimes I wonder. I saw real deep down low poverty when I went south. No one down there cares about the New Negro movement. Maybe we New Yorkers are really the provincials." Langston said this too thoughtfully; all he could really think was: wait til me and Zora get to do *our* blues opera.

Charles let Langston's thought hang around there in the air like a third person for a while.

"Have you thought any more about the Gurdjieff Work, Langston?"

Langston hesitated. "Oh. I don't know. Not so much, I guess. I mean it's interesting."

"I still hold meetings. Not as often as before, but there are others from our group who hold them regularly. You should give it some more consideration."

"Ain't it kind of just a cult?"

Charles laughed. "Yeah, sure, if you're a cult kind of person. But you don't strike me as that type, so I wouldn't worry about that too much. Just check out a meeting or two."

"Yeah, maybe." Langston glanced quickly at Charles. "You see the February *New Masses*?"

Charles looked back at Langston. "Yeah. That's right. I saw it. You had a poem in there." Charles paused to smoke. "You going Red, Langston?"

"Well, I'm considering social issues more, at least. *Sunset – Coney Island* is kind of a declaration of that. All my old stuff's old hat now anyhow. Making the trip to Jean's Sparta kind of laid that down on me."

"Well, it's a good poem. The imagery is strong, and the propaganda isn't, and that's good. It's subtle, when it's not so concerned with its symbolism, at least. I don't know. Maybe the direction will work for you, maybe not. But you really think you're a socialist?"

"I didn't say I was all that. But I don't want to get caught in the same circle Dunbar did. I can't be a folksy Negro forever. So I don't know where my poetry's gonna go from here." Langston tossed off his cigarette. "Speaking of, where are we off to anyway?"

"Uptown, of course. Jessie's place. She's having a party for -," here Charles swept an arm upward and wriggled his fingers – "*Salvador de Madariaga!*" He puffed his cigarette magnificently.

"Who?"

"Salvador de Madariaga."

"No kidding… Who's he?"

"Some Spanish diplomat."

For a moment there was this confusing silence, and then they both started laughing. Charles was strange that way, a strange one, sure.

"Everyone will be there – the whole Harlem set. Bruce and Wallie, of course."

"Bruce is in *Porgy*. I even saw him in it when Wallie was still part of it."

"Why wasn't he there tonight?"

"He's an extra or something. They don't need him every performance."

"How was he? How was Wallie?"

"Acting comes more natural to Bruce."

"Oh, I could have guessed that, I guess."

They laughed.

"Countee will be there tonight," Charles said after a while.

"It will be good to see him."

They were quiet for a spell.

"Been a while?"

"We've had our problems."

"No kidding. You basically called him an Uncle Tom in *The Nation* last year."

Langston grinned. "Aw, I never said I was talking about him."

They were walking north up Broadway now. Ahead of them, the entrance to the subway. It was real chilly, and they looked at each other with the same question.

"Subway or taxi?" A duet.

"Taxi," said Charles. "It's on me."

"No, I miss the New York subway. Let's do it."

"Indeed."

They got off at 116th Street, and walked north up Harlem's wide Seventh Avenue, discussing the future of Negro art. Charles seemed cynical.

"Things are complicated," Charles said, catching Langston's look. "I think we've done a lot of important work here, and now it's just what it is. We've launched the careers of lots of new artists, and they'll have to sink or swim on their own merit at some point. I think we've reached that point. This vogue with Negroes won't last forever. If we're going to have an artistic legacy, it's time for us to stop being a movement, and just be individual artists."

They were coming up to Jessie's building when Charles kicked at the sidewalk, muttering: "Anyway, if I seem to sound jaded these days, I am a little. I'm probably going to be leaving the Urban League, Langston."

Langston opened his mouth, closed it again. Then managed, "Why would you – What about *Opportunity*?"

"I've been offered a position at Fisk," said Charles. "Sociology department." He puffed hard on his cigarette, and threw it down on the steps leading up to Jessie's building. "*Opportunity's* a sinking ship. It won't last. It's not like *The Crisis*, where the organization really takes advantage of all the magazine's – heh – opportunities, as it were."

"Well, gee. I don't know how I feel about that."

"My work here's finished. We've started something, and now it needs to build off its own momentum. I know how folks talk. Some say I forced the literary thing into being, instead of letting it develop organically, but that's a lot of hokum. Little literary magazines out of New York, well that's the way every literary community builds and supports itself. Why shouldn't we have ours, too? Anyway, there are a lot of you who are ready to start publishing books regularly. This year we'll have far more books coming out by black authors than any previous year. So, the ball is already rolling. And there's a lot of good I can do at Fisk."

"No one can argue with that. But you think you're ready to live down south?"

"I've actually been ready to leave the city for a while. Anyway, not a word of this once we're inside. It's still not finalized, and it's bound to rouse up some controversy."

"My lips are sealed, and mum's the word. The business begs silence."

Jessie's apartment overlooked Seventh Avenue between 117th and 118th. The apartment was large and old, with light hardwood floors that creaked when walked upon, and the whole place smelled like soap and scented candles.

"Charles, you've brought Langston!" Jessie greeted them each with a kiss on both cheeks. "Oh, it's so good to see you again."

"Gang's all here," said Langston. "You got some gin?"

"Oh Langston," Jessie sighed. "What a way to greet an old friend. You just walked in, for shame's sake. Let me look at you. Tell me about school."

"Aw, it's all right. I'm kinda cutting class right as we speak." Langston winked, checked his watch. "Well, not right as we speak, so to speak, but I sneaked here to New York to hang out in speaks and see *Porgy*."

"How was it tonight?"

"They're not vampires, darling," Bruce called from across the room. "Aren't you going to invite them in?"

45

"Oh, ignore him," said Jessie, taking their coats. "Take a seat. What can I get you to drink? Oh, well, we know what you want, Lank. How about you Charles? What's your poison?"

"You came just in time to break the tension," Bruce winked at Langston as he took a seat.

"Oh Bruce," said Jessie, bringing drinks, but she left it at that.

"Nothing controversial, I hope," said Langston, looking from Jessie to Bruce. Alain frowned. Charles smiled. Langston caught Charles' smile, and a look passed between them.

"Do Negroes smile?" Georgia Douglas asked quietly, fumbling with her blouse sleeve.

"Of course Negroes smile!" Jessie frowned. "That's rather simplifying what's a complex issue."

"Which is why poetry's superior to prose." Georgia looked up from her sleeve to reveal that soft lovely face of hers. The face of a poetess, if ever there was. "Prose is European by design. You have to play by European rules. It's a prison, prose. Poetry's more engaged with life and language. It's more universal. You can't tell our story in prose. It only demeans us. You have to tell it in poetry."

"Superior?" Jessie sat up straight, like a beanstalk. "When you consider the prose of Dickens, or Austen, or *Du Bois*." This last name was served up with an extra helping of emphasis.

"Every art form has its native aesthetic advantages and disadvantages," Alain offered evenly. "But certainly, there is a *joie de vivre* in the Negro spirit, is there not, that writers like Du Bois have referenced, without making the Negro ridiculous. I believe *The Souls of Black Folk* allows for the sorrow and joy of the sorrow songs."

"I heard he's writing a novel," said Wallie.

"Speak up," Bruce nudged him.

"I heard Du Bois is writing another novel."

"That's right," said Jessie.

"Should be something to see," said Langston. "You read any of it yet?"

Jessie folded her hands across her stomach. "No." A beat. Then, "I heard you're writing a novel yourself, Langston. Now *that* should be something to see."

"Aw, I've just barely started on it yet." A lie, you could say, since he hadn't started on it at all.

"What's it about?" Madariaga had been watching the conversation quietly for a while, and the thick Spanish accent startled Langston, along with the directness of a question he had no ready answer for.

"It's about…" Now everyone was real quiet and looking at him. "It's about me, Kansas, I guess. I don't know… what it's like for someone to come to learn they live in a world where white folks hate Negroes and Negroes hate white folks and how you learn to live in that kind of a world."

"Well arguably, all Negro literature is about that." Countee caught Langston's eye in a flash like a Chicago drive-by. "A novel needs a story."

"Well, it's like I say Countee. I've barely started on it."

"No reason to get defensive Langston. You might want to try outlining your plot first, before you begin work on it. Countee makes a good point." Alain was looking at Langston inscrutably. Langston figured he knew there was no work on the novel yet.

"Aw, who's defensive? Listen, look – the book's the story of our people like my poems are the story of our people, like Georgia was just getting at. It's like a series of blues songs that tell a story. I can give you a piece from it now." Langston took a drink of gin, continued. "There's this bluesman in it, and he sings a lyric. I'll recite that, if I may."

"By all means," said Jessie. "Please do."

Langston hopped off the loveseat and took center stage in the circle of sofas. "This is from a part in the book where folks are singing, laughing and playing guitar. And this one bluesman starts in to sing in that down south gator gravel way they have. Here goes:

Down in 'ouisiana
They got peppers round and raw
Down in 'ouisiana
Where the peppers round and raw
There's this spicy little pepper,
Well, there ought to be a law!

The Blindman told the Preacher,
Preacher, you can not see
The Blindman told the Preacher,
Lawd knows you blind as me.
The Preacher told the Blindman,
Your woman don't agree!

I've traveled and I've traveled
Just to find a good old gal.
I've traveled and I've traveled
Jes to find a good old gal.
Well, I come cross plenty women,
But ain't never had a pal.

The sweeter is the juice,
The blacker is the berry.

Said the sweeter is the juice,
The blacker is the berry,
The coolest of my blues
Can warm up January.

Langston beamed and sat down to laughter and applause. All of it was improvised, he even impressed himself. "So that's what I have to say about that!"

"*You* are the diplomat," said the diplomat. "I've heard a lot about you Langston Hughes. It's good to finally meet you, and hear you read."

"Langston's a genius," said Jessie. "No one's denying that. But here's my challenge. The black artist has had her image twisted and distorted by the white world ever since we were brought here. And in order to participate in entertainment, black artists have had to pander to these stereotypes. Bert Williams was a genius too, but he was also an Uncle Tom."

Suddenly no one was laughing anymore.

"So as black artists we have a responsibility to our people," Jessie continued. "We have to consider whether our art hurts our race or helps the race. The white, the European artist, their concerns are necessarily different. But a Negro artist is a preacher and poet at the same time, because after all, our preachers are poets, so our poets must be preachers. White people will always reward images of our people that conform with their idea of us as simple, shiftless, unsophisticated, unintelligent people. So long as we just sing and dance and laugh and jive and drink moonshine and gin, white folks are happy and call us great artists. But I'd like to see real artists who have the courage to challenge those conventions."

For a while no one said anything. The room went still and silent and just a little bit cold. Langston lit a cigarette. He opened his mouth to respond to Jessie, and just closed it again in a petulant puff of smoke. Every time he thought to start, he worried he'd just sound naïve. He could imagine Du Bois pulling some heavy history book down from the shelf with a deep frown. "Actually, Langston…"

"Well someone needs to speak for the lowdown folks," Wallie said after a while. "We're not all Talented Tenth Negroes."

"Well we are we are we are," said Bruce, throwing his feet up on the table and gesticulating in an all-embracing manner. Bruce grinned a sleepy grin, and sank into his oversized gray suit; he had no socks on and was wearing dress shoes, so his bare ankles rested against the edge of the table.

"And Bruce is right about that much," said Jessie. "You are not from a poor, uneducated, deep south family, Langston. You are a relative of John Mercer Langston and Charles Henry Langston. Even though you weren't well-to-do growing up, in your last book of poems, you were simply aping a people you know nothing about. Why don't you write something from the heart, something you know? After all, you yourself wrote in *The Nation* that no great artist is afraid to be herself."

"Why not let real blues and jazz speak for the lowdown folks?" Alain suggested helpfully, with a delicious dollop of irony. Langston frowned.

"And in the meantime we get these sensationalist novels, like – like *Nigger Heaven*, of all things. Sure, they sell; but they do more harm than good. They're cheap, sentimental trash, perpetuating stereotypes, masquerading as art. And when Van Vechten deigns to show Negroes acting civil, well – My God! He writes it like it's a revelation. Like some Negroes aren't savages, speak French, discuss ideas! He makes it seem unnatural, and that just makes us the exception that proves the rule. I can't stand him or that novel of his."

"Well it wasn't so bad as all that. Not Carlo's best book, admittedly, but a noble effort," said Walter White.

Jessie snorted. "A noble effort indeed. It just goes to show. Everyone wants to be blacker than they really are. The white writers want to write about shines and the black writers want to write about shines, too. How can you glorify a social catastrophe and believe you hold to the standards of high art."

"High art, pie chart," said Bruce. "Ain't you just mad at that book because you're Mary Love in it? As for high art, I never heard of the thing, and the fella who coined such a concept must've been a high tart, sure."

"The Mary Love character is a grossly distorted caricature at best." Jessie Fauset blushed cherry brown red. "And Van Vechten certainly has no understanding of the inner lives of black women. Which is precisely why the Negro artist has a responsibility to write honestly about herself. Van Vechten, as an over-privileged white man isn't up to that task. Why don't you understand that you can't possibly separate culture from politics?"

"I don't see why a poet should have to identify himself as a Negro anyway," said Countee. "You all know how I feel already, and I know how some of you feel about that." Countee gave Langston a meaning look, and then, "But I am proud to say that I am a poet first and foremost. I just happen to be a Negro."

"How is that different than a Negro who just happens to be a poet?" asked Charles.

"Because I don't define myself by my race. I define myself by my vocation."

"And what defines your vocation? I always thought a poet wrote from experience."

"A poet writes for universal truths."

"And how does he arrive at them?"

"Through particulars."

"You mean like being a Negro."

"That's one of many."

"Which is why I say you're a Negro who happens to be a poet. Like it or not Countee, being a Negro has defined more than a small part of your experience."

"Clever sophistry, Charles, but it is sophistry. Poetry is about revealing universals through particulars, yes. And of course my experiences as a Negro play a large role in my poetry. But I don't limit myself to being a Negro poet. That's what I won't do. Segregate myself into some subsection of literature. I want to write work that's timeless and particular at the same time like all great poets do."

"Aw, go on back to Europe where you belong," said Langston.

"And which you do quite well," said Alain, tempering the growing tension. "And if you don't mind, I'd like to make a request, since we just heard Langston read. Will you recite, *Yet Do I Marvel?* I think it states your case beautifully."

"Man, haven't we all already heard that thing to death?" Bruce protested.

"Get over yourself, Ricardo," said Wallie. "It's a great poem. Read it Countee."

But an hour later, Wallie and Langston and Bruce and Charles were up at Small's, listening to jazz and drinking likker. The diplomat Salvador de Madariaga had come with them, making hilarious apologies on the way out the door.

"But Salvador, it's your party."

"He needs to see the real Harlem," Langston shrugged. "We're the best of the best to show him."

"In the interests of diplomacy, you understand."

Now a skinny deep black woman in a green sequin dress was singing:

Dat thing, I dig a liverlipped jig,
Inky dark viper makes me hyper, you dig?
I don't love the man, and I don't love his gin,
But I do love the state his gage puts me in.

Small's Paradise was a dank basement speakeasy, space about the size of a walk-in closet. The band played on an elevated stage, dancers squeezed tight hot sweating right smack in front, while all around the chairs and quarter size tables, waitresses shuffled along the floor in short skirts and rollerskates, delivering drinks and dancing the Charleston.

"You dance the Charleston, Salvador?" Bruce couldn't stop teasing the distracted diplomat.

"This is really too too incredible."

"Nope, not too incredible, and hell, if you wanna have it, Jessie's right. It's all just theater you know. We do it up big for the white folks. Most these Harlem cabarets are Jim Crow anyway."

This cheering observation was made by Wallie.

"Hell, at least they let Negroes in here. Sometimes they won't even let Negroes in; places like the Cotton Club."

"But why wouldn't they let Negroes into a jazz club in Harlem?"

"Man could go crazy pondering those kinds of questions," warned Bruce.

"You know. I think you guys were too hard on poor Jessie tonight," said Charles. "I may not agree with her completely, but she makes a good point. That preacher and poet bit. And then, the thing about Van Vechten's book is-,"

Go on, Charlie Johnson!

Salvador looked over at the singer, startled, and then at Charles Johnson, who just winked. Langston and Wallie and Bruce almost upset the table and bottles and ashtray with laughter. Salvador looked back at them, eyes big as, what's going on?

"Go on, Charlie Johnson!" Wallie called out, real sharp and loud, and another voice from the crowd growled:

"Go on, Charlie Johnson!"

Go on, Charlie Johnson!

Which broke the band out into a swinging sweeping sway of a blues parade.

Go on, Charlie Johnson!

The glasses rattled against the shivering table, and spinning on their rims suddenly gave off the sound of a sharp crash of shattering glass, then a rolling groan, followed by a few words from the corner, thrown like a callback to the chorus:

I don't love the man, and I don't love his gin
But I do love the state his gage puts me in.

"Say that shit again!"

But I do love the state his gage puts me in.

Away in a corner by the stage, a table overturned. There was a final crescendo of glass, and then the damp dull reek of likker.

"Nigger, say that shit again."

Langston strained to see through the smoke, the rollerskating waitresses, the dim light and the dancers, all still in full swing. Two dark shadows lumbered back and forth, from foot to foot over the upturned table.

"Is this typical?" asked Salvador, leaning into him.

"It can happen."

"This is precisely why the Cotton Club will not allow Negroes into its fine establishment!" Bruce declared.

Swift from the sides of the stage a couple other shadows swept to the scene. The club had hushed, but slightly. The Charlie Johnson Band kept right on playing, Charlie kept ragging the piano, and the singer sang:

Viping sweet gage, I love Georgia Brown fine
When I'm viping sweet gage,I love Georgia Brown fine
When I don't have my gage
Georgia's on my mind

Well, like a shift between bridge and melody, the fighting was finished, vanished, in a rush of lumbering shadows, and when the music crooned back the time, the titter shushed with a hush.

"Now who do you think acted as the diplomat there?" Charles smiled, lit a cigarette, and pushed his glasses up the damp bridge of his nose.

"That's what diplomacy is," said Wallie sourly. He took a drink and flagged a waitress for another. "Sweeping niggers under the carpet. Or our souls at least."

Wallie had been drinking more than anyone realized. The table got quiet. Wallie opened his mouth to keep on talking and noticed he suddenly had more than just their casual attention. "Aw, get over it," lighting a cigarette. "The whole thing's artificial is all I'm saying. All Harlem's a stage. And all the Niggers and Ofays merely players."

They stayed late into the early morning, put the diplomat in a cab back to his hotel, and walked wearily up Lenox in the bleak early breaking day. Charles lived close enough to walk home, but Langston figured he'd join Wallie and Bruce for a nightcap back at the Manor.

Langston had lived in old Niggerati Manor on West 136th for a spell a couple years back. That was back when they all thought they were really part of an important Negro Arts Movement. Wallie was the editor of their magazine, *Fire!!*, and they'd named it after Langston's

Fire! Lord
Fire gonna burn ma soul!

O, they'd been naïve.

They didn't write much, but they drank lots of gin and talked a lot of nonsense. Langston and Zora would sometimes lean into each other out in the hallway, sitting on the steps, smoking cigarettes. They'd sit and wonder about the future, and wonder about themselves, and Zora seemed lost back in those days in a way she never seemed again. She needed to get out of New York maybe. Reconnect with the south. Langston needed to get back out of New York maybe. Reconnect with – what?

The Manor, with its wide sprawling living room of an entrance wound around into several passages leading to back rooms. It was dark, the light was poor in the daytime, and an unsteady amber at night. Bruce's pornographic phantasmagorias hung leering in unsettling choirs around the walls, comfortable in the likker and stale smoke atmosphere sweating through the apartment. Walking back into it brought up rotten memories fresh. The rent parties, the writing, the endless gin soaked arguments. Everything looked and felt the same, and Langston wondered if that was negative or positive, which made him think back to his talk with Charles Johnson.

"I'll make some gin and gingers," said Wallie.

Bruce went over to the victrola, and Langston, exhausted, slumped on the old familiar blue couch.

"What you been listening to these days, Bruce?" Langston lit a Lucky, and felt it rush right to his head, making him nauseous and dizzy. He put it out. "Zora's husband keeps saying Chicago jazz is what's really happening right now."

"Ha! Chicago jazz!" Bruce giggled. "Chicago jazz is all reet, but listen to this: it's some ofay, but he's o-kay. Named Eric Satie."

II

Langston woke to a sallow sliver of sunlight and the smell of highballs. Bruce and Wallie were wandering around the apartment chattering back and forth, smoking cigarettes, making the sweet incense heavy room heavier with dun colored smoke.

"Lazarus Hughes rises from the dead." Bruce peered over at him, highball in one hand, cigarette in the other.

"What time is it?"

"Negroes have no concept of time."

Langston shuffled upright. "Then consult that Nordic blood of yours."

Bruce shrugged. "My Nordic blood is wide and varied, and doesn't agree with itself on abstractions like time."

"God, I don't feel too great. How the hell are you two?"

"Drunk again, bless us!" Wallie called from somewhere.

"Where'd we get money?" For a moment it almost felt like he was living at the Manor again, waking from a convincing dream after a long night. He rubbed the back of his head. "I had the strangest dream. I dreamt I was a college student."

"Now that would take money," said Bruce, turning to wind up the victrola.

"Where's Zora?"

"Gone to measure the bootleggers head, I gather. She'll be back soon enough with more gin."

"You know what I think," Wallie gliding into the room. "I think there's something up with the two of youse, Lank. You and Zora, I do."

"Aw, Wallie. You've been drinking."

Something French classical, slightly jazz infused issued into the ambience.

"That's true," Wallie agreed. "The fact of which does not preclude the veracity of my previous statement."

Bruce looked from Wallie to Langston. "I think you're wrong there Wallie."

"See now, there's some sense at long last. Besides, if we're gonna do this, I'm gonna need some gin."

"Darling, I brought you a gin and ginger already." Bruce handed Langston a drink that had been idling on the table.

"What makes you think I'm wrong? They're always together, always asking after each other, always-,"

"Completing each other's thoughts? I know, Wallie. It's uncanny. We do the same thing, you and I."

"So?"

"I think they're just doppelgangers. We all have ours in the group. You're mine, obviously: the blacker version of me, both in temperament and in tint; Zora and Langston are each other's, they're the folksy ones; Nella Larsen and Dorothy Peterson, the Gurdjieff girls."

"And who's Jean's?"

"I heard he hangs out with some white poet in the Village. That guy, maybe. Jeans' would have to be an ofay anyway."

"Or Wallie, and go the opposite extreme..."

"Enough with all that," Wallie said, colorless. He finished his drink and skulked back toward the alcove for another.

"Besides," Bruce said as Wallie passed him, winking at Langston. "You ever see the brother with a woman before?"

Bruce's observation halted Wallie in his progress towards his next drink; just long enough for him to give Langston Hughes a long regard. "Hmm." Pondered a beat longer, and passed.

"I been with plenty women!" Langston tasted his drink quickly, and sat it on the table. He smiled. "But I ain't never found a pal." He winked. "What are we listening to anyway? I'm liking this."

"Anyone need a refill?" from the alcove.

"Naw, Wallie, and you might consider slowing down yourself."

"I'm just starting to get right."

Bruce took a moment of pause in their exchange to loll luxuriously into a large armchair by the records. "It's Gershwin," he said, picking up an album cover. "*Rhapsody in Blue.*"

"You have *Rhapsody in Blue?*"

"Have it?" said Bruce. "I wrote it."

"Come again?"

"Well, I feel like I wrote it every time I hear it."

Wallie returned weaving. "Ricardo's right though, Lank. What's up with you anyway?"

Langston shrugged, picked up his drink and looked at it a moment. "How do you mean?"

"I think what Wallie means," Bruce crossing his legs in the armchair, "is: is you queer or what?"

Langston giggled and took another quick sip of his drink.

"He's queer, all reet. I can tell. We can always tell another brother, don't you think, Ricardo?"

"Ha! A moment ago you thought I had something going on with Zora."

"No, now that was a red-herring, my friend. I'm afraid I set you up."

Bruce turned and nodded Langston a long up and down look of a nod, while the clip of jazz like Walt Whitman and Debussy filled the room, a blues opera. "I don't know about him," haltingly. "He might be asexual even."

"Not a chance, nobody's that."

"Oh, don't be so sure. He just might be that rare bird"

"I am sitting right here," Langston smiled an easy reminder.

"So which one are you?" asked Wallie. "Straight? Queer? All of the above? None of the above?"

"What a question! I figured you were above those kinds of easy labels."

"Well, then Langston, which do you prefer? Lads or lasses?"

"Howsabout you? Which do you prefer?"

"I rather like lads and lassies alike."

"Well, I would say the same."

Wallie giggled. "Which do you prefer to *coucher* with?"

"Aw, I'll sleep in bed with any old body so long's it's a warm safe place to stay for the night."

"I don't know about him," Wallie looked at Bruce. "Always dissembling."

"And quite possibly not in an enlightened way, like I do. I think he may even dissemble with himself."

"You two are crazy, you know that? Women don't leave me alone. I don't need to care about chasing after them."

"Youth, alas, is fleeting. I have the same problem, it's true, with beautiful young men. You seem to be carving yourself in my image. Of course if you want to do that, you'll have to admit that you're queer. And if you're not queer, who and what exactly do you fornicate with?"

"Check the ego, Ricardo," Wallie lit a cigarette. "Langston's more conservative than us. I think that's why he can't admit he's queer. That's what's going on with him."

"That's what Countee thinks."

"All right, that's enough now! Christ, who gives a fast fuck what Countee thinks? When he's marrying Du Bois daughter? When's he's as queer as a black president? Are you kidding? And he said what about me?" Langston stubbed out his cigarette and lit another. He laughed, but it was hollow, obviously forced. "And what about you two? You have your own problems. Wallie, you're the one that can't fess up; and as for you, Bruce – Well!"

Bruce uncrossed his legs and crossed them again. "We do have our issues, Langston, however when we talk about yours it doesn't seem like it anymore. But yes. Please. Let's hurry on to mine."

"You're not really comfortable with other black folk. That's always been your issue. That's why you're always reposing in a pose. It's fear, I say. That's what it is." Langston puffed his Lucky triumphantly, "That's why you don't like black men. You're only attracted to white men, and that's why."

Bruce's comfort shifted into stiffness. "Well Langston, it's not so much a question of who I like, but sexual preference. One which goes back to my experiences in DC. We've talked about this."

"It says a lot about who you really are you find, deep down inside I mean, when you analyze your preferences. You learn stuff about yourself you couldn't come to face before."

"Clever Langston, turning my own rhetoric against me. Like I said, I really think you want to create yourself in my image."

"Jokes again! Always the same deflection with you to the point where it's a predictable cliché. Get a new character to play. Why can't you admit you don't like black men, and you yourself are one, and -,"

"Why am I a Negro any more than a Nord, Langston? I have more Nordic blood than Negro blood, and I love both my Nordic and my Negro blood. What – ha! – I don't love so much are the standard labels of race people apply to each other, when if you count all the permutations of blood and racial mix out there as different races, then there are as many races as there are individuals living at any given moment."

A quiet roll of piano blues and a low moaning tempo melted against the soft sound of a small rain coming in with the western wind.

"You're right maybe, Bruce, but when we talk about our people, you know what we mean, because we know what we've been through. However you want to divvy up the races, there's a bunch of us in this country that share a heritage and a history, and it's awful and ugly, and you're afraid to look at that. So you never learn to see the beauty and redemption our people made of it all. I don't know. Hell, kids it's raining." Langston gulped down his drink and put out his cigarette. "And I should get going. Tell Zora to measure your own thick skulls while she's at it." Langston smiled, winked and stood; put on his hat. There was a very strange still in the air where Gershwin's fantasia turned eerie with the soft pitying pitterpatter rain. It was awkward and uncomfortable. Not knowing the words to dispel it, Langston turned and walked out the door.

"And don't do anything like in that fool dream of yours and enroll in college."

Outside in the slow cold drizzle, Langston walked south on Lenox. He was feeling a way he'd never felt before: plain awful, downright down and out blue; and yet, there was no poetry in his heart. No poetry coming to him at all, soothing friend in his sadness. Spend the afternoon staring at a page, listening to Bessie, blue as you can be. Told you so.

CHAPTER FOUR

A summer morning in a motel room in an unmapped town somewhere in Alabama, and Zora awoke in a dizzy map of sweat. Her head whirled in the middle of a wheel, what with the remnants of dreams and the remnants of nightmares, and the realization that the soul only makes progress through catastrophe.

And there was an essay on the desk: *How It Feels To Be Colored Me!*

She'd gone down through the south in a shiny new Chevrolet paid for by Mrs. Mason, and she drove it through seasons thinking back on her past, thinking on Kudjo Lewis thinking back on his past and thinking that this time she'd got her interview with him just right, had brought something of herself to it, had taken something back away from it again. Not like last summer, right before she'd met up with Langston in Tuskegee; last summer she hadn't written about her interview with Kudjo one way or the next: she'd plagiarized an obscure old article no one would ever know about, and sent it along to Boas like her own.

Wheel whirling in the middle of a wheel.

"Where you get that shiny silver car at, Zora?" folks crowding round the corner as she came honking up the old Eatonville street.

Folks could watch you in the south; make sure you didn't get too ahead of yourself. But they could teach you something too, and teach you through trial. Last time here she talked pure Barnadese til folks thought she sounded too dicty to live, but she'd since fixed all that.

"Where you get that shiny silver car at, Zora?"

"Oh you know. Trial and error and a little bit of trickery."

Well, I'll tell you about trial. Hadn't Miss Becky Moore told her a colored girl had no business fussing about school? And why, you gone and chose to leave your home your self.

Well, what did she know?

Home shrieked with the image of her brother and her father facing each other, faces drawn like bloodlusty hound dogs, knife in brother's hand, hands trembling; Mattie, Pop's new gal, sassy and sloppy and slatternly lying all over the house, Preacher John, do me this, Preacher John do me that. Living there was no choice, no choice more than walking up the hill and lying astride the railroad tracks.

Communities turn into spirits, spirits turn into personalities. Take a walk through any town and the houses have faces; the buildings have faces, and some have whole families; the faces tell you a tale about the town. Some towns have houses where the faces are all the same: bland, blank and astonishingly stupid, like people can have, with wide vacant window eyes and a mouth like a baffled retort.

Eatonville wasn't like that.

The houses in Eatonville had faces with history, and the faces could change day by day.

Zora's old home had gone from sweet and cheerful and warm to dull, vapid and miserable, leering and bitter so that the windows shuttered up into a cruel squint, and the doorway lurched ajar, banging the screen, a smirk.

Leaving home, she worked. Black woman black man's mule. She stayed with friends of the family, and played perpetual maid. The family had more and more friends by the day, too. What with Zora gone, and Mattie running the show, Pop had got the big idea to run for mayor, and he was making a big noise. He would visit folks at home, and make speeches in church, and chat folks up at the jook.

The day he won, Zora left town.

Astride the railroad tracks late one summer twilight, Zora stared up at the blinking stars and wandered with them where they went, way up north. She followed the North Star, and the oases of constellations spanning the seas, while the rumble of a train rolled around in her imagination. What she wanted was to travel. And she wanted to go to school; she wanted to see the world, introduce herself to important people.

Five years gone by since she left home. Five years behind her, disappearing beneath her feet with the dirty wet slop of a mop. Real good times, what with crushed beneath pale, fat, flabby, sweaty Mr. Moncrieff, a slovenly white man who smelled like a shaggy dog wet with whisky. Zora shivered a shiver like the slick sweet southern summer wind poured into her every pore. She was desperately lonely.

The quickening wind across the tracks presaged a train. Zora rolled off the tracks and on to her feet. She scanned the long run of track, crabbing backwards down the hill road. The light of the train was a speck of a star, traveling up north. She turned back to see the town. It had gotten darker, later than she'd thought. Her thoughts went back to the inanities of her life. With the secretary wages, she could stay at the boarding house for a while, for as long as she kept the job that was. Eventually the girl she was filling in for would come back. Then it was back out going house to house, face to face, a perpetually aging maid, without a face of her own. Tears wet on her cheeks, bitterly, maybe she even shoulda run off with Mr. Moncrieff to Canada and been his kept Negress. She tried to imagine it, and laughed for a long time; laughed at the image, and laughed at feeling so sorry for herself.

Back in the sickly bluish white light of the boarding room, Zora stared at the walls a while and wished she had something to read. She chain smoked Pall Malls halfway down, and crushed them in a large red ashtray, so they looked like joints of skeleton fingers, caked in red wax and ash.

Nights pass all the same. The repetition of working hours renders the repetition of free time inane. The next morning Zora stirred to the toll of the sound of the town at seven in the morning, and the brittle seven in the morning sun, wrapping its gleaming knuckles around the windowsills, ruffling the pillows warm and light.

Waking is a beauty, those first few moments rediscovering the world; then you remember everything about it, and that ruins the whole thing.

Zora sat up blinking, thinking about another day. She frowned and lit a Pall Mall.

"Miss Hurston?" It was the landlady.

"Yes?" Now what was this about? Rent? No, that was paid. "I- I'm not dressed just yet. I'm only just now getting up."

"Oh, Miss Hurston, don't trouble yourself. It's a letter for you. I'll leave it under the door."

The envelope slipped below the crack and Zora listened to the landlady's footfalls fall softer and softer down the stairs. Finally she got out of bed and picked up the envelope. It was from Bobby, her brother, the oldest of the three. Zora opened the letter and smiled to see Bob's familiar scratchy penmanship:

Zora!

I'm a doctor now! Officially! I've graduated Meharry, and I've really gotten my doctorate. I can't believe it myself, but it just shows how times are changing. Anyway, we have a big house in Memphis now, and I want to see you get your education. I know how much it's meant to you, and now that I'm over the fence, I want to throw back the rope. We all know how things were with Big Nigger Pop around. Anyway, that's all behind us now. I've been worried about you. I'm enclosing ticket money with this letter.

Come just as soon as you can. We'll have you enrolled in school by the next semester.

Love,
Bob

Well! If that wasn't Big Moose come down from the mountain! If Zora were a white woman, she probably would have swooned.

School meant more than education; school meant friends. The friends she'd known growing up in Eatonville had gone, grown, got married, or the really lucky ones were in school. A fickle jealous shadow of sadness and loneliness passed over her watching other young people learn and play.

So imagine how she felt when it turned out the whole thing was just a trap! Zora went to live with Bob and his wife, worked as a maid in the house, and the semester came and went, while Bob said, "be patient Zora, next semester after this. Time's not good right now." So she worked as a maid, and another semester came and went, and Bob said, "be patient Zora. Now's not good. We'll get you in school yet." He gave her that silly grin, and tried to be big about it, but it was just a trap. She was working for nothing.

Zora shivered again, because that's what happens when someone walks over your grave, even if it's your own self. Remembering the life she lived at Bob's was treading the grave of a dead woman.

And so, education comes all kinds of ways. No, Bob never did send Zora to school. What else was there to do then, but up and run away with theater folk?

It all happened when she met Molly, an actress and singer with lovely dove skin and a cloud of blonde hair. Molly was part of a traveling Gilbert and Sullivan Theater troupe. They were passing through town, and Molly was looking for a maid. Zora had been working for her just a couple weeks, when Molly sat her down after a show.

"You'll be coming with us, won't you Zora?" Molly asked her, casual as a spring day.

"I'd already figured that for understood."

"Good. We leave tomorrow."

"Where to?"

"Back up north."

So not on a train after all, but on an enchanting rolling coach, Zora finally went Harriet Tubman way up north with the Gilbert and Sullivan group as they stopped town to town to perform the *HMS Pinafore*. Zora laughed to hear the songs they sang, like

Bad language or abuse,
I never never use.
Whatever the emergency;
Though 'Bother it' I may
Occasionally say,
I never use a big, big D

What, never?
No, never!
What, never?
Well, hardly ever!

And driving along the blooming spring roads in the ascending south, Zora countered their songs with songs she knew from back at the jooks, those suited for polite company only of course, like,

Oh you like my peaches
But you don't like me.
Don't you like my peaches
Don't you shake my tree.
Well you may go, but this will bring you back:
Hoodoo
Hoodoo
Hoodoo

Leaving the south at last! Zora let the days and nights disappear watching the south vanish behind her. Tony, one of the actors was a Harvard fella, and he had all kinds of books. He sure was surprised when Zora showed interest in what he had up on his little makeshift shelf, but he got wise to it. They'd talk about them after she read them, and he'd give her suggestions based on what she said she liked and didn't like. If she couldn't get an education the regular way, she'd get it on her own terms, the world be damned, brother and fathers and neighbors and all.

One morning they were in a town in Maryland, colonial old Annapolis, like Zora had read about in books. It looked just like it did in pictures, and the way she imagined it would look, like straight out of George Washington days. Molly suggested they all have breakfast together. Everyone went quiet, and looked around without knowing what to say. Finally Tony spoke up.

"This is still the south, Molly."

"Aw, if they won't serve us, we'll just march right back out," said Zora. "I'm not concerned. Let's do it."

"Where should we go?"

They ended up at a small diner next to a large red Northern looking church. When they walked in everyone in the joint stared. A couple people looked over at the waiters and staff to see if there'd be trouble.

Zora lit a Pall Mall. "Say, let's grab a table."

No one said a word. No one moved a beat. The whole room went tense with history for one split second, and then Molly pushed on forward and seated herself in a booth. The rest followed in a clutter. But that was all for show, anyhow. The whole thing was, sure. Molly leaned in, huddled the team: "Let's leave the south with a little show, something to remember us by. Whaddya say?"

"Well, the south sure is beautiful," Tony, leaning back loud in the booth, "but it's oppressive as an August afternoon in Georgia. Fella can't even say God doesn't exist down here."

A few people glanced over. The whole restaurant was buzzing with flies and titter.

"You got that wrong," Zora corrected him. "It's just we got us a way of saying things is all. I know it's a lot of runaway Negroes up north, spent they lives apin down the road away from the south, and I don't necessarily blame them. Running the same game myself as a matter of fact, for a spell. But make no mistake: there's plenty of undertalking and overtalking and talking at de gate down south, too. That's just it. You talk at the gate."

"What's talking at the gate?"

"It's talking at the wall, talking at the stairs, talking at the pillow. It's talking at the stars; it's talking at the window; it's an old Negro proverb about slavery days. You don't give a piece of your mind to massa, you give it to de gate."

"That's another thing," said Molly. "The south makes me think too much of slavery. It just drips from everywhere here. Ick!"

"The north should remind you of slavery too," said Tony. "When you consider the slums and the condition of the proletariat, Negro and white alike."

"Tony's a Marxist," said Amy, a sarcastic girl with really small green eyes, but a wide skinny mouth that bloomed into brilliant soft peach cheeks, curtained by a flapper haircut. She rolled her eyes.

"And Amy's an Anarchist."

"Well!" Amy lighting a cigarette, batting her eyelashes dramatically. "Freedom frightens the weaker minds."

"Marxism is the only political philosophy that actually confronts the problem of human freedom."

"So what's a Marxist do?" asked Zora.

"Oh well." Tony smiled bashfully, and lit a cigarette. A swirling cocoon of smoke swaddled the booth. "Lots of things. Personally, I haven't had an opportunity to join-,"

"What he means is he means nothing," said Amy, and Tony flushed deep red like a Russian flag.

"It's an Anarchist who does nothing!"

"Or an actress, thank God, though I still maintain His non-existence," said Molly.

"Well if you're going to blaspheme the good Lord, Molly," Zora smiling slyly, "you might as well lay the dozens on Him, and really put your foot up and get to specifyin'. Lay down the particulars, and tell Him how you really feel. Tell Him you think He's nothing but a garrulous, battle-hammed old jig, beating up His gums in a book full of bad lies and loud talk; Negro so inky dink black ain't no one even seen him, so black He's invisible, and only handkerchief-head Negroes get down on they knees and pray to Him like massa, though the occasional ofay goes through the motions to keep the Negroes convinced. When I die, don't take the pillow from under my head, I'd rather lay there a-suffering than spend one more minute than I have to in the afterlife with Him and His. Send me on down to Scratch."

Zora had the table's attention now, and the restaurant's.

"I've never heard anything quite like that before," said Tony. "Can you write that down?"

"What? A few words for Sweet Jesus? Sure. Hand me a pen and pad."

Pen and pad in hand, Zora went right to work. First she sketched up a picture of an old man with a long beard sitting Indian-style. The she started specifyin' right underneath, like she'd done out loud. When she was finished, she passed it over to Tony.

Tony couldn't stop laughing, but he was studying it too, while everyone else leaned in for a look. "So these compounds," he asked. "Do you just improvise them? Or is there a standard lexicon people use?"

"It's mostly improvised, but folks got their old stand-bys, of course." Zora lit a Pall Mall. "Go on, give it a shot."

"I'm gonna do Amy," he flipped the page.

"In your dreams," Amy said.

Tony ignored this slight and went right to work drawing a caricature of her. Once he finished he looked over at Amy, then at Zora.

"Well, go on, Tony," said Zora. "Just speak your mind and put it all out there."

They were having such a good time, they didn't even notice the red-faced manager storming his way up to the booth.

II

Traveling north with Gilbert and Sullivan had the wonderful new spirit of adventure novels; all major life changes do when you're young. They got as far as Boston, a colonial town like Annapolis, only this town was a big old city. Molly showed Zora all the winding labyrinth streets downtown and around regal Faneuil Hall. They walked along the Charles River and let the clear wind wrap around their coats, crossed over to Cambridge, and strolled the Harvard quad together, a white woman and a black woman, and no one said a word. They got lots of funny looks, though.

"We'll have to stay at my place in Southie," said Molly. "It's just for two weeks, and we'll go back on the road again."

"Sounds just fine to me."

"My family's a little crazy, just so you know," said Molly. "You know. So you're warned and all."

"How crazy?" Zora arched an eyebrow. She knew enough to know crazy white folk could be bad news.

"They're harmless," Molly reading her face. "It's not that. Just that, well, we're a big old Irish family, and the Irish are crazy."

"Heck, folks say that about Negroes."

Houses have faces, and every face betrays a personality. Molly lived in an old shotgun house in Dorchester, faded out against a row of others just like it, except they were all a little brighter. The poor peeling face was just begging for a fresh mask. Zora wondered about this crazy Irish family. Sometimes Molly would receive long letters from Post Offices while they were out on the road, and these were always from Molly's mum. Molly would read them over sullen a few times, fold them up carefully, lovingly almost, and tear them into tiny squares, which she let flutter over the side of the coach. Then she would go off by herself to cry for a while. The way Molly's face looked as she read those letters: that's what the house looked like. Beautiful Molly.

On the other hand, Molly had two older brothers, and they weren't much to look at, let's be blunt, not even handsome. Johnnie, the oldest, looked like a broke-down old townhouse from the Jackson Administration, a crockery of crooked teeth and all. The younger, Charlie was a lumpy man like an old sofa with the stuffing coming out. Their mum was frail and thin, unsteady on her feet so she was always sitting or reclining. The whole family smoked constantly, and the front and back doors were always open or opening, so drafts of smoke haunted the hallway and rooms like ghostly swifts. Charlie was a firefighter and had a family of his own. Johnnie didn't seem good for much at all but telling stories, but he was a world-class storyteller when it came down to it, and Zora had grown up with the best of them. He would tell her old Irish fables, like the story of the Prince of the Lonesome Isle and the well of fire. How the Prince had gone in search of this well, whose healing waters were guarded by a Queen in the palace of Tubber Tintye. None had achieved this feat before, but the Queen of Erin would die if she did not get three bottles of this firewater. So off the prince went, across a river of fire and through poisonous forests, and into the palace. All through the palace were lions and tigers and bears, and the Prince passed them by with no fear. Up he went into a hallway, and entered a chamber. There he saw the most beautiful woman in the world. But he was not to be distracted. On he went to the next chamber, where he saw a woman even more beautiful than the last. And so on through twelve chambers, until he came to the thirteenth. When he walked in he saw a sight no mortal had ever lived to see before.

"What? What'd he see?"

"You want me to tell you? Because what he saw, well, he stayed a good six days and six nights there, forgetting all about his quest."

They traded tall tales back and forth, trying to outdo each other in outrageousness. They traded folk tales and superstitions and spells. Zora learned all about Druid spells and Celtic mythology, and she told Johnnie all about Hoodoo and Conjure and the loas. Molly's mum didn't like to see them together, and neither did Molly for that matter.

"He's wonderful, I love Johnnie of course." Molly would say. "He is my brother after all. But you just have to watch out for him sometimes, is all."

Well! Another thing they had in common. How many times had she heard that about herself?

"I'll be sure to keep that in mind," Zora'd reply, and go right on off to see what Johnnie had to say about the matter.

"Ay, they like to hang me with a bad reputation," Johnnie said. He looked pensive, his large jaw sliding to one side. All of a sudden he brightened. "Well, what's with the long face?" he asked himself. "I've got a story for you Zora. Let's walk a ways and talk."

Spring in Boston is in no way like spring in Eatonville. Everything felt sharp and clear and bright, like the smell of freshly chopped cedar. None of the sweet languorous drowsiness of the earth. Zora and Johnnie walked out of the garden, and down the homely road of rowhouses. They talked and laughed and exchanged stories. Zora felt like she'd come into her own a little bit, in her own way, in the telling of them, what with traveling and talking with the Gilbert and Sullivaners, so she'd perfected her storytelling to a precise pitch. She skipped gaily along with Johnnie acting out her stories like a dizzy child. She got Johnnie into it too, so he was a-lumbering on down the road miming his stories, like – "a man takes a drink, looks over at the fella next to him; takes another long drink, and looks at the fella again, this time longer. Then he goes and drinks again, this time real long, draining the glass. He puts it down on the bar, and turns to look at the fella again. This time the fella looks back."

"Oooh. What happened then?"

The sun went down dusky orange on a golden afternoon. Zora and Johnnie walked up the noisy Dorchester street slowly for two people racing the setting of the sun. They picked dandelions as they went, blowing dandelion parachutes and making wishes along the way like a couple superstitious kids. Occasionally Johnnie would pick a yellow dandelion and pocket it.

"What you doing that for?"

"I'm pocketing sunshine."

Yellow dandelions sprouted from Zora's panties in the morning sun. They were hanging from the clothesline outside the window when Zora sleepily went to make her morning coffee. She shrieked, and ran half naked to a roaring applause. Men were standing around the front yard laughing and nudging and pointing at her panties on the clothesline with the flowers tucked around them like halos. Zora eeped and dashed back inside to more laughter and applause.

"What – what – what?" she sputtered.

Johnnie lumbered by her and poured himself a large mug of coffee. "Morning Zora."

Molly peeked around the corner to see what all the commotion was about, followed by Mum a moment later.

"So what's with all the fuss?" Molly dabbed her eyes and pouted.

"My panties -," Zora panted, and seeing what Zora was gesturing at out the open door, Molly burst into laughter like a song.

"Oh my!"

Even Mum was laughing.

"Let me go clear this all up," Johnnie cleared his throat, gulped down some coffee and lit a cigarette. He grinned and strode strutting out the door, right out into the front yard, where he accepted his cheering laughter with a wave and a flourish. Then, cigarette dangling from his mouth, he turned Zora's panties about, rotating them slowly, one by one, and plucked the dandelions from them.

Everyone inside and outside the house laughed and laughed and laughed themselves hoarse, except for Zora who stood mortified, until the laughing sickness caught her too. They laughed about it all morning over coffee and breakfast, and after breakfast Zora and Johnnie walked off again to watch the tulips bloom in spring.

"Why'd you play that prank on me Johnnie?"

"Maybe I just like to get your attention." Johnnie grinned, looked straight ahead, chin up.

"Oh, you did that all reet."

They walked a ways and spent all day in their peculiar haze of sunlight, telling tall tales, just like they'd done the day before.

"I was a rich man once," said Johnnie. They were sitting on a lawn of tulips, smoking cigarettes.

"Oh yeah?" Zora looked him up and down. "What happened?"

"I came upon hard times, but I've been blessed by God, so that didn't bother me. This was back in Dublin, where I was known as a poet and pucker. I'd been a pucker since birth, I pucked out my own Da' the day he ducked out on Mum. I became a poet shortly after. I was six then. I would go to the taverns in me teens and puck and declaim. I'd knock a fellow out, and recite something righteous once I'd whooped him. It turned into a sport, actually. They still play it in Dublin pubs to this day; pucketry, it's called. And for the first six years, I was unbeatable. But that was before Kelly Frazier. Kelly Frazier changed the way they play the game."

"Who's Kelly Frazier. What did she do?"

"He." Johnnie lit a cigarette. "What did *he* do. It'll cost you two dollars to hear it."

"Oh, go on."

"I'm serious. Two dollars. Otherwise, balls to ya."

"Fine. Two dollars. When we get back to the house."

"Promise?"

"Yeah, of course. Go on. Tell it. This better be good. I'll be livid if it's not two dollars worth of good. And that's a whole lotta good."

"Well," said Johnnie, and he took her hand, inched in close to her so she could smell him warm and heavy, his cologne, tobacco, tall blue tulips, all tall tales all morning long.

Back at the house the afternoon weaseled into evening. Zora couldn't believe it, but Johnnie was serious about the two dollars. As soon as they got back he asked for it, and then she didn't see him again for a couple hours. When she asked Molly about it, Molly went pale, and ran from the room. Zora stood in the middle of Molly's room befuddled, wondering what was afoot. Following Molly out the door, she ended up in Mum's room, where Mum was crying, and Molly was crying, and then Molly turned and ran out the front door, saying she'd be right back with Charlie.

"What's – What did I do?" Zora stuttered.

Mum just shook her sad old head slow and said, "Oh, Zora. You shouldn't have given him that money."

The hours passed, and no sign of Johnnie. Zora went to bed with her head swimming with worries. She couldn't sleep so she tried to read herself to sleep, even read a copy of *The Crisis* and everything, but she couldn't keep her thoughts still. She smoked Pall Malls and stared out the window at the stars until their blinking hypnotic spell finally made her drowsy, and she vanished.

Somewhere where the night had no walls, and darkness stretched back and forth and back again, a crash and a scream startled Zora awake. She sat upright in bed, propped on an elbow, her eyes blinking in the black like the stars. Outside her door she heard the pounding of feet on the stairs and loud male and female voices hollering over each other. She hesitated a moment, looking blank in the direction of the night lamp. She strained to listen, but couldn't hear anything distinct. A door slammed – shouting – the slamming door.

Zora rolled back the covers and lowered her legs over the side of the bed. She crept up to the door, listened. She leaned into it, listening to the vibrations of yelling through the wood. Then she backed off, whispered herself into some clothes, and out of her room, all without turning on the lights.

Down the stairs light harried the narrow passageway, erupting garish around the stairwell wall. Zora hurried down and around the steps, finding herself in Mum's room, where Molly was tending to her. There was a nasty gash on Mum's shoulder, and the flesh was rich with blood.

"What happened?" all Zora could mumble and repeat.

A moment later Charlie came through the door lugging Johnnie with him. Johnnie was trussed up like a Thanksgiving turkey, and his skin was blood red, just like the veins bursting out of his wild stretched eyes, which bobbed lazy in the sockets with likker.

"Balls to Mum, and to you too, ya cunt!" Johnnie writhed in the ropes binding him. "Give me my money!"

"He gets this way," Charlie, helplessly, "Damn it, Zora. You should have asked someone first before you gave him anything." And for a moment Charlie stood there, a grown man, and blubbered like a baby. Then he shrugged it off. "It's no fault of yours. He's no good, Zora. He never has been. He's ruined all our lives. He should be locked up, but Mum won't have it. It's no fault of yours. He'll use anyone to get his way. Next time it will be someone else."

Zora walked over to Johnnie and looked him right in the eyes – those glassy watery things had none of the warm humor Zora had come to exult in. "What happened Johnnie?"

"The fucking cunt is sitting on a goldmine of useless shit," Johnnie spat on the floor.

"What shit?"

"Art, you stupid fucking nigger."

Zora froze. She felt Charlie try to guide her away, but she shook him off violently. "You know better than to talk to me like that, Johnnie."

"Don't tell me what I know, you idiot fucking nigger." He glared at her stupidly a moment, then his eyes glazed over completely, and went for a swim. He threw his head back and roared a horrible groan like Satan screaming from the depths of Hell, Paradise Lost.

Our lives are too thin not to make meaning out of those banalities that wound us. Zora cried up a whole rainy season. She cried all the next couple days, and she and Molly both cried when they left to go back on the road; they kept up their weeping session all the way back south to meet up with the other Gilbert and Sullivaners in New York.

Johnnie had a problem with his likker, Molly told her. He'd been in jail for armed robbery cuz of it and everything. But Mum loved him best of them all, and couldn't bear to see him locked up. She'd visited him all the time, and eventually arranged for an early release with the Mayor; but that doomed the rest of the family. You see, they say love saves you, but time and again you find love really just destroys people.

III

God bless Molly. She still believed love could save her despite everything. She had a fella in Baltimore, and he proposed to her almost as soon as they got to town.

"Well, Zora. I thought about that old house in Dorchester, and Johnnie and Charlie and Mum, and how I'm getting no younger. I didn't even hesitate. I told him yes yes yes, right then and there."

"You still gonna act?"

"There's younger, cuter girls at every show nowadays. It's a young girl's racket, this acting business. I'm marrying off and leaving it to them. You should do the same."

Well Zora respectfully disagreed. She'd lost sight of her quest, let her education slip. So she shaved ten years off her age, and enrolled in Morgan High School.

She dazzled her teachers during the day and worked as a waitress at night.

In dizzy blurry years of learning, she devoured books. You can't hope for anything in this world without the help of other people who respect how you help yourself. When she heard Pop was dead she felt nothing at all. His car got stuck on a railroad track in Memphis. It was a fitting end. He never did figure out how to get unstuck in life once her mother passed.

Now, Zora, on the other hand, she was going places.

With some help from her teachers and with the money she'd saved, she enrolled in Morgan College, and just two years later she met Mae Miller, who was going to Howard.

Mae and Zora were the best of friends, and right from the get.

"Say, Zora. Why aren't you up at Howard with us? You're Howard material if anyone is."

"I guess I'll give it a shot," Zora said with a sheepishly sly smile.

Well and naturally, she was accepted with enthusiasm.

She moved to Washington and found work right away. She stayed with the parents of the girl from Morgan who introduced her to Mae. They quite conveniently had a house by Cleveland Park, and it was a quick trip to and from campus. She took classes to make up missing credits, and by the fall, with the trees in Cleveland Park lighting the auburn sky a melodious mauve, Zora was fully enrolled at Howard.

On weekends she'd go discuss literature and love and stuff with Mae. They would walk down to the diner on the corner, drink coffee and talk up the books they'd been assigned for class. One afternoon Mae brought a magazine along.

"It's Howard's Magazine," Mae's lovely wide brown eyes lit up like saucers in the sun, splashed with coffee. "*The Stylus*. They're holding a writing competition. The best writers get to join the staff. We should try for it, Zora. I've been reading through it, and I think we can write as well as most of what they got here."

Mae had a way of talking Zora into these things. She'd talked her into transferring from Morgan to Howard in the first place, and now here she was reading Zora's mind again, convincing her to be a writer.

"Let's do it," said Zora. "I don't see what we've got to lose."

After that they met almost every day for coffee and conversation. They would show each other what they were working on and discuss ideas, exchange criticism. Mae was writing a play about a couple Englishmen in Africa.

"I want it to be almost a tragedy of errors," said Mae, "You know, like a Greek tragedy. Where all the players are connected, and they don't even realize it."

"Have you been to Africa?" Zora asked a little too earnestly, and Mae's brown cheeks flushed a royal purple blush.

"I've heard a lot about it."

"Aw, you've heard a lot about everywhere."

Mae rubbed her frizzled hair, looked around. "Yeah. Say, when we graduate, you and me, Zora. We gotta travel for real. See the world and then we can really write about it."

Mae's father was a dean at Howard, so Mae knew important people like Du Bois, and Georgia Douglas Johnson. She knew James Weldon Johnson; she'd even met Booker T. Washington when she was little.

"What about you? How's your short story coming along?"

"Oh, it's coming along, okay. Like a freight train coming along the bend, barreling along, but it's got no direction. Been trying to write about Eatonville, but nothing happens but folks set and talk the day down. Maybe

I should do like you and write a play."

"But then it'll be like we're competing." Mae frowned into her coffee.

"Well I'm just like my freight train of a story, casting some light around in the dark. I'm not really gonna write a play." She laughed at Mae pouting. "What I really mean is my story just needs more action. I think maybe there needs to be some travel in it, like yours has, just for the adventure of it. I don't know. Maybe I'll write in a couple characters like us, who are just itching to get out and see the world."

Mae turned her play into Black Medea, and Zora wrote a story about a man with a wandering spell upon him. They spent the weeks of winter vacation writing, meeting every afternoon in the warm café, while outside the streets of Washington went gray and cold. They would drink coffee and then switch to tea. They ate pastries and discussed literature. They wrote poetry. Poetry was awkward; too sentimental and repressed really, to get right at it. If you got something to say, why, just come on out and say it how you mean it.

"You're just not trying hard enough," Mae shrugged. "Come on, you like poetry. Whose poetry do you like? James Weldon Johnson? Vachel Lindsay? Claude McKay?"

Zora had been reading a lot of Claude Mckay lately. In Washington wandering from street to street, she debated poetics with herself, and whispered his sonnets. She knew half of *Harlem Shadows* by heart, and she decided she would take the poetry of the people she grew up with and mix it with the languorous lyricism of southern prose, the way Mckay dipped in and out of West Indian dialect and high Victorian verse. Then she'd write it around a parable about a man who just can't seem to get unstuck.

When philosophy professor Alain Locke read her and Mae's submissions, he arranged a meeting with them in his office. Dr. Locke already knew Mae and her family, but he didn't know Zora.

"How do you find Howard, Miss Hurston?" he asked after they were settled.

"Please, Zora."

"Very well. Zora."

A ladder of blushing sunlight crept across the desk. Dr. Locke leaned back in his chair, and clasped his fingers. He smiled a tight, thin-lipped smile.

"I couldn't be happier to be here," Zora said.

"And it seems you have a way with words."

"Well, I grew up listening to folks tell stories. That's all. I guess it's just natural with me."

"I can see that. I liked the story you submitted quite a bit. It has flaws.

It's pacing is awkward, and the transitions – well, they need a lot of work, but-,"

Zora flushed. She pulled up, looked sidelong at Mae, then back at Dr. Locke. "Well, I just wrote it the way folks tell the stories."

"Of course." Locke pressed his fingers down, and lowered his head like he was thinking very hard on something. Mae shot Zora a funny glance, like yeah, meet Dr. Locke, and Zora almost laughed outright.

"What do you like to read?" Dr. Locke lifted his head.

"Anything but poetry," Mae tittered a repressed laugh.

Zora giggled back, "Aw, don't listen to her."

Locke looked between the two young women, puzzled.

"I read everything," Zora went on. "And don't let her tell you I don't. I love poetry. Take for example, Milton's *Paradise Lost*. That's probably one of my favorite books of all time."

"*Paradise Lost!*" Locke brightened. "Yes."

"Now there's a book every Negro needs to read."

The tips of Locke's fingers pranced against each other. "I suppose that's so. I suppose that's so. A wonderful essay could be written about how the book can act as a symbol for the race problem."

"Maybe I'll write it."

Locke's smile broadened. "I like you Zora. There's a literary society we hold every Saturday night over on S Street, at Georgia Douglas Johnson's apartment. I'd really like the two of you to come this Saturday."

Zora had heard mention of literary societies in the dicty Negro enclaves of Washington, but she'd never actually been to one. Going to see one of those would be something. She was sure to meet all sorts of interesting and important people there too. "We wouldn't miss it for the world, would we Mae?"

"Of course not. We'll be there." The two girls exchanged glances and giggled again.

"All right. Enough silliness. I'm very proud of you both. I'm really quite impressed with the quality of your work. I look forward to seeing you at the next *Stylus* meeting, and again on Saturday night. I think you'll like Mrs. Johnson's salon quite a bit. It's a very dialectic experience. And I look forward to reading more from you both."

Eatonville was a world of fables, and residents who turned their lives into a tapestry of art and history. So it was just natural when Zora turned her talents toward writing, the stories from her childhood town would serve her fiction. Only she wondered how Washington society would take them.

She decided to shock everyone with a story about two friends, Dave Carter and Jim Weston who shoot at the same turkey. They both claim the shot, and have a falling out over it. The falling out leads to Jim Weston whopping Dave Carter over the head with the hind-bone of the meanest old mule in town history. Dave takes Jim to court, and the case is decided in church with the Baptists and the Methodists arguing the matter to satisfaction. She wrote it all at once, out loud, while Mae typed furiously after her.

Dr. Locke was not quite as impressed with this sophomore effort.

"It needs work," he said the next Saturday night, setting the manuscript down. "The transitions, again the transitions aren't working. And when the transitions don't work, the humor doesn't work. You also need to work on the dynamic between Dave Carter and Jim Weston. They don't have one right now, and so the reader's interest in the dramatic action flags." Dr. Locke took a sip of his coffee; Zora took a measured sip of her tea. She smiled from behind her cup, glancing around the room to see if the general consensus was with Dr. Locke.

"Anything worth keeping in?"

Locke frowned. "As it is, I'm afraid I don't see..."

So this was the fabled Saturday night with the Saturday Nighters, Georgia Douglas Johnson's literary salon. Georgia lived in a large Washington townhouse in Northwest, right on S Street, an artsy frilly apartment, but a home, too, where Georgia had raised two boys. The Saturday Nighters were sitting in a small den, the room designated for their meetings. Locke was looking around the room more confidently than Zora, looking to find his sentiments confirmed in the expressions of the others present. He partially raised his right hand to his lapel, then dropped it to his lap again.

"I don't understand its purpose," he said finally. "Or rather – I do. I do understand that you're trying to tell an old Eatonville story. But why *this* story? The writing doesn't feel urgent."

"Oh." Zora slowly lowered the cup.

"Well, nonsense! It was a scream. You're over intellectualizing it, Dr. Locke. You and your transitions. Zora builds beautiful tapestries of life."

Mae was a sweetheart. Zora glanced at her, and Mae caught her glance with a sidelong grin.

"No, Dr. Locke's right. Something isn't quite coming together. Something's missing from it," said Georgia, leaning toward the manuscript on the table. She picked it up, and Zora reclined, lifting the teacup to her lips again. Georgia was always so reasonable. If she said it needed work, it probably did.

"But I like it more than Dr. Locke does," she hastened to add. "I think it's worth keeping. Maybe play with it some. Improvise on the story and make it more your own. That's what's missing." Georgia brightened like she lit on something suddenly. "That's what works about your best short stories."

"It's why Dr. Locke says the writing doesn't feel urgent," said a dapper, pale young man. To look at him you'd think at first he was white, and then you'd think Negro, then white, then Negro, and then you'd just be flabbergasted trying to figure it out; but then there were a lot of Mulattos like that. No, there was something different, other-worldly about Jean Toomer. Not black, not white, not Mulatto, not Spanish, not Arab, not of this planet, when you get right down to it, but he wrote dense, difficult, beautiful, image soaked poetry that somehow managed to sound like the blues.

"Well, it's written just how folks tell it."

"That may well be. But verisimilitude does not verse make," said Locke.

"I'd suggest changing the ending," a husky, earnest young man, Waldo Frank, a novelist and self-proclaimed polemicist, suggested. Waldo was a handsome man in the English 19th Century style; a dapper suit, finely combed mustache, parted hair and all. He also had the distinction of being the only white man in the room. "The whole thing about Judges 15:16, Samson slaying a thousand Philistines with the jawbone of an ass, well is…"

Everyone started to giggle, like a little epidemic passed through the window. Even Waldo caught it and coughed a chuckle.

"See! It was funny! Admit it!" Zora, triumphant.

"But it wasn't quite an ending – or not a particularly strong one," Waldo countered.

Zora lit a Pall Mall, looked around the room a moment, supplicating, then sank back defeated. "Well, I'll see what can be done with it." She shot Dr. Locke a meaning look. "If anything."

"Oh, it's worth saving, all right," this, emphatically stated by Lewis Alexander, a young poet from Washington high Negro society, and a fellow student at Howard. "I've experimented with folk literature in my own writing, but it didn't work with me. I've seen other poets try it too, but it doesn't work with them either. No – no – Zora's the real deal with this stuff. This story may need some work, but all the stories she's given us so far have been keepers. No doubt about it."

Zora beamed. "So what's to be done with it?"

Lewis folded his long brown fingers into each other like lines of poetry. "You're being true to the story, but I don't think you're being true to the spirit of the story."

"All of your stories have the spirit of the theater," observed Waldo.

"That's true," Mae said.

Zora considered the thing as a play. "No – I see what you mean, Waldo, but not this one. This one's a teller. Like something to be read aloud, not so much acted out. There are others better for that."

"I agree," said Angelina Grimké, a lovely, rich brown poetess and playwright. She looked at Zora. "There's not enough dramatic action and tension to sustain a play."

"Well, that all comes down to how it ends again," said Waldo. "I think the problem's not with the form, it's with the way it all comes together, or rather fails to do so."

One of those eerie communal spaces of silence slumped through the room.

"Well, Gwen, Frank, you two haven't said much. What do you think?"

Gwendolyn Bennett was a painter and poetess, younger than Angelina, and not from quite as cultured a background, but Zora found her poetry the better for it. Frank Horne was a young poet, athlete and optometrist, who to all appearances looked white and not black at all. But he wrote fierce, racially charged poetry that could make Zora's skin prickle in goosebumps.

"I like this discussion," Gwendolyn said. "Because I think the question of form's an especially urgent one for the Negro artist. I don't have an answer. I think it will come to you. The debate itself convinces me you shouldn't give up on it."

"I say turn it into a poem!" Frank declared decisively, and everybody laughed.

IV

That wandering story she wrote got to some wandering of its own. It wandered its way on up to New York through *The Stylus,* and into the hands of Charles S. Johnson, who was busy orchestrating a Negro Arts Movement. Well that changed everything. From there things just went along with their own momentum, like a train soaring through the Adirondacks. Zora moved to New York, got a job with the famous novelist Fannie Hurst, enrolled in Barnard College, and was taken under the wing of Dr. Franz Boas, the world's leading Anthropologist, all just like that.

The good life had softened her up more than she let on. When Boas suggested fieldwork, she felt the familiar tingle of wanderlust, and agreed to it right away. She would go out, collect folklore from Florida, and in the meantime interview Kudjo Lewis, the last living man who'd come over on the slave ships, and come back with a full report.

Well life is full of trial and error, and a little bit of trickery. Turn the trickery into poetry, and disarm disaster. What Zora couldn't tell the folks back in Eatonville was still eating away at her. What she couldn't tell anyone. How being an anthropologist is like making a deal at the crossroads dumb to the fact.

Honestly, she was still haunted by the day

an afternoon sun reached down two long roads intersecting four directions. Zora stepped out of *Sassy Susie* in a dizzy map of sweat. She reached in the car and pulled out her notebook. The thought of writing anything in it was agony. She looked again down the four long roads and started to cry. She, Zora Neale Herself! She didn't have a thing in her to say.

The whole expedition had been much harder than anticipated. When she was driving into Eatonville she was sure she'd just go on over to Joe Clarke's porch and get stories upon stories and they'd even let her in on Hoodoo too, you know? But no one seemed to say much.

"You got to go down to Loughman's for that kind of spooky superstitious parlay. Or better yet, clean out to New Orleans," Joe Clarke told her. "We good God-fearing people here in Eatonville. You know that, Zora."

"But I've heard folks tell all these stories."

"Oh those is just stories, and they mostly just parables for the gospels, matter of fact."

"So where's Loughman's camp?"

"It's kinda rough out there, and you really ought not go alone, Zora."

"I'll be all right, I reckon."

"Well, you know the song we sometimes sing, *Polk County Blues,* where the water tastes like cherry wine? You got to decipher the code in those lyrics if you want to find Loughman's camp. But I don't like the idea of you going, so I won't say no more."

She'd even tried to talk to Kudjo Lewis, but Kudjo was harder to comprehend than Big Nigger Pop peeping through his likker. The old African slave may as well have been speaking Swahili for all she could tell, and now she had to go back to Barnard with nothing to show for all her hard fieldwork down south. After everything she'd been through, the chances she'd managed to conjure up somehow, to blow it all out here in the field, and all alone. She kept on crying. She should write a story about what a failure she was, only it would be too depressing, and even she wouldn't want to read it. That made her laugh.

Zora got back in *Sassy Susie* and started driving. A good hour or so passed before she realized she didn't know where she was. The road was thinning and everything looked unfamiliar. She hadn't seen another car in ages. She turned off onto a tiny unmarked road, looking for the nearest town.

She found one, but it wasn't much. There was a travel lodge at least, and an old motel too. That was about it. She went to the travel lodge and asked a sullen looking kid behind the counter where she was, and if they were far from Orlando.

"Maps is right over there," he shrugged.

Zora went to inspect the rack of maps and brochures. She ran her fingers across the literature, looking at the county names, when her finger hit a brochure for the Mobile Historical Society. Something in it called to her. She opened it and started reading. The first thing she saw was Kazoola – Kudjo Lewis' African name. *Historical Sketches of the South.* The title of a book. She read on. And possibly a way out of her present dilemma. Not that she would ever think of passing someone else's work off as her own.

Notational research.

V

Research is an exercise in self-revision. Each new discovery slightly alters your methodology, and suddenly you've found you've changed your approach to how you satisfy your own curiosity. The second time Zora drove into Eatonville, this time in Mrs. Mason's Chevrolet, she didn't even bother talk about anthropology.

"Where you get that shiny new Chevrolet at, Zora?"

"Oh, you know. Trial and error and a little bit of trickery."

Well, every anthropologist worth her salt is a crack cryptologist, too. Zora spent the afternoons in Eatonville listening to folks tell and retell the same old stories and sing the same old songs, until the *Polk County Blues* yielded its mysteries and unfolded into a landscape.

She arrived in Loughman's on a rainy late January afternoon. A dull pool of light lolled along the clouds. Mud splashed up over the wheels of the brand new Chevy and the headlights flickered unsteady through a bend of trees like a beacon.

Zora stopped the car when she got to the town square. She rolled down the window and looked out. The faces of the houses looked back a little beat down, but merry. This would do just fine. Striding up the road in the rain, a big black woman looking like mayor of the town, hippily approached the vehicle like she was looking for a showdown. Zora fumbled on her straw hat and stepped out into the rain.

"I'm Big Sweet," the woman coming up right to Zora, face to face, to greet her. "Who's you, and what's your business?"

"Zora. Zora Hurston from Eatonville. I'm looking for a room a while." Zora looked right into Sweet's wide, complicated, weary lined eyes square on. Sweet studied her a while.

"All right then. G'wan down that road, and you'll see a house at the end of it, light blue. That's Mrs. Allen's boarding house. Tell her you need a room and Big Sweet sent you."

Zora smiled. "Thanks. I'll do that."

Zora drove down the road watching the faces of the houses for the one where she'd be staying. She didn't even need Sweet's directions. She was sure she'd know it to see it. In the rain, the faces all seemed to be streaked with tears and sweat, repositories of memories, and memories are answers.

Memories are answers, because they're the conversations the soul has with itself. On Joe Clarke's front porch, the men from Eatonville liked to congregate in the long hot afternoon with gin and lies. The lies come from memories of lies heard before, and the memories of the man telling them, and the gin gets to get its say, too. By telling stories, you learned the story of your own life and the lies folks tell tell true stories all on their own. The storytellers down at Loughman's camp told ribald tales to match Rabelais, in language studied to startle.

"A woman ain't fit to lissen to them cussin all day," Big Sweet once muttered, walking past the men in Loughman's as they sat on benches around the town square of an early evening, just before the jooks. Now, Big Sweet was never known to withhold a spicy word or two of her own, truth of the fact she pretty much used them on the regular, so folks just laughed to hear it, saying, "Big Sweet, g'wan putting on high and mighty airs for the new girl. Look at you."

All the same, folks didn't seem to say much whenever Zora was around. They were cooling things down for her, sure, but she didn't know why. She'd hear an edge in the work songs they sang that wasn't there when she heard them tell tales, and you can tell what type of storyteller a fella is by the songs he sings.

Uncle Bud got a wife,
Big and fat-
She got a cunt like a Stetson hat!
Uncle Bud,
Uncle Bud.

And when Zora came around, their faces would tense warmly, and they'd smile and exchange glances, and that's when all the fun seemed to deflate from their eyes as well as their lies, so that Zora felt like she was bringing everyone down every time she came around.

One night out at the jook, Zora had been dancing hard, and stumbled out into the crisp winter night air for a Pall Mall. A couple cats standing by got quiet, and Zora knew they'd been laying down some real talk.

"Say, what's the angle," said Zora. "You won't talk rough with a woman around? Seen you do it enough around Big Sweet."

"Aw, Zora, we wasn't saying nothing," said one of the men, and having said that much, threw down his cigarette and sauntered back to the door. In a blast of call and response, he swung it open, and let it shut right behind him.

"What's with him?"

The night was cool; a humid breeze wandered down from the trees up the hill, and when Zora lifted her cigarette to her lips, the remaining fellow leaned in, cupped his hands, struck a match and lit it for her.

"You know you can't just drop in on black folk, Zora." He tossed down his cigarette, screwed up his face, and brushed right past her. For a moment Zora was sure he was headed for the door just like the other fella, but then he stopped just upstage. He turned and lit another cigarette. They were face to face now, and very close. "Where, 'zactly in Florida you say you was from?"

"Eatonville."

"Hm. Eatonville. All black town, sure I know of it. That's a ways off." He stopped to think a moment. Then: "Come on, Zora. Let's take a walk."

"Okay." Zora hesitated. "Where to?"

"Just a walk. Maybe up that hill into the trees."

The moon loomed mauve, lording the midnight sky like a warning. The breeze chilly now, walking uphill where the wind mazed a jagged prating gathering of black trees.

"So how's it you come to our camp in your fancy car and clothes? Woman like you with your means got nothing better to do with her time, I 'spose."

Zora didn't like the acid in his voice. She tensed. "Say, what's your name anyway, fella?"

"Clifford." He dragged on his cigarette. "Folks just call me Cliff. But you ain't answered the question."

"Is that why folks clam up when I come around, Cliff? They're not used to strange women dropping in?" She smiled, and sassed with her cigarette like she wasn't the least bit nervous. "Sounds awful lonesome."

Cliff considered this for a while. "Well, Zora. See, we get women stomping on down the hill to the camp, great big dirty skirts billowing like a bellflower about 'em; but we don't have too many drive up in shiny silver Chevys wearing expensive city clothes like you. What's your beat? You the law or something?" He let that drop, and then stopped and threw down his cigarette. When he stomped it out, the woods went cool, quiet and dark. "If you is, you better say so to me now, and g'wan and go about your business elsewhere. It'll be worse if folks come to find out later."

"What, well that's what it is then?" Zora fumbled unsteadily for a Pall Mall. Now her turn to tell a lie. "Baby, I'm much too much of a lady to be the Man. And too much of a lady to come on clomping down the hill in my skirts and petticoats. My man's locked up; they got him in Miami, and I've been laying low. Which is why I'm here. You got me figured on the wrong side of things if you think I'm the law." Zora puffed nonchalantly. "All of which is more than you need to know anyway."

Cliff studied her a moment; then he lit another cigarette to a great leaping flame. "All right. Le's go on back. You stick with me if folks give you any trouble. You dance the black bottom?"

"Question is, do you?"

Education comes all kinds of ways. Zora could get the good graces of Big Sweet and the Loughmen men easy enough, but the women were a different story entirely. Frails can turn on each other, and sharp too. She even came clean, told Cliff she'd just made up all that stuff about her being a pimp's woman as posturing. She wasn't exactly eager to drop her cover, mind you, these were some unpredictable Negroes, but circumstances called for the occasion. One afternoon she was shooting dice with Cliff, and they were casting conjures on each other seeing would the bones bear the conjures up, when moving into a roll, Zora slid up and gave Cliff a kiss.

After a while Cliff leaned back and said, "Well I don't intend to be getting in trouble with some pimp from Miami, or his people."

"Well, you ain't gotta worry about that," said Zora.

"Yeah? And why not?"

"I just made all that up." And Zora proceeded to tell him about her work and her writing and how she was collecting folk tales from the race, and that next she was going to go deep down into the murky south and learn about Hoodoo proper and for real.

"Well!" Cliff laughed. "I don't know who sounds more dangerous; the old you or the new."

They lounged the day off, and then the next one and the next one after that, and as the days went along, they got real close. Zora would sit next to Clifford at the lying sessions, lean up into him with her notebook open, and her pen poised motionless above it. Only you couldn't take notes when folks like that got to lying. You just had to listen and take it in, and hope you soaked enough of it in to put it back out there again.

One evening after a lying session Big Sweet took step with Zora as she walked back to her room.

"Say," said Sweet. "You and Clifford mighty close, huh?"

The question startled Zora. A blood red moon rode the horizon.

"Well, sure. I guess so."

"Lucy used to be sweet on him, too," Sweet said solemnly.

Lucy was a woman a little younger than Zora, round the age Zora proclaimed to be. She was small and black and slinky like a little black panther, and just as fierce too. She'd get in hollering matches with the men, and most of the women plum wouldn't mess with her. Lucy never made motions at Big Sweet, though, cuz no one did that. Most towns are like that:

there may be more strong men than women in it, but you can bet your daddy's Cadillac the strongest person in town's gonna be a black woman.

"So what about it?"

"So Lucy's been studying about cutting you, Zora. She ain't kilt nobody yet, and she's losing some status on account of that. She's been saying she's gonna fix that by fixing you." Big Sweet gave Zora a powerful meaning look. "Not if I'm around she ain't gonna do a damn thing. But you should jes be warned and be on guard."

"Aw, I ain't scared of that old scarecrow hag."

But really Zora was petrified. She turned out the lights that night only late, late into the wee hours, reading, blinking, sleepy and terrified. When she finally curled up in the dark, the shadows came prating through the windows, and she sat up, staring at them, looking for them. A shadow darted quick across the walls, and Zora's mind whirled. She stood up, and walked carefully over to the window. She didn't see anything. All she could think about was Johnnie climbing through Mum's window with a knife, her own brother, knife in hand, facing Big Nigger Pop. There was a creak at the door, and Zora nearly shrieked, spinning. She stifled it – there was no one there. Then she sat on the bed and cried for a very long time. She was going to leave Loughman's that night. Call her a coward, call her what you will. She'd find out who she really was in the spellbound swamps of Louisiana. She'd had enough of traveling around Florida asking people to tell her stories even they were bored with. Besides, she had enough folk stories now. She even had enough songs. What she wanted was to learn about Hoodoo; after all, this was both a scientific and spiritual hegira from New York, and so there was only one logical place to go: clean out to New Orleans.

Old memories can haunt you like Scratch, so you have to scratch that itch and move on. Zora drove all through the night chain smoking Pall Malls and pulling over, shaking, crying, recovering. She drove all through the morning until she reached a town somewhere in Alabama. She got a room and paced for an hour, smoking Pall Malls in a room the color of the light of the lunatic morning moon. She felt like she could scream. She sat down and wrote an exuberant essay, all in one furious flurry. She stood up and paced for another couple minutes. She sat back down. She scrawled *How It Feels To Be Colored Me!* across the top. She got up again and paced.

Wheel whirling in the middle of a wheel. The soul only makes progress through catastrophe. It was a spirituality she would awake with.

CHAPTER FIVE

A spell was in the air the spring of 1928. Langston didn't know if it bode well or ill, but it was surely there, he could feel it like a recurring itch he couldn't scratch. Maybe Uncle Monday was behind it. He'd put old Monday's hat in a bank safe almost a year ago. Come last Tuesday, he'd gone back to the safe for some of his southern notes, and imagine his surprise to find that hat had transformed into a flock of moths! Afterwards he itched for days, and when the itch went away from his skin it turned inward.

Zora's letters were getting strange, too. The last one, Langston opened it to find a love letter tumbling out, written in frightfully convincing dialect. Found poetry, as it turned out. But her own accompanying letter jived with that itchy feeling he had, tingle on the back of the inside of the neck.

Zora was getting divorced, that was news. Good for her. Herb just made her miserable. And she'd been wandering around lumber camps reading Langston's poetry? Very strange, sure. He wondered what they thought of it, and wondering, lit a Lucky.

"It's time for a change in my life anyway." Enter Louise Thompson, as she returned to her seat.

The two were having lunch. Langston folded Zora's letter back into his pocket. It was early March, back in the south again briefly, and he felt as if he'd been able to hear Zora's voice like she was right there, reading her letter to him. He kept finding himself distracted by thoughts of her wherever he went. Once he thought he spotted her in a bus station in New York, and announced himself to an astonished young lady who just blushed and asked for his autograph.

"Something's in the air."

Louise sipped her tea and nodded. She was a lovely young lady, easy to look at and easy to listen to, too. She was quick witted and funny, even though she was unhappy, and Langston admired that.

"You're gonna love New York." Langston leaned forward. "Is it you think you'll miss teaching? Negro colleges aren't going anywhere anymore anyway. Even at Lincoln. They're all complacent over there; it's as bad as everywhere else. You did the right thing. Something had to be said." Langston winked at her. "It's in the air."

Louise smiled. "Well, that's true." She started to say something, changed her mind: "I will miss teaching. Though Bohemian black Harlem does sound exciting. If maybe a trifle decadent."

Langston laughed, shrugged, and kept on laughing.

"See!" Louise, triumphantly.

They were brand new best friends, Louise and Langston. She was an English teacher at Hampton, and Langston had come down to the school for a reading. They'd only been introduced a few days before, but they'd made a point of having lunch at the local diner every day since. Louise was light skinned, girlish, brooding. She'd written an anonymous letter to *The Crisis* about the oppressive white administration at Hampton, and Du Bois published it. She loved and respected the Great Crusader, but that published letter cost her her job. When she saw it in print she didn't know whether to be horrified or elated. Maybe no one would figure out she wrote it. Maybe she could deny it. All sorts of crazy ideas. In the end she just marched into the president's office, and presented it to him herself.

"You're gonna love New York." Langston repeated, like he was trying to convince himself more than her. "It's the perfect time to go. Spring – rebirth – love is in the air, and all that."

Seated on an outdoor terrace, the air carried with it the rolling, murky smell of the Chesapeake.

Louise tapped her fork against her plate thoughtfully. "Wedding bells tolling from the Harlem churches, I'm sure."

"Countee's getting married," said Langston. "To Du Bois daughter, Yolande." He started to laugh again.

"I heard about that. What's so funny? It sounds romantic, like out of a novel or something."

"Oh, it would make a great novel," Langston agreed. He pictured pouting, porky black Countee Cullen, squat and sad and panting, Langston's arm around him, poor, heartbroken Countee Cullen, the black, the gay, the Keats of Harlem. "But it might make for a really sad novel. Listen – maybe I can take you."

"Oh, I won't be up there yet." She hesitated. "I should just go though, shouldn't I, Langston? Why would I miss Cullen's wedding for this place, when I know I'm done with this place forever anyway? What's motivating me to do that? That's what worries me."

"Aw, you're overthinking things."

"Maybe. Probably. Contemplating the next stage in my life, is all, I guess. More and more I wonder if we're doing any good anyway, us so called Talented Tenth, when there are so many of our people out there really suffering."

"Wait till you see Harlem."

"What about you, Langston? Where's your poetry headed? Do you ever think about maybe taking your poetry in a more political direction? Like your poem *Sunset – Coney Island* in the *New Masses* a couple months ago."

"See, I've been wondering about that myself. Especially being at Lincoln, and studying sociology. And I think Socialist theory makes a lot of sense. It's certainly the only way to make for a racially tolerant world. Plus, I don't know, but it seems the only direction left to me as a poet. I can't just re-hash the blues thing forever. But it's probably not as open to me as I'd like either."

"Why's that?"

"Oh." Langston frowned. "It's complicated."

Louise took a sip of her tea, and looked off at the Chesapeake. "I understand complicated." She smiled to herself. "Like I should go to the wedding with you. I'd like nothing more. Everyone – even here – everyone's been talking about it. But I guess I won't." She sighed. "Why were you laughing about the wedding anyway? You sure are an oddity, Langston Hughes."

"I think you must have me mixed up with someone else."

They both smiled.

"Well, the offer stands," said Langston. "The marriage of the 20th Century is the marriage of the Du Bois – Cullen line. You wouldn't want to miss that."

Langston, of course, wished dearly he could miss it; but he was an important guest, a member of the wedding party in fact. So a month later, Easter Monday, found him shivering in a cheap rented tuxedo, as the last wisps of a cool, cloudy day softened into night. That southern summery spring he'd fallen in love with, those afternoons with Louise, vanished in a mist of chilly Harlem April rain. Were the memories even his own? A mirror of his own thoughts, Langston looked at his friend Arna Bontemps while proceeding down the aisle with stately, frail Nina Du Bois, wife to the Great Man Himself. Arna smiled politely, a smile Langston himself might have given, the two looked like spitting images of each other, doppelgangers smiling at a funeral. Negroes sure had a gift for the theatrical, but where did the theatrics end and reality begin?

After the ceremony was the dinner reception at Madame Walker's. Madame A'leila Walker was a wealthy socialite who lived in a decadent town house on 136th Street, affectionately known as the Dark Tower, named after Countee Cullen's poem painted on the wall in the main salon. On the opposite wall Langston Hughes' *The Weary Blues* challenged Cullen's poem in large, elegant letters. Through most of the reception Langston and Arna sat with the wedding party, listlessly watching the various groups of attendees chatter at tables scattered around the room.

"Hear anything from Zora yet?" Arna asked.

"Last letter I got from her she was back in Eatonville. Figures she'd just go on home instead of coming up to New York for this charade."

A group of the blues women were gathered together leaning in close, giggling. Across from them a group of male writers were doing the same.

"You think Du Bois knows?"

"About Countee? How can't he? All you got to do is meet the brother to know he's queer as a talking duck. Du Bois has to know."

The Dark Tower was filling up. A clutter of dark bodies, light bodies, pink and brown and black and yellow and beige bodies, all in a colorful array of suits and dresses. The room was vast and vastly crowded, lit golden brown by the glow of the large African papyrus chandelier glowing against the faces. An elegant modern classical waltz, sounded like Strauss, a live quartet.

"Let's first chance we get, get out of here and check out Niggerati Manor," Langston suggested.

"That old crew of smart-alecks?"

"Well, what of it? It sure beats being stuck here."

"Got me there."

An hour later they were laying around 267 with Bruce and Wallie and Aaron Douglas, drinking gin and ice cream and listening to the funkiest, dirtiest, muddiest jazz they could find. Aaron had done the illustrations for *Fire!!*, and to Langton's thinking, was well on his way to reinventing African American Modernist painting.

"All that decadence; it's aesthetically, spiritually backwards, you ask me," Aaron was saying. "It's a cliché riddled facsimile of European decadence, and that damns that Dark Tower for sure. No disrespect to your poem on the wall, Langston."

"They shoulda just let me go ahead and paint the place," Bruce decided. He'd been commissioned to do just that, but like with many things with Bruce, it had mysteriously fallen through. "Whole atmosphere would be different there." Bruce was laying on the floor, smoking a cigarette and looking up at a painting he'd done on a far wall of two naked white figures, women, entwined with two naked black figures, men. The whites were painted with exaggerated lips and kinky hair, and the blacks with long flowing hair and sharp thin facial features.

"No arguing with that," Langston was sitting in the same seat on the same couch as the last time he'd been here, and he was trying very hard to ignore the déjà vu feeling this was giving him. "What happened with that anyway?"

"It was never gonna happen." A truism Bruce delivered philosophically. "Can you imagine it?" He laughed. "A'lelia's seen this place. She knew what she'd be in for."

"Maybe she figured you'd grown more respectable in your old age," said Wallie.

"Rubbish."

"Hogwash."

"Bunkum."

"Speaking of," said Wallie, "I'm putting together another magazine, like *Fire!!*, for those of you not already initiated. I'm gonna call it *Harlem*. It'll be more broad and respectable than *Fire!!*, only it won't be respectable at all. So give me pieces if you got 'em."

"You know I'm in," said Langston.

"And Bruce and I can do illustrations," said Aaron.

"I might write me a little something, too," Bruce mused. "If *Smoke, Lilies and Jade* shocked Old Man Du Bois, I'm like to write something that'll finish him off for good."

"Oh Bruce, when will you grow up?"

"Can it, Wallie. Let's all have another round of gin and ice cream."

"We should go out after that," Arna, fidgeting, looking as restless at Niggerati Manor as he did at the Dark Tower. "Besides, I can't be staying out too late."

"The family man!" Wallie got up to make drinks. "Countee's in a family way himself now – well, not in that kind of a family way yet, by your smiles!"

Not smiling, everyone was laughing. "A toast to the Newlyweds!" Aaron roared, and they all drained their glasses.

"You think Countee can handle a woman?" Langston asked no one in particular. "I doubt he even knows what to do."

"He'll start ass backwards, no doubt," Bruce, from the floor.

"Hey, nothing better than a fine black woman's bottom," said Aaron, lecherous grin and all. "Maybe she'll turn 'im."

That set everyone to laughing again. Wallie returned with the drinks on a tray. He passed them around the room. "Countee'll be all right. Once he's given Du Bois a baby genius or two the pressure's off." A joke only Wallie laughed at, he said it in such an awkward way, which he followed with his own awful and nervous roar of a laugh.

"Well, we got new drinks, so we need a new toast," Arna said after a while. "Let's toast to Countee and Yolanda's baby Du Bois."

"Cheers!" Bruce lifted his glass. "And here's to the baby being queer!"

"Here! Here!" All around.

"Now let's finish these drinks and get outta here. I want to see some real dancing," Arna was a little more drunk than usual now, "You fellas are like a lotta ladies when it comes to getting out the door!"

"Here! Here!"

They ended up at the Congo, a divedown jook joint spot, steps descending to a large metal door, where the concrete shook underfoot with drums and bass. Bruce buzzed the buzzer, a latch slid open, and then so did the door.

"Fellas!" a large black man ushered them in with a couple furtive glances. Then a whirlwind of saxophones and drums and cymbals, a dervish of sound where sense of time and place evaporated, and the company found themselves mid-set a screaming swinging jazz session. Langston lit a Lucky and Wallie tipped a tin of gin. The thrum of the drums dragged them across the crowded floor – no tables open, no seats, no surprise – a crush of bodies rocking sexually locked back and forth between.

"Nowhere to sit!" Arna yelled back. "What do we do?"

The place smelled like booze and cigarettes and the thick stink of a hundred hot, sweating, likkerlivered bodies. The smoke was so thick the crush of dancing, shuffling faces were all a hazy periwinkle. Langston thought he saw Zora for a moment – impossible, of course – he wondered how this compared to those jooks in the south she constantly wrote him about. No white folk down there, there was a difference, and maybe all the difference. Harlem was just a theater, all show, not the real deal, not at all. Negroes sure had a gift for the theatrical, but where did the theatrics end and reality begin?

"We losing you over there?" Aaron nudged him. "You look just like a black *The Thinker*."

"Naw."

"Because I was about to say -,"

"Brother seems a trifle pensive."

A waitress appeared with a tray of White Rock. Wallie paid and passed drinks around.

"To the wild, untamable African spirit!"

"Rah! Rah!"

"Of course, there is no such thing, but sometimes I wonder," Wallie raised his glass, and with a group roar, they crashed in cheer.

The gin got Langston in a spin where he branched out into the crowd and didn't fight the hypnotic rock of the rolling jazz thundering shrieks and peals and complaints and laments and laughter, the black sax soul, the hunger and the haunting lack of melody playing around a melody, a suggestion, like a suggestion of sex. A dark brown girl with a body like a black panther slinked around a stranded seat, and up to Langston. She draped her arms around his neck, and arm around her waist now, one nursing his drink by her thigh, the two did a slow, sexy, close Black Bottom.

Ain't my baby just too cute,
Aint't my baby just too cute,
Ain't my baby just too cute,
I'm percussion, she's the flute.

I'm percussion, she's the flute
Ain't my baby just too much?
I lay my baby down a beat,
How she whistles to the touch!

Ain't my baby just too cute,
Aint't my baby just too cute,
Ain't my baby just too cute,
I'm percussion, she's the flute.

Percussions of motion into and around each other as the jazz blared Langston and lady in a melting mix of sweat. She made Langston dream back to a dark brown girl he'd been sweet on as a child, and dissolving with the wandering of the saxophone, as soon as she twined herself around him, the lights went up, the music stopped, and Langston found himself alone in a dizzy, waking crowd, still humming in his head

Ain't my baby just too cute?
I'm percussion, she's the flute.

Late night later, maybe early morning, the five of them, Langston, Arna, Aaron, Wallie and Bruce, staggered a Charleston shoulder to shoulder, soldier to soldier, through the metal doors and back up the short flight of stairs. They were singing and jigging and taking discrete drinks of gin.

"Where next?" Wallie staggered a few steps ahead on Lenox Avenue, waved his arms. "The night's young yet!"

They ended up at a speakeasy on 129th Street, a low-key place where an old bluesman sat on stage, wrapped up in his own world of down home acoustics. They grabbed a table and ordered a round of gin and ginger ales. The speakeasy was relatively quiet and cool, in a haze of blue smoky cobwebs. Bruce passed a round of cigars around.

"Where did you get these?" asked Wallie.

"Compliments of Madame Walker, gentleman. And let me be the first to congratulate us. We've finally done done it."

"Done what now, Bruce?" Aaron lit the cigar, and brought it to life with eager fresh puffs.

"Done got rid o' Countee!"

Langston belted out a laugh a little too loudly.

"Well, someone's glad to see him go."

"Aw, it's not that Wallie." Langston puffed thoughtfully on his cigar. "Countee's a good guy."

"Say, you and Countee never - ?" Bruce slyly to Langston, then down to light his cigar.

"This again."

"No, Langston's straight all reet," said Aaron. "He's sweet on his old Godmother, ain't that it Langston?"

Bruce and Wallie started giggling.

"Aw, what her? Look, a brother's gotta eat in this world."

"*What's* he gotta eat, methinks be the question."

"Dat's your Mammy. I just get money to write books like I've *been* doing. Anyway, look, here's the ginger ale."

Ginger ales passed around and fortified with gin, Langston continued. "Besides, she's not so bad as all that, anyhow. Some Negrotarians are all right. Carlo's cool. So why not Godmother? She's kooky sometimes, sure, but overall, she's okay for an ofay."

"Says I don't paint primitive enough when I do anything but the same old Africa thing," Aaron muttered, drinking quickly. "I really don't like that ol' Miss Anne Slavedriver."

"Well there's something to it, after all, our appreciation as a people of the primitive energy – the bright primary colors, white America doesn't have it. Compare Harlem to anywhere else in the city. We have our own way."

"However it may be, a white lady shouldn't be the one to dictate to you what it is, is what I think Aaron's saying," said Arna.

"No, see – I challenge the very premise still," said Bruce. "That the Negro has an intrinsic primitive spirit. Folderol! In this country maybe, because folks get brainwashed so easy, most of them sleeping or machines or worse."

"Come on, now. You ever seen a white boy try to dance?"

They laughed all around.

"Seriously though. I heard Zora's not even allowed to publish anything," said Wallie.

"Where'd you hear that?"

"I just heard it. Is it true?"

"Yeah." Langston shrugged. "It's true."

"Which means she can't be in my new magazine."

"Yeah, I guess. I mean – you could always use something old, probably."

"Who is this Godmother that tells a writer she can't publish? Does she tell birds they can't sing and fish they can't swim?" Bruce again.

"That's between them."

"I bet," said Bruce. He lit a cigarette. "Ten to one old Alain has his hand in it somehow. The long fingers of Doctor Locke." Bruce shuddered.

Ezekiel saw the wheel of time
Wheel whirling in the middle of a wheel,
And each spoke spoke of human kind,
Way in the middle of the air.

Now hypocrites may slander you,
Wheel whirling in the middle of a wheel,
Well slander back, and you're one too,
Way in the middle of the air.

"There's something in the air, too," said Arna. "Stirring creativity. Everyone's coming out with a book, or writing one."

"What are you writing, Arna?" asked Wallie.

"Trying to write about California, and growing up there. It's rough going so far. I keep scrapping fragments of drafts. How's your book coming?"

"It's coming." Wallie shrugged. "Bruce is writing one too. So is Langston."

Aaron smiled, puffed his cigar. "You fellas and your books. My paintings tell better stories, and with less words."

They all laughed. Langston puffed his cigar a little uncomfortably. He still hadn't done any work on his book yet. "Claude McKay's first novel's supposed to be out any day now."

"Now that should light a fire!" said Bruce. "I'm looking forward to reading that book."

"Here! Here!"

"Rah! Rah!"

"Still," after they all toasted, added a little sadly, "It's not the same if Zora can't publish."

"Hey," said Aaron. "She's your beloved Godmother."

The sky was a hue of twilight blue by the time they slumped home.

They dropped off in a diner wending their way around the streets of Harlem, trying to chase a thought or maybe just an idea. It had been a long day and night and morning, and they'd run out of things to say to one another. Wearily, with the rising sun, they broke fast and continued to drink gin. A round of watchmen, they woke each other up as they dozed in turn.

Turning the hours forward, broad daylight in the diner, Langston alone, homeless resident of the Harlem Y, last man in the booth, coffee and gin, and feeling like hell. He thought about Zora, and he thought about Louise and he thought about the girl in the Congo, and he thought about Countee Cullen getting married to Yolande Du Bois, and Langston felt about as low as could be. And didn't even know why. Lonesome, so lonesome I could cry. A blue confusion, like the sky. Something in the air.

The trip to New York wasn't all fun and games, either. Godmother wanted to see him while he was in town to discuss his plans for the summer, once Lincoln let out. But a crisis had arisen.

Zora had published something.

A short article appeared in the May issue of *The World Tomorrow* called "How It Feels To Be Colored Me." Really good, too. Zora ended the essay with this wonderful metaphor, an image of a colorful row of bags, each filled with the treasures of an individual life. It was a wonderful essay, full of harmony. And how did Godmother react?

"What did either of you know about this?" she demanded from her throne. Her whole face was flushed a deep ruddy red, and her eyes watered wide open all bursting veins. Langston and Alain exchanged glances.

"Don't look at each other, you monkeys! Look at me! What did you know about this Alain?"

"I didn't know a thing about it."

"And Langston?"

"How would I know anything about it? I'm sure it's just a misunderstanding."

"And after all," reasoned Alain, "It has nothing to do with the field research work she's doing for you. So technically -,"

"Don't get smart with me, young man. It states quite clearly in the contract that Zora shall not publish. At all. Nothing. Whatsoever. You, of all people, should appreciate this, Alain."

Langston remembered what Bruce said in the speakeasy, and suddenly found the whole situation somewhat comic; like he was removed from it and watching from a distance.

"Is something funny, Langston?" Godmother whirled his way.

"Nothing Godmother. I'm only just sure Zora has a hilarious explanation for the whole debacle, and all this melodrama here is for nothing."

Godmother frowned at him a while. Then she said, "What are your plans after Lincoln lets out, Langston?"

He'd been thinking about that, and thinking about traveling again. Going south maybe with Zora, though that was looking less and less like a possibility. So maybe he'd go back west, to Kansas, where he could reconnect with the landscape of his childhood, finally get some work done on his novel. Maybe head out to Quebec. He was feeling more down and out by the day, and the wanderlust was tugging at him again.

"Well," said Langston. He considered what to say. "I've been meaning to write this book. So I was thinking of maybe traveling back out west to Kansas for material."

Godmother looked at Langston, then at Alain, then she reclined in her throne, and put her head back. "That may be feasible. Dr. Locke and I will discuss it – and the appropriate amount of money you should be allotted. In the meantime, I'll need a detailed summary of all your financial transactions this year."

"Excuse me?"

Godmother raised her head from the back of the throne and gave Langston a chilling glare. "I will remind you again this week through post. That way you will have time to prepare it."

"But Godmother, I've given you monthly -,"

"Don't start with me, boy. Now I've been more than generous. And ask very little in return. Zora makes me wonder if I can trust any of you Negroes to begin with, and I'm certainly not going to renew her contract at the end of the year. The primitive has no sense of the moral, after all. And in a civilization like ours, the lack of a moral center perverts the primitive mind. Negroes in this country may be doomed to a duplicitous nature." Godmother bowed her head to contemplate this new insight a moment. "Please have a detailed financial transaction report ready by the time school is out," she said after some time. "There can be no further discussion on this matter."

Langston glanced resentfully over at Alain, whose head was bowed at an angle, almost as if in meditation, or prayer.

April passed and May passed and then somehow Langston's plans for travel changed, though he'd done nothing but dream of travel: of the summer out west, and up north in Canada. Northwest Territory! Somewhere he'd never been before. He made plans to see his Aunt out in Kansas, and thought mebbe he'd just keep on going west til he hit California, Hollywood and strange old San Francisco. But at the last minute he received a letter from Godmother. She would be going to Europe for the summer, but she was banishing him just where he was stuck already: Lincoln, Pennsylvania.

When Langston read that letter, he collapsed weak into the chair in his room. It was unthinkable, it was prison, worse – slavery! To have to stay in Lincoln after school let out, when he'd been dreaming of a western sojourn? He lit a Lucky; he didn't feel so lucky. Lincoln! Not even New York. Could she even do that?

He thought about the still incomplete expense report Godmother demanded, and realized, awfully, that she could. She could even keep Zora from publishing. Imagine that. Not that she actually kept Zora from publishing! Langston laughed, got up, crossed the room and poured himself a glass of gin.

It helped.

Moments later, feeling immensely better, if still disappointed.

Hell, Lincoln wouldn't be so bad. He could write his novel after all, and no distractions. Travel would be all distractions. This disappointment he felt was a good thing, all things considered. He could channel it. He always said he had to feel bad to write well. Well, he felt like hell now. He might just write a masterpiece. He took another drink of gin.

Ten to one it was Alain who'd orchestrated the whole thing. No doubt about it, he could see sly Dr. Locke now, appealing to Godmother:

"Godmother, Langston's easily distracted. And admits he writes best when he's unhappy. Why not keep him at Lincoln?"

Langston laughed to imagine it, but it probably really did happen something like that, so he was also hurt and confused and angry. He puffed hard on his cigarette and paced the room, following that same silly image of Dr. Locke's treachery over and over again in his mind.

Staying somewhere stranded feels like wearing traveling shoes while awaiting an urgent letter. The first few quiet weeks after Lincoln let out Langston took long walks. At first the walks were familiar. He'd walk out to the campus, stroll around the grounds, and then wander his way around the neighborhood streets. The spring had blossomed into a dizzy blend of trees and clusters of purple and yellow flowers. The afternoons had the honey heavy odor of late spring and after a while, he even got to enjoy it. He started venturing off into the woods, noting the slant of the sun as it arched breaking into evening. He would circle the woods, a little lost, following the falling sun, and emerge from the woods in another part of town. The walks helped him think, especially the slow walks through the woods, crushing his way through brambles, branches, leaves, muddy hills and wet, clingy flowers, remembering being a boy in Kansas. Remembering a thunderstorm he witnessed as a nine-year old boy, running indoors just as it was breaking. Nature's power was pugnacious and untamable. Stopping a moment in the thicket of a copse, the sun going a jelly July evening orange, Langston sat down and considered. That, he decided, was how he would begin his novel.

He'd begin it with that storm right there, and out of the storm construct the world he knew as a boy. The storm removes little Langston, it's the moment of crossing over – Langston smiled at that – and then I can make the book really about everybody else. I've just crossed over, like Moses. Langston's grin grew to a chuckle, and looking up, taking a chuckling puff of his Lucky, he saw a puff of wooly black hair disappear behind a tree, and shuffling feet.

Langston stood, and approached the trees cautiously. He looked around. Hadn't it looked a bit like Uncle Monday from back in Alabamy? Naw. Langston let his face relax in a grin again. Impossible. That old kook! Maybe Zora'd hoodoo'd him up to Lincoln. Which made him laugh outright. As soon as he let the laugh go, he caught it, but too late. It echoed weirdly against the silent trees.

"Hello?" Langston called. "Anyone there?"

Eerily, eerily, the woods echoed back, repeating:

"Hello? Anyone there?"

Work began on the novel right away. Langston started with the storm, wrote himself as a boy named Sandy, and from there, he began to pull together sketches of family, family friends, setting, remembering Kansas again through the muse of Pennsylvania woods and Uncle Monday. He set a routine for himself: breakfast at the diner near campus, followed by a long early morning walk. He loved the dawn at daybreak, the mildewed campus lawn, and the streets waking up to another summer day; walking down the hill to where the woods were just stirring awake in sunlight. He wandered the woods and wondered about his book. He'd worry about getting back to his room and having to actually write it. He smoked cigarettes, one after the other, came home, had a glass of gin for nerves and spirits, and then wrote into the afternoon. Carlo had suggested he do three hundred words a day. No lie, even that was hard at first. He dodged writing by writing sketches and an outline, which he drafted and redrafted until he finally gave up and tore the thing up. When he couldn't write fiction or character sketches, he wrote to Zora. Zora was sending him the most fascinating letters. She was traveling through Alabama, still reading his poetry to low-down folks. They were singing his poetry to guitar, and did *Fine Clothes* cover to cover. They called it the Party Book.

Zora would also send Langston character sketches and bits of stories and folklore, because she couldn't do anything with them herself. She was really growing as a writer. Of course she'd caught hell for "How It Feels To Be Colored Me," she said. But she'd beat old Alain at his own game, and manipulated him into manipulating Godmother, and made him convince her she'd sent the article in for publication before the contract. That made Langston laugh out loud, all alone, even slap the table, and he looked up from the letter and missed the hell out of Zora.

Zora was an inspiration and muse to him as much as his walks through the woods, as much as his own memories even. It was wonderful to have a confidante. And as the weeks went on the number of words he wrote in his book increased. It got easier and easier to lose himself in his world, and flow. After a while Langston was doing a thousand words a day easy. And then something uncanny happened. The characters began to take care of the writing of the book themselves, the way the characters in his best poems did. The book was the characters, and nothing more. There was no plot, because he was a poet, and poets don't concern themselves with plots. He thought this ironically, of course, but he meant it too, because that summer Claude McKay's *Home to Harlem* appeared, and it was like a revelation. McKay's book was about nothing but the people in it, and the social circumstances they were stuck in. Langston's poetry had always been just that way too, and so why shouldn't his novel be? Besides, *Home to Harlem* was the best novel ever written by a Negro.

Zora wasn't his only light, either. Langston often thought about Louise Thompson, the girl he met in March down in Hampton, Virginia. He thought about her all the time, about that something in the air, about their discussions on politics, and he thought about the direction of his work, and so he structured his book as a loose social satire based around the character sketches.

With Louise's political inspiration as structural lodestar, a Socialist's keen sense of satire, McKay's novel as spiritual center, and Zora's letters as pure storytelling inspiration, and in the growing comfort of a routine, Langston's work on the book doubled, and then tripled. On his best days, he was writing three thousand words a day. Editing at this point became unthinkable. He'd worry about all that later. For now he just had to get the draft finished.

It surprised him how quickly it all came together. On a sultry afternoon in August Langston rushed through the final pages of the last chapter. He thought about Zora as an actress, singing and dancing, Princess of the Blues, like conflating her with Bessie, and turning her into the most remarkable singer of all time, and transposed the image onto Harriet, Sandy's sister. When he finally wrote the words THE END, he just stared down at his notebook, blinking, and wondered what he'd created. He lit a Lucky and poured himself a tall gin and ginger. He didn't stop at one either, but sat and drank and smoked sitting in the window, sweating like a steampipe all afternoon, while listening to blues records. He watched the sun set over the sleepy streets of Lincoln as it turned from high yellow to orange to gold to red to purple. He drank more gin and sang improvised blues, like

I got a lot of songs,
And I ain't got a frail.

I got a lot of songs,
And I ain't got a frail.

I done a lot of wrongs,
And I ain't gone to jail!

Twilight turned to evening and Langston, strangely blue and real drunk, too, crawled into bed and wondered what spell he'd cast, and how it'd look to him come morning.

II

Finishing the book meant returning to civilization. That civilization was still there at all almost seemed inconceivable. Godmother sent money, and Langston sent her his manuscript. Then he hopped the first bus out of Lincoln, and got to wandering from there. He bushopped to Boston, then to Cape Cod, walked the rocky New England beaches and thought maybe he'd just avoid civilization. That it was still there at all almost seemed inconceivable. Funny how he'd fought against seclusion, tooth and nail, and it was all he'd ever really wanted. He was blue, sure, but it was a kind of lonely, solitary blue you could grow to love. He could write. All he wanted to do was write. And read of course. He'd been reading about the history of Haiti, and maybe he'd write about that next. The New England beaches with their turbulent, suicide waves crashing desperately against the rocks like poets against society (and themselves), inspired him. Haiti's history was turbulent and dramatic; it would even make a great play. The subject matter was weighty enough for an opera.

Langston hopped a bus back to Boston and went straight to the Boston Public Library in Copley Square, where he researched the material until he exhausted himself. He listened to Haitian music, and read Haitian folklore, read about hoodoo and smiled to think of Zora. Was he writing their black opera now without her? It almost felt like a betrayal. Well, it wasn't, because a Haitian opera wasn't a blues opera, and he and Zora had agreed on a blues opera.

The days after leaving Lincoln stuck together like a damp pack of cigarette papers. Langston could flip through them in his memory, but couldn't seem to separate them, without tearing them into fragments. He arrived in Grand Central Station dazed and feeling disembodied, especially being back in New York.

Bruce met him at the station. "You look awful."

"Thanks. You too."

Bruce was dressed conservatively for Bruce: a loose fitting short sleeve dark blue button down and slacks. He looked pretty put together, actually.

"How's the novel?"

"Aw, I don't know. It's done, but it needs work. I'm just glad to get a draft banged out. How about you? Working on anything?"

"Distractions."

"Distractions?"

"Something like that."

"Esoteric. How's the old crew? The Manor?"

"The Manor's gone."

"Gone? Really?"

"The end of an era."

"No kidding. What happened?"

"Landlady finally got tired of us. It was just a matter of time. She wants to turn it into a rooming house for colored girls."

"Well, gee."

The two walked out into the roaring heat of Manhattan of a late August afternoon. They lit cigarettes.

"So where you staying these days?"

"Around." Bruce shrugged. "Mostly downtown."

"Downtown? So you pass?"

"I can if I like. Ricardo, you know. Where to?"

"Let's get a drink in Harlem."

"How'd I know you'd say that?"

They turned the corner and made toward the subway. Langston laughed and shook his head. "So you're downtown passing, huh. Well, that's no option for Wallie. Where's he staying?"

"Now that's a funny story. You remember Countee?"

"Naw. Not really."

"Well just to say that Wallie went the way of Countee." He cast a curious glance at Langston. "We lost another one, brother."

"Wait-," Langston halted mid-step, took a hard drag of his cigarette. "You're not telling me-,"

"That's right."

"So he's just engaged then, right?"

"No. No. He's all married up." Bruce giggled with delight.

"Jesus! He's married? Who the hell to?"

"You wouldn't know her. She's awful anyway. She just moved up here from the south. She was teaching at Hampton University or something. A real dicty lass. Her name's Louise. Louise Thompson. Or Louise Thompson Thurman now, I guess. She'll drive poor Wallie to his death."

"Louise Thompson?" Langston hollered it.

"Why? Don't tell me you know her?" Bruce regarded Langston curiously. "Small world, they say. Say, Lank, you really don't look so swell, do you?"

They ended up at Pocket Billiards on 138th and Seventh. Pocket was dropped on the corner, a wide glass storefront window below a stack of elegant apartments. Inside, the glow of light from windows facing south and west made the place crawl with humidity. Langston and Bruce shot pool and parlayed up the politics like they hadn't done since years ago, back in Washington, when they would walk block to block, engaged in long talk.

"It just happened, you know," said Bruce. "They got married last week."

"What's Wallie thinking?"

Bruce sipped some gin. "Of destroying himself."

"No doubt."

"She's good for him too, though." Bruce scratched his head. "It's weird. She's typing his book. He's not doing so well, you know. Says it's the book and this new show he's got going that's killing him, but we all know it's the gin."

Langston didn't know where to begin. He lit a cigarette.

"We'll go see him," Bruce decided. "Play a couple games and go over there. I stay there sometimes, too, when I stay in Harlem. But it's small – you'll see. It's just a rooming house down on 128th. It's like death in there."

"How so?"

"Oh, I don't know. Like I say, you'll see."

They walked down to Wallie's in the late afternoon. It was turning into a very hot and humid day. They sweated gin and laughed and smoked walking the hazy Harlem landscape.

"How's Wallie's book? You read any of it?"

"Just bits and pieces. It's about this real coal black sister."

"Near and dear to Wallie's heart."

"No doubt. He says it's killing him, but he hopes it will save him, too."

"Huh."

"I don't see how that's gonna happen when he's so hell bent on destroying himself first. I worry about him some."

Fifteen minutes later they were at Wallie's. Bruce let them in, and called out as they came through the door.

A large electric fan roared in the corner. Wallie propped up by pillows on a sofa taken from the Manor. For someone so dark, he looked a little pale. His eyes sagged, and a glass of gin sat sweating on the table directly beside him. Next to the sofa, Louise sat at a small desk with nothing but a typewriter, a dictionary and a stack of pages. She looked up as the two men walked in. Wallie didn't; he was stretched out with his eyes closed.

"Langston!" Louise chirped with genuine surprise and delight. Wallie opened his eyes and looked.

"So it is." He glanced from Langston to Louise. "How do you two know each other?"

"We met a couple months ago back at Hampton," said Louise.

"I see you finally made it to New York," said Langston. "How are you finding it?"

Louise and Wallie exchanged a glance and giggles. "Well, I'm married now. So we shall see."

"So soon…" said Langston.

"We know, it's fast, it's unprecedented. All that." Wallie waved a limp hand. "But I believe if you're going to go in for an institution like marriage, it should be done with the same artistic recklessness with which the artist approaches all ventures. Besides, Louise and I are soul mates. That was obvious to us both right away."

"I always thought of you and Bruce as soul mates," Langston laughed, perhaps a little tactlessly, and he took a seat on the floor next to Bruce.

"'No. Not in the same way," Wallie said, some of the color momentarily flushing back through him. He raised up off the couch. "Drinks?"

"All around," said Bruce.

"So how's the book coming?" Langston asked Wallie when he returned with a tray of gin and ice cream.

"Oh, I don't know. Ask Louise. She can be more objective about it than I can. How's your book? Word in the percolator is that your Evil Old Godmother had you banished to the woods of Pennsylvania to make sure you actually wrote it."

"Aw, well, I think that was Locke's idea, really. But it worked. I got a draft of the book done, so no complaining."

"Everyone's published a book this year," said Wallie. "It's like something's in the air. Bud has a book out; there's McKay's novel; even Du Bois has his new novel out this year. And then there's Nella's book, though it's not quite a novel, is it? Honestly I don't know if I have enough for a whole novel myself." Wallie took a long drink, lit a cigarette, stabbed it in the air at Langston. "How long is your book?"

"Oh, not that long. Maybe about the same as McKay's."

"Well, that's a novel at least."

"It's not something you should worry about," said Louise. She looked appealingly at Langston. "I keep telling him just tell the story the way it needs to be told, and it doesn't matter what the length is."

"Yes, but there are certain standards to form," said Wallie. He blushed black as a blackberry for a moment. "I mean – just that – a novel should be of a certain length – certain expectations from the reader – if it's going to feel novelistic, and I worry that I don't have that certain novelistic facility as a writer that I need."

"Neither do I," admitted Langston. "I am a poet, after all."

"So what did you do?"

"I just wrote around the weakness. I styled my novel like McKay's. It's kind of plotless."

"That's not the book I want to write," said Wallie miserably. "I have certain problems in mind this novel has to solve."

"Oh."

"When are you gonna write a book Bruce?"

"Who says I haven't? My books won't be published in my lifetime."

"And are you a writer too?" Langston asked Louise.

"The only thing I've published cost me my career." Louise smiled thinly. "No. I'm not a writer. Though I wouldn't mind writing pieces for *The Crisis* and *Opportunity*. But no novels. Wallie's too hard on himself. You should read some of the Harlem set pieces he's written."

"Balderdash!" said Wallie.

"Folderol!" Bruce.

"Hokum!" Langston.

They laughed as the sun clipped the room, lighting a slightly discombobulated Louise high golden, the fan ruffling her hair like a flush of autumn clouds at sunset. She looked lovely. For a moment Langston could see what Wallie saw in her. And then the oddest idea occurred to him: he wondered if Wallie was hoping she would turn him straight.

III

That image of Louise stayed with Langston a long time, and he wondered why. As soon as he returned to his room in Lincoln, he was miserable again. The blues hit him so hard seeing that familiar old room, the first few days he just sat, its captive, drinking gin and listening to Bessie. After that he picked up the Haitian opera, just to be working on something, but he'd lost all the prior enthusiasm for it. It didn't really touch his heart; it was all intellect and no inspiration. What's Haiti to he, or he to Haiti? Hell. Worse, he'd heard nothing from Godmother about his novel. Maybe it was no good. Maybe it was too radical. Godmother didn't really like his radical politics. It was definitely too radical. He recalled passages, and winced. Langston brooded, and considered the even worse possibility that she'd just found it far too damn dull to read.

Intending then, to blend into college life that year, Langston did it well, and was now an experienced senior at it. Maybe he could forget about worries a while around campus life: going to parties, games, seminars, functions. Participating in life.

After a while he wondered what he'd even been trying to distract himself from.

Autumn came in with an unsteady hand, always on the quick retreat. The first week of September flushed in a blush of crisp, cool blue air, but then it was hot again for weeks. One weekend in Richmond, at a Richmond vs. Lincoln ballgame, Langston even met a girl! It was a cool early October morning, finally the promise of fall returning, and the leaves dark verdant threads of the trees. A group of students from Lincoln and Richmond were standing outside a diner. Langston recognized some of them, so he slowed his step as he walked by. Laudee stopped his step complete. She was bright walnut brown, and had dark waves of curls cascading down her shoulders. Love is only love if it happens at first sight. Dark eyelashes like romantic epics. He caught her eyes in a blink behind the poetics, and she caught his. Something in the air made him feel bold. The boys all around her were talking loud and gesticulating wild and all that jazz. Cool as the morning, Langston strolled up to where she stood quietly watching him, and introduced himself.

"Hi. Pleasure to meet you. I'm Langston Hughes."

She smiled a little bit. "Laudee Williams. Nice to meet you Langston."

"Laudee Williams? What a name! I believe the pleasure's all mine." He paused to look around, up at the wide blue sky, survey the day. "Would you like to go on a walk with me? Enjoy the morning? We can get lost in Richmond."

"Don't be silly. I go to school here," Laudee said, taking Langston's arm, while the group of boys was slowly going quietly puzzled.

They walked the lane beneath the linden trees and talked of little things.

"So which one of those boys back there is your boyfriend?"

Laudee blushed between the blushes of sunshine and shade. "I don't have a boyfriend."

"Oh."

"I've read you, you know?"

"You've read me?"

Laudee giggled. "Of course. In *The Crisis*."

"Of course."

"You're a very good poet."

"Oh, I don't know."

"Don't be bashful."

"Bashful! What a word. Maybe you're the poet."

"Declaim me something."

So Langston recited Swinburne and Shakespeare, Walt Whitman and Claude McKay. Laudee listened and smiled the whole way through. She kept her hand around Langston's; squeezed it lightly occasionally. When he finished she said, "That last one was Claude McKay. Have you read his new novel?"

"Oh, of course."

"Of course."

"It's wonderful."

"I'm surprised you like it."

"Really!" Langston laughed, and straightened into a silly, dignified strut. "And why would that be?"

"Because you seem so innocent and refined."

Which only encouraged Langston's strut. "No doubt about that," he laughed. "But seriously. You know what I like so much about *Home to Harlem*?

Laudee was giving Langston an adorably curious look, like a kitten recognizing a friend. "Why's that?"

"It's a work of poetry; a pastiche like John Dos Passos' book, *Manhattan Transfer*. It's really new and modern, like Jean's book, but not as coded as Jean's." This set Langston on a thought. "That Jean…"

"Jean Toomer?"

"You're really caught up on things, huh?"

"What's he like?"

Langston lit a Lucky and by doing so slipped slipping into a spell of strange memories. "Aw, why talk about him? Let's talk about you. Who's your favorite poet?"

"You are, silly."

"Great answer!" said Langston, and turning slightly on his heel, between two shadows of trees, he kissed her.

Everyone else was doing it; he was going to do it too: Langston Hughes was going to have a girlfriend. Maybe he'd even get married!

Easy. Easy there.

He loved her a little, all the same. They strolled around the whole day through the afternoon and into early evening, They picnicked for lunch in a large field. Langston bought a copy of Plato's *Dialogues* from an old bookstore downtown, and then they spent the hours on the lawn after lunch with Langston reading *Phaedrus* to Laudee. When they parted, Langston kissed her and kissed her and kissed her, and walking home smelled her hair in his clothes.

Oh Laudee Williams,
Oh Laudee Williams
Oh Lawd, Miss Williams
She said we'd meet

Beneath the apple tree.

He saw her again the very next day. And the day after that. Every day brought beautiful crisp blue skies and every day they did pretty much the same thing. They walked and talked and held hands kissing; they strolled down old Penrose Hill into the field where they picnicked and Langston read romantic adventure stories and plays and love poems.

"Have you written any plays?" Laudee asked him.

"Not the one I'd like to, no." Langston looked up at the sky, blew smoke rings at it, his head resting in Laudee's lap. She sat overtop him Indian style, and toyed with his hair.

"What's the one you'd like to write?"

"I'm writing something now -," Langston was about to mention Zora, but then, not sure why, decided against it. "I'm writing a play now."

"Yeah? What about?"

"Well, I'm writing two plays actually. I mean one's an opera, and," but now he didn't know himself what he was writing anymore, or with whom. For just the briefest moment he was confused like the sky. "It's complicated."

"You're writing an opera?" Laudee looked genuinely impressed.

"Well – yeah. A blues opera. The first ever."

"They say Scott Joplin tried to write a Negro opera, and it killed him." Laudee looked off, then down at Langston. She smiled. "You know Langston, you're even cuter than you look in all your pictures."

Three swift sweet days, unbelievably blissful, Langston returned to Lincoln in a bittersweet mood. The first week back he couldn't concentrate on anything, only Laudee. He wrote her love letters as responses to the found love letters Zora sent him. He never sent these to her. He listened to records by Debussy and remembered their few days together in a gush of impressions. He wrote her love letters, real ones, small prose poems, and sent them. He doted on thoughts of her, and doted on his doting, all in a whirl of a circle of desire. He told all his friends he was in love. He tried to read Rimbaud in the original French.

No one's serious at twenty-six.

The next week her image was less luminescent than the last. What he'd perceived as a glow over the memory of her turned out to be a blur. There were parties to go to, and there were lots of beautiful people to dote on for a night, eyes to get lost in. Sure, he'd loved Laudee, in his way, but he was Langston Hughes, and Langston loved all his people. A funny thing to tell yourself. Besides, what had Laudee meant – surprised that he liked Claude's book? Laudee was gorgeous, no argument there, a man who didn't like her didn't like women, but she was dicty to the depths of her. He imagined Zora playing the dozens on Laudee one evening while he was alone, listening to jazzmen go back and forth at each other on the street below. He thought about that and laughed like a man gone mad for a good half an hour.

Then there were more important things to think about. All foolishness aside, Langston had been relieved to have Godmother away in Europe. Every time he pictured her, he pictured her as he'd last seen her: her face bloated in anger, wild eyes a'rolling, screaming at him and spineless Alain for something Zora did; like all Negroes answered for all other Negroes. He winced every time he thought about it. The way she'd talked to them – well, that had definitely soured the sweetness of her bank account; Bessie's warning came back to him all the time.

But Godmother returned in October, and with her the first review of his novel.

On an overcast, blustery Sunday afternoon he returned again to 399 Park Avenue, right back to those same humiliating stools in that humiliating room beneath Godmother's humiliating gaze. Being back there gave him creeps and chills all over. He had hoped a summer in Europe might've done the old girl some good, but once Godmother had assumed her throne, her tone immediately set things in a gloomy light:

"Langston, I'm going to need monthly statements of your expenses from this past summer. How much money have you currently got?"

"Oh."

"Oh is not an answer, boy. I want those statements by the end of the week."

"Of course, Godmother. But why begin this way? What about – Hi, Langston, let me tell you about my trip? Let's start there."

"Pleasantries are for pedestrian minds. My trip had moments I shall never be able to describe. I have learned things through the ancient architecture of foreign cities I could never heave learned had I not gone. I channeled the spirit of Paul Robeson, and found civilization has damaged his world-soul too deeply. He may be able to heal, but it will take him a very long time. I learned that there are some things out of our control; that some must learn their own way through fire and suffering."

"Oh." Langston paused cautiously. "And my manuscript?"

Godmother sighed. "The writing is exquisite. You're a born poet. But as a novel, it's a mess. Your own voice intercedes far too often. I will write you in detail what needs to be changed, and how, and why. Have patience, Langston. And as you see, I am exhausted. So that will be all for now. Please have those statements ready for me by our meeting next Sunday."

Leaving the apartment, finding himself back on Park Avenue, Langston lit a cigarette and considered his position. He'd put everything he had into that book. Notes and suggestions were okay – like Dr. Locke might give him. But what Godmother was proposing, surely that was preposterous. She could only mean the voice of social satire underlying the story. How much was her money worth to his artistic integrity? Of course, without her money, he would have to work as a completely unskilled, slightly effete, small statured colored man. That meant elevator boy at best, and surely that would compromise his artistic integrity as well. He walked up Fifth Avenue considering it all. At least he could still publish. Poor Zora! He missed her terribly. And then he almost envied her because away on her southern sojourn she never had to deal with Godmother face to face in that awful room. She could travel and write freely, and if she couldn't publish – well, she wasn't the first black writer to find herself in that conundrum; a thought which made him laugh. Well, he would see what specifically Godmother had to say about his manuscript, and decide what to do from there.

Thanksgiving and Christmas were bittersweet. Godmother wouldn't lessen her hold on him: the notes for his novel never came. He could think of nothing but his book; read through his copy and finally, he came to the conclusion that it was unsalvageable. It would be nice to say Godmother just objected to the politics. But it was more than that. He compared his book to Claude's. Oh boy.

But Zora made him happy. They exchanged confidential letters like secret lovers. She sent him money and stories and character sketches and random writings weird and wonderful. She was getting good.

For Christmas Godmother sent Langston some dicty old black leather bag with African designs on it or something. It was hideous. The ugliest old accessory he'd ever seen in his life, and it just made him like Godmother less than ever. Especially when he had his trusty old satchel, and it had never once let him down. He spent Christmas night in a particularly sour mood, drinking gin and listening to Bessie sing good cheer.

It was a cold, white Christmas in Lincoln, snowflakes falling slow and heavy, like a layer of clouds beneath the town. He thought about Zora, and thought about Louise, and thought about Laudee, and thinking about her, he yawned a powerful mouthful of smoke. Laudee bored him now, she always had, really. He had just needed a distraction, and there she was. Laughing, taking a drink, he remembered: something was in the air. Countee's marriage, Wallie's marriage. Love was in the air: the love of acting and illusions, that is. Oh, all Harlem's a stage, said Wallie.

An evil omen in the air, too. Langston passed the New Year listlessly; he passed the cold barren January days listless. There was class and there was wistfulness. Wistfulness for what he wasn't sure. He was getting older, he knew that. He spent his twenty-seventh birthday drinking gin and writing poetry. That was a habit. Always a poem on his birthday, the requisite

February 2nd poem. It was a tradition he started ten years earlier, and kept to, watching himself in evolution.

All the same, he enjoyed being lost in his last days of Lincoln. He knew he enjoyed it because he had nightmares about leaving. Nightmares about Godmother and Dr. Locke getting control of him, devolution, a wired up Langston Frankenstein. Lincoln was sanctuary from all that madness, and that sanctuary would be gone, and very soon. Langston wrote a deranged poem that February 2nd in his room at Lincoln, thinking about graduation and the future, still hoping to believe in the heart's bright flower, and he passed out in a pile of books and notebooks, feeling deranged himself.

Deranged evening followed by deranged morning followed by a barrage of deranged days, all soaked in gin. Leading two weeks later to a bright Monday morning in Manhattan. A car took him to 399 Park Avenue, where he was happy to have lunch in Godmother's parlor, and not back in that horrible room. He felt half-dead; he'd been drinking gin every day for a couple weeks straight; his head felt cluttered, disarranged, like a messy room. He'd had a bunch of questions – things to discuss with Godmother, but he couldn't recall any of them. The parlor throbbed with the pulsing light in the passing shadows of clouds. He was glad to eat, but it made him feel mentally sluggish. They spoke about little things, Langston's birthday, life at Lincoln, Europe and art. Godmother refused to speak about Langston's novel. "Your novel's not ready yet child, and neither are my notes for it," was all she would say. "I expect you'll be working on it again this coming summer. I expect you'll be staying at Lincoln this summer again, too. It's the only way someone with your temperament will ever have the focus to do the work on the book it still so badly needs."

This woke Langston up. "What – you mean? The summer after I graduate? Stay in Lincoln?"

"Yes. That's right."

"You really want me to stay in that same old room in that same old town you exiled me to last year? I was so miserable there, Godmother. I can't possibly do it again. It doesn't even make any sense. Why would I stay in Lincoln after graduation?"

Godmother glared at Langston through her pince-nez for a moment. Her eyes burned grey blue pale fire. Langston blinked.

"You're the one that insisted on going to school with that yapping crowd to begin with, Langston." She paused, took a breath, and drew herself up, like she was assuming her position on the throne. Her whole body shifted into itself, so her face flattened like an ancient mask. "All that I've given you, Langston, and you refuse to make the smallest sacrifices. What a despicable ingrate. All you Negroes – you! Zora!" She laughed triumphantly. "Ha! Alain too. Why does he always talk in circles? Why can't

Negroes be trusted? Is it some remainder from slavery? Is it like I surmised before, the primitive is perverted by the civilized because the primitive lacks a moral center?" She glared accusingly at Langston. "Consider that leather bag I sent you for Christmas. Where is it? You don't even think to wear it? You don't even do me that *one* common courtesy? Instead you bring that same old beat up bag you've had since you were just another dirty nigger." Godmother looked off, out the window, while a dazed and hurt Langston looked at her helplessly, full of despair and shame and rage, and he felt like doing nothing but crying.

"The more I think on it, the angrier it makes me, Langston. You're nothing but a spoiled little pickaninny. You know that? You sit there with your boyish good looks and ever-ready smile, your folksy aw-shucks routine, but behind it all is the heart and soul of a scoundrel. Out of my sight. Our lunch here is finished."

And so saying, Godmother lifted herself out of the chair and disappeared into the hall. Cordelia came out immediately after, looking flustered and embarrassed.

"Can I show you the door, Mr. Hughes?"

Langston plummeted the elevator from the Penthouse falling like a body swinging, the wire stretch vertical plunge, colored elevator boy looking curiously at him like a body length mirror.

Outside on Park Avenue, mists and clouds. Langston wandered north up Park, west, north and west, just walk towards Harlem. Stumbling into the crush of Columbus Circle, he saw Uncle Monday descend into the subway. He tried to make sense of what just happened. He followed Monday into the subway station. He would call Godmother as soon as he got back to the Y. He would call her and beg her forgiveness for what he'd done. He'd beg her forgiveness for what America had done. For what America had done to Negroes and ofays and for what could maybe never be undone. That's what he would do.

But what had he done?

The subway shuttled north, ascended over Seventh Avenue where New York rushed past a crush of tall strivers of buildings, and squat pedestrians. There would be no more money. There would be no more help from Alain either; all those channels were cut off now forever. Locke would never choose Langston over Godmother, and rightly so. Godmother had all the money and power. Stomach tight, and getting tighter, Langston leaned over and shook sobbing into his knees a great choke of tears that misted his eyes as misty as the misty subway windows. Langston cried and the city stared back, terrible and expressionless with tears. His stomach began to feel soft, mushy, like ice cream dissolving in gin, oozing through his intestines, like he might vomit. The thought made him suddenly dizzy, queasy, faint. He staggered out of the train at the next stop, and up the stairs, into the street. Corner groceries and pharmacies. Broken brick red row houses down Seventh Avenue. Nothing was familiar anymore: not the billiard halls or the movie houses, the theatres or the speakeasies. Even the restaurants and diners looked different, and turning he saw Monday disappear into a flower-shop – Monday caught pale and gold, a glow from a Woolworth's marquee, the frock of hair shocking Langston into the realization that he was not just having a novelistic moment of despair, but that he was actually lost, and had no idea where in New York City he was.

CHAPTER SIX

How do two people find each other?

Zora was lost in a puzzle of her own. Puzzled that having finished collecting research, here she sat one April afternoon contemplating just how she was to put all this mess together. On the one hand, she had enough material for Mrs. Mason, and enough for Boas too; most important, she had enough for her and Langston's play, which she had decided would be simply called *Jook*.

On the other hand, all this was impossible to be perfectly happy about with Mrs. Mason herself still in the picture. None of this research or writing even belonged to Zora as things stood. The only way she could keep anything was by giving it to Langston.

If the old lady really did have psychic abilities, to hell with it all, Zora's were stronger. The months in New Orleans were instructive enough in that. Instructive enough for her to know there was something hidden at the crossroads of all religions, and psychic ability was just an increased understanding of these elementals and how they functioned. Action was what mattered. But Mrs. Mason was still a problematic force in her life for the time being, and might have to remain one for a while. Maybe she'd break with Mason come the end of the year, refuse to renew the contract, and live off Langston's money.

See, there you go. People find each other.

She missed Langston achingly. Not like a love ache, mind you, but a blood ache, he was dearer to her than she'd realized. She considered his presence acting out scenes for their play. She wrote scenes and characters, scrapped some, sent others to him to critique, auditioned them with him right there in her room. He was with her all the time now, because somehow his spirit had fused with hers.

Still, spiritually, she felt stuck.

She started a letter to Langston, and stopped after a few sentences. The early spring sun lit the corner of her desk a mauve color, like her skin in the shadows. She put down the pen, lay her hand flat palm down on the desk, and then lay her head on the desk, on top of her hand on top of the letter. She didn't know what to do. The only reason she was writing Langston was cuz she was too shook up to write Boas. Was she really afraid of that old lady, and her powers? Or was it just Mrs. Mason's money halting her hand? She listened to the pulse of her blood through her veins. She should write to Boas, and get his feedback and advice. Boas was a scientist and Mrs. Mason was just a superstitious old lady. She considered Mason bent over the notebooks of anthropology, pince-nez dangling above her nose, the occasional remark about the spiritual primitive beauty of the Negro, and Zora laughed herself breathless. Should she send her work to Boas or not? Was it even a question? The fact that she'd even considered otherwise made her laugh even harder.

But laughter all alone rarely lasts. Catching her reflection in the window against the sun going down, a dusky shadow across the glass, she saw the arch of her arms, stiffer now, almost like the Tin Woodsman, heartless, and thought about how she wasn't so young no more.

The early spring months had been difficult for Langston, too, but they'd also been a learning experience. He was determined to become a stronger, more forthright individual. He wanted the courage of his convictions like Du Bois. Like Sandy in his novel, he wanted to do great things for his people, only it seemed too many personal failings would prevent him from ever becoming that person. He thought about Zora in the south collecting stories and songs, and how she published something against Godmother's direct orders, and he felt ashamed of himself.

So with college life coming to an end, and Zora's indomitable spirit inspiring him, and Louise's brave letter inspiring him, (another shaming example of how everyone seemed to have more courage than he did) Langston committed himself to doing something daring and dangerous and political and important.

Only he didn't know what.

An idea began to take shape in his head over the next few weeks. Spring was in bloom; it was hard to believe a whole year had elapsed since those restless dogday dawns in Lincoln. Those mornings, being so close to school, but not attending it, he'd managed to reflect on things about this place. If Louise had been brave enough to write about the conditions of things at Hampton, why shouldn't he write about Lincoln? Black colleges nationwide were up in arms about the stultifying white patronage that kept them in check. Lincoln was no different; they just knew how to keep things a little quieter. Well, he could change all that. He could write a sociological study of the administration in the style of Du Bois, with arguments and figures and refutations and all.

He first cast the idea off a Junior friend of his, a brother named Thurgood Marshall, a Humanities Major. Thurgood was the perfect person to ask about something like this: he had a sharp, critical mind like old George Schuyler back in Harlem, but Thurgood was more fun and friendly and approachable.

Thurgood had been passing through the Sociology Department when Langston spotted him, and caught pace. They passed through Sociology, turned downstairs and headed into Economics. Economics led to a wide hall that opened into a foyer, and then out through two large red doors.

"Well yeah, Lankston," Thurgood gave him a curious look. "I do think white patronage can hurt just as much as it can help. Howzabout you?"

"Well, yeah. I mean, cuz that's what I'm getting at."

They were both quiet a little while.

"You probably think I'm talking about myself I guess. I know folks have been talking."

"Well, I didn't say it." Thurgood took another searching look at Langston. "Say, did Van Vechten ruin you or what, brother?"

"That's all poppycock."

"Poppycock. Huh."

They walked out into a warm green Pennsylvania spring. Langston lit a Lucky. "Most of *Weary Blues* was written before I even met Carlo. Lot of *Fine Clothes,* too."

"Well maybe not your poetry, but that awful book. What was it called? *Niggers' Heaven*? It's influenced damn near every black book since."

"*Nigger Heaven.* Well, and yeah. It's been influential, you could say."

"Don't write another Van Vechten novel, Langston. I mean, they say you're writing a book now, right?"

"I am." Langston puffed thoughtfully. They were headed across the quad. Langston wondered if he was following Thurgood or vice versa. "I can't write a novel like Van Vechten's," he said after a while. "Scandalous and all that. I'm just a kid from Kansas, so that's what I'm writing about."

"There you go."

"But hold up. Here's the thing, cause somehow you tricked me and got me distracted. Thought you had me there, didn't you? See, I wasn't asking about white patronage because of me. I was asking about Lincoln. I want to do a study of Lincoln; interview the students and faculty. Have folks talk on and off the record, as they please, just so's they speak honestly. And demonstrate in a sociological deconstruction what's wrong with the white patronage here."

"What in particular do you find wrong with it?"

"Well, no black professors just to begin with."

"Well. Okay. Go on."

"The buildings are old. The books are old. The classes aren't challenging. It's hardly even a school. It's just a giant fraternity!"

"Let me ask you something, Langston."

"Shoot."

"Do you believe an artist has to tell the truth?"

"Of course I do."

"Because the truth about the older generation of black professors. They simply weren't given the educational opportunities the white teachers were. It's tragic, but it's true. Which makes the white professors more qualified."

Langston shook his head. "I can't believe you'd say that, Thurgood."

"Just something to think about. It might come up in your study."

They walked on in silence for a while.

"Don't get me wrong," Thurgood said. "I think you're onto something. Lincoln's no grade A school. I like it here, but I'm thinking University of Maryland for my real education, once I graduate."

"What would you do that for?" Langston smiled. "Why not come to Harlem and be a writer? It's all the rage."

"There's that..." Thurgood looked up ahead where the music department loomed leering into view. "Or maybe I'll just run for president."

"Me too."

"Very funny. No, hell. I mean there's as much chance as me being the first Negro president as me being interested in being a great writer. Or even being in New York. No, I can get more done in Washington, that's for sure."

"Well, I guess we wind up who we've been," Langston, philosophically, as they walked up the steps to the music hall. "Anyway, I'm off to get some work done on this thing. Figure I'll draw up an outline, and go from there. You done with class for the day?"

"Yep," said Thurgood. "There's this jazz cat, Cabell, has ties to the school, thinking of coming here, but he's not exactly the college type. But every blue moon he drops by to play some deep blues on the piano. He's a friend of mine. You should come check him out."

"Normally, you know, I would. But I'm really excited to get to work on this."

"Your call. You only live the once, I'm told." Thurgood turned to go, paused on the step, turned back to Langston. "Speaking of -." Fumbling in his coat for a moment, he produced a small cigarillo. "It's from Cuba," said Thurgood. "My dad gets them. These just came in. Congratulations on your project, brother. Get yourself a good brandy to go with it."

"Thanks, Thurgood." Langston took the little cigarillo and slipped it in with his Luckys. "I'll go smoke it now. For inspiration."

"You do that."

There was something funny about Thurgood's cigarillo. Langston lit it just as soon as he got himself situated: some blues on the victrola, notebook and pen, a glass of gin and ginger – not quite the brandy Thurgood recommended, but it would do. He was thinking through the title of what he figured would be the first chapter when he noticed the cigarillo tasted and smelled strangely sweet. Citrusy almost. A Cuban blend, eh? He grinned and gave another glance to the twist. Thurgood, that joker. He wouldn't have, would he? Langston took another long puff of the thing, and breathed it in good and deep. It burned, but he held it right down in his lungs, then spilled it out in a wobbly wash of smoke. Not bad. He took another puff. Hmmm. Liking this Cuban stuff.

Langston remembered he still had some of Herb's Chicago jazz. He flipped through the records, and put on Jelly Roll Morton. He puffed the Cuban, picked his pen back up, and listened to Jelly slide into a stride piano rag with a swing, and could almost hear Alberta Hunter coo,

Someday, Sweetheart
You're gonna be sorry
When you realize
What you have done,
To a true heart
That always loved you,
Then you start trying to mend your broken vows.

Somewhere in the hum of the strings and horns and the buzz of a blue smoke now misting up like fog, Langston reconnected with something distant, like something thick and primitive in his blood. Outside, the streets of Lincoln blinked, one by one, in the spring's periwinkle twilight; old oak trees leaned toward the receding sun, a shimmering slice of clementine behind the clouds; the Cuban smoke sinking up-side down, the thrum of Jelly's Roll on the piano, like the thrum of the drumming of tom-toms; every new thought reopened the world, like a child lost in the Pennsylvania woods. It was here, in the primitive, where you found your true moral center, and everything built over that was just sociological conditioning. So if he was going to write a sociological study of Lincoln, and the conditioning imposed by the white patronage, he'd have to give the piece some proper moral authority, right from the start. State his premise outright. He puffed another puff of the good old Cuban stuff, poised his pen, and looked at the notepad intent.

Suddenly self-conscious. Remember what Thurgood said, and it was true: a whole lot of the new Negro novels owe a whole lot to *Nigger Heaven*. Don't write you another *Nigger Heaven* Langston. Another puff of the Cuban stuff. Langston laughed. No, he was a higher soul from the lower orders. No *Nigger Heaven*, but something deep down from the souls of black folk. If he had any influence it was Du Bois. One more little tasty-taste of that Cuban, and now here we go, by way of introduction, a little poetic foreword…

You are happy now
And you can't see how
That the weary blues
Should ever come to you.
But as you sow, so shall you reap, dear,
And you're bound to reap sorrow
Someday, Sweetheart.

He penned a short paragraph about the profound simplicity of the primitive and looked away across the campus, through the window where dusk was coming cobalt behind swollen purple clouds, laughed, and shook his head. Maybe he should have a talk with Dr. Locke about this study. To think he'd gone to that rascal Thurgood Marshall!

The brother was like to shake some things up, though, if he ever did get his act together, and get himself on down to Washington.

One day amidst the now constant flurry of letters back and forth with Boas and Langston and Ruth Benedict and Dr. Locke and Mrs. Mason, Zora received an invitation to speak at the Jacksonville convention of the Association for the Study of Negro Life and History (ASNLH for short) signed, Carter G. Woodson Himself. Zora, caught up in the massive amount of work she had to sort through, was starting to rediscover her long lost respect for academia – all within limits, of course.

So against her natural instincts, she drove all the way out there from Miami. She figured maybe preparing a speech and working with the boys through some of her material might give her ideas for the structure of her book. There was of course the sticky issue that this could quite easily get back to old dame Mason, and old dame Mason was sure to be displeased should she hear about it. Well, let her be displeased. Zora herself was displeased with the arrangement. Misery loves company.

And she could've used some. The night before the convention there was a – shall we say – banquet, with all the formal speakers, and the Venerable Carter G. had Zora sit right next to him. All she could think was how great it would be to have Langston there, because he'd worked for the good doctor before, and so had Zora, and they both knew what a slave-driver he was, stubborn as Brazzle's mule. You'd probably be better off down on some Georgia plantation somewhere than working for him.

"So, Zora." He was a middle-aged man with a severe frown of a chin and a jut of a forehead. He looked serious and seriously upset all the time, even when trying to smile, which he was doing now. "You must be excited to speak tonight, knowing you."

"Oh. Well."

"Say, why don't I let you open? I've been thinking it over. Your energy would be a perfect launch into the evening. Don't you think?"

Now all evening he'd grown more and more animated about his newfound discovery, Imhotep, an Egyptian super-genius who built the pyramids. Zora knew all about Imhotep, but her education on him was different than Carter G.'s miseducation. Imhotep, as a spiritual prophet parallel to Christ would have wanted nothing to do with this reclamation of him as a Great Negro Leader. What could possibly be more ridiculous than dragging a visionary into this American race argument, which had no basis in anything but collective insanity?

Don't let that stop this windbag. Carter G. continued on into a discussion of how the mathematical intricacies of the pyramids proved the black man's intelligence, all of which led to a panegyric about the African soul, the black race, the New Negro and a whole lot of other hokum. Not to discount the history, mind you; but what chimerical African soul was he talking about exactly? And what could this abstract history mean to folks who needed a logical spiritual philosophy, not a list of funny-sounding African names? So just who was his audience supposed to be but these other purblind intellectuals? And here he was, having these discussions with what were supposedly the best Negro minds alive; one of the best white minds too, since Schlesinger was there. Arthur Schlesinger, a handsome sort of ordinary looking man with thin, watery intelligent eyes mostly nodded and took notes as the others talked. He was the quietest of them all.

The loudest and most loquacious of the group was Mary McLeod Bethune, as big and black and bold as her name. She would lean in, one heavy arm anchored to the table, large fingers gripping the ledge.

"You know I'm with you there," she said in her large, confident voice. "So long as you include something about us black women. A black man will make a sack cloth of a black woman faster than a white man will."

"And if we ignore the black woman's voice," Rayford Logan, a light skinned young man probably just a few years older than Langston, leaned forward, "then we're no better than those who would ignore the black man's voice."

That was when Carter G. turned to Zora and offered to have her open the floor. "Your energy would be a perfect launch into the evening. Don't you think?"

"Well," Zora considered her next statement. "I don't think there are any racial histories. Or that it even makes sense to contextualize things in terms of race and not culture, since race is just a social fiction. And we seem to be building on that social fiction instead of tearing it down. So if I speak first, I'll probably say something the likes of that."

The professor smiled like a patron. "Zora! Certainly! Cultural histories as opposed to racial histories – you're making a purely semantic argument. African culture necessarily informs Aframerican culture, and it's important for the New Negro to take pride in his racial ancestry."

Zora flushed. This man could try her patience. "The history of all African people isn't our history. Our people only come from a handful of Western African countries. Each of our individual histories is even more specific than that, and in many cases, hopelessly lost. The American Negro's history as a people and our culture begins with this country, and our history as an entire race of colored folks begins with balderdash."

Carter peered at Zora intently, adjusted his glasses.

"Those are just the facts," she insisted.

"Maybe you're right. Maybe you aren't ready to speak just yet. I'd hoped -," He leaned back in his seat, and looked around at the other guests, like a shrug. "Well, but maybe you're just not ready."

"Even if you deny everything else," Rayford Logan said after a long silence, "you still have to admit that the colored people world over have been exploited and persecuted by Europeans for centuries. That's a common denominator."

"As have the Jews. But we don't include them."

"Well!" This throatily uttered by Schlesinger. "Part of the reason so many from the Jewish community have joined with the Negro is because of our similar predicament. There's a reason Moses is so often invoked in the spirituals. The histories of the African people, and yes, histories is plural, and the Jewish people are more interconnected than most people realize – both historically, and metahistorically…"

At which point Schlesinger launched into a philosophy he would expound upon in more detail the next day at the convention. Each of them in turn, in fact, had their moment to drag out their particular pet studies: Rayford Logan on the failures of Reconstruction, and the long lasting consequences of such; the great black statesmen who'd been part of the Reconstruction movement, right down to John Mercer Langston, Langston's great uncle, and Governor Pinchback of Louisiana, Jean Toomer's grandfather; Mary McLeod Bethune delivered a powerful jeremiad on racism and decadence and the iniquities of the black community, before going on to give brief biographies of various great black women, some of them truly great like Sojourner Truth and Harriet

Tubman; though she made no mention, thank you very much of Ma Rainey or Ethel Waters or the great Bessie Smith either, and they made one pale frail of the likes of the oft-mentioned Phyllis Weeply. But the ice-cream on the apple-pie was Carter G. Woodson's forty-five minute long encomium to the Great Black Men and Women of the Past. The kings Akhcnaton, Benhazin Hassu Bouelle, Hannibal; his misunderstood favorite, Imhotep, of course, and Jaja and Khama; he dragged poor Phyllis back up again from the dead, called Olaudah Equiano the father of American literature, heaped praise on old Frederick Douglas, who had to be feeling a little left out, and then launched into a discussion of African painters, sculptors, musicians, philosophers, statesmen, poets. "The Negro in Africa had kings and scholars and philosophers and prophets while Europe wallowed in barbarism. The African soul informs all the great cultural and moral achievements of our society, and it will be the Negro worldwide, who will provide this world's salvation."

Zora's salvation lay out the window where the warm Florida day folded softly away behind the clouds, and a clean, dusky orange light flooded the hall. The meeting had gone on all day, and she was the only one who'd been invited to speak, but not allowed to. So much for freedom of speech in the black community. Propagandists weren't interested in the truth, only in better ways to deliver their propaganda, and the truth, with all its subtleties and complexities and confounding shades of gray had no place in propaganda. What with the dinner the night before and the long, ponderous speeches, and now Carter G. droning on and on, dropping more names than a runaway slave, it felt like it had gone on longer than an African empire. She yawned and nodded through the whole thing, and when they finally emerged into a warm teal twilight, Zora felt like she'd been sleeping a very long time, her eyes just finally blinking open like the night's new stars.

Langston had nightmares about leaving academia. He walked up and down the busy Manhattan avenues and watched the bourgeois business folk and the workers rush blindly about, bumping into each other like bumper cars, had tried to picture himself as actively engaged in this mass insanity, and it gave him nightmares; always the same theme, Langston and the elevator boy in Godmother's building, Langston as an elevator boy in some other building, wandering the streets of Harlem ratty and hungry like Bruce Nugent, a failure right at the start of a career which once had limitless potential. And yet his degree was supposed to be a safeguard from that kind of thing; poetry couldn't pay forever, after all, the Negro vogue was bound to pass. Besides, no Negro in history had ever made his living solely off his writing. Not even the wise old William Edward Burghardt Du Bois could do that.

Langston stepped off the platform at Grand Central. Now here he was, school finished. A summer lay ahead of him in Lincoln to finish off that pesky novel as well, and then – the rest of his life, for whatever that may hold.

New York had changed; at least as he'd remembered it, though his last memory of it wasn't particularly pleasant, what with Godmother's rebuke, and Wallie's breakdown, the end of Niggerati Manor, the end of an era, as Bruce had put it. Langston walked the stairs to the terminal leading to the main hall, where Louise was waiting for him, looking as changed as Manhattan herself. Some of the gaiety around her mouth and eyes had slivered, shaded, relaxed into a more mature cynically smiling frown. Well, New York could do that to you, a fella lets his guard down. He approached her, took her hands, and gave her a kiss on the cheek.

"Louise! You look lovely."

Louise pulled back from Langston and gave him a good once over.

"You don't look so bad yourself, college man. How's it feel to be an educated Negro?"

Langston winked at her. "I'm like Dr. Du Bois now."

They walked out to the street, and Langston hailed a taxi. "Where to?"

"I suppose you're rich these days?"

They hopped in a cab and Louise gave an address on Edgecombe Avenue.

"Have you been introduced to Mrs. Mason?" Langston asked her.

"I've heard enough about her." Louise made a face. "I don't know how I feel about these white philanthropists. I mean, Carl Van Vechten's a blast, but Mrs. Mason?" Louise shrugged. "I don't know."

"Well, she's got money," Langston said after a while.

"Yeah, I know. Money's always nice. Wallie's doing everything he can to avoid paying me anything."

"How are you getting along, anyway?"

"Well," Louise folded her hands over her lap, and looked out the window. "I'm doing okay. Wallie could be more cooperative, though."

"So are you working in the mean time?"

For a long time New York passed by in a quiet atmospheric rush.

"New York's changed since you left, Langston."

"It seems different."

"Wallie's gone now, you know. Bruce, too."

"I heard. Bruce is in, what is it, England? With the crew of *Porgy*?"

Louise nodded. "He seems happy at least."

They stopped at a small gray building on Edgecombe, right near City College. Upstairs, the apartment reminded Langston of a tidier version of the rooming house where he'd last visited Wallie and Louise. The couch was still there, the writing table; the place smelled the same, like stale cigarettes, gin and ginger ale, and the typewriter sat upright like a character of its own, singularly occupying the room.

Louise poured Langston a gin and ginger, and then poured one for herself.

"What do you listen to these days? Sit down. Make yourself comfortable. I'll be right over." Without waiting for Langston to respond, Louise put on a Gershwin record, sighed and sat next to him on the couch. Out the window the campus of City College in the high afternoon sun unexpectedly made Langston feel a pang of yearning for Lincoln. He looked at Louise, squinted her a half-cocked smile, maybe a little sadder than he meant it. "And how are you Louise?"

Louise choked on a chuckle. "Getting along I guess."

"Do you not want to talk about it?"

She looked away. For a while she didn't say anything. Then: "Can you answer me something honestly."

"Sure. Shoot."

"Is Wallie gay, Langston?"

Just like that. Langston didn't know what to say.

"You know what? I'm sorry. You don't have to answer that, and I know the answer anyway, or I wouldn't be asking in the first place."

Langston opened his mouth; closed it.

"He won't admit it. Why won't he just admit it? He's such a coward!"

"Wallie really does love you, Louise."

She snorted. "Wallie doesn't love anybody or anything, and I don't think he knows how to. All he knows how to do is tear things down."

The room around them shuffled unsteadily in the waning daylight to *Rhapsody in Blue.*

"I read his book," said Langston after a while. "It's good."

"I know it is. He hates it too, though. He really hates that book. I mean it's not perfect, but it's not like it's the worst novel ever written."

"It's that mind of his. Like a pocket razor, quick and clean and deadly, and he uses it like a weapon on everything, even himself."

"So why can't he just admit to being a homosexual? It's not like I care. I mean. Not all that much. Not all that much." Louise was starting to quiver, and her cheeks misted. "All I want is for him to be honest with me. Some soul mates, huh? Lies and recriminations between us, that's all it ever is, and whenever he-,"

"Slow down there, little lady," said Langston, and he touched her hand. "Slow down. Wallie's had a tough year too, remember. What with that book and the new magazine, and the play on Broadway – your marriage – Hollywood, and on top of all that, his health's been poor."

"Well," Louise calming like a lake after a storm, "it's over anyway, and Wallie's gone. I don't know where he is, and frankly, I don't much care.

California or something like that, like you say." She looked over at Langston and attempted something like a smile. "Never get married Langston." She misted over all over again. "Oh, that's just my bitterness, though!"

Langston tried something like a smile himself. "So whatcha gon' do, baby blue?"

Louise smiled, genuinely. "Who knows?"

Langston winked at her. "Why not type my novel? Lord knows I need a competent typist. I'll bet I can get Godmother to pay you really well for it. What do you say?"

"I don't know, Langston."

"Well, think it over. Really, you'd be doing me the favor."

"So tell me about it."

"What? The book?"

"What else, silly?"

"Aw, I don't know. It's about people I knew, and people I knew of when I was growing up in Kansas."

Louise gave Langston a searching glance. "What was that like? Growing up in Kansas? What was your family like?"

"Well, I don't know. Everyone else's family, I guess."

Louise laughed and Langston laughed too.

"Oh no, young man. You don't get off that easy."

"Well, I don't talk about my family all that much." Quickly adding: "Besides, the book's not so much about my immediate family anyway."

"No? Why not? What's your immediate family like? Tell me about your mother."

Langston smiled. "Well. Howsabout yours?"

"No fair. I asked first."

"Well." Taking a drink. "She's lonely a lot, I think. She always wanted to be an actress, you know."

"That's like half the black women in Harlem," Louise said quietly. "Provided they're light enough." She quietly contemplated her drink. "So is she all alone, your mother?"

"Well, there's my step-father, but they're on and off. And then there's my little brother. He's a handful, but the two of them, they just egg each other on. I worry about them both a lot, and I guess maybe that's why I don't like to talk much about them."

"Oh. Where are they now?"

"Mom's in New Jersey – Atlantic City, actually. Kit, well his real name is Gwyn, but everyone calls him Kit, he's – I don't know. Godmother was paying for him to be settled and in school and all, but that didn't really take." Langston smiled sideways. "You know, it's like I say. It's not so bully to talk about."

"Sorry. Didn't mean to pry."

"So tell me about you," said Langston, relaxing a bit. He took a long drink of gin and ginger.

"Oh." Louise considered something. "Well. I feel a little rootless right now, you know. I don't know what to do. I thought I'd be in Reno right now, if you asked me a couple weeks ago."

"So where do you hail from originally?"

"Well, I say I'm from Chicago sometimes, and Oakland others." Louise laughed. "I guess just depending on how I feel. But I grew up in Chicago for the most part."

"Sounds complicated."

"It was my folks. Dad mostly. He hated Northern cities back east here. He said they were the most racist of all, because they couldn't even admit it, so they were meaner and sneakier about it. I have to say he turned me off to New York for a long time."

Louise, then Langston looked around the room, Langston trailing Louise's line of thought. Then they caught each other's eyes.

"Chicago was a real city, though, and Dad had to live in the big city. He couldn't work anywhere else."

"What'd he do?"

"He was a cook most of the time. It's funny. It's what he called himself, but he just fell into it, like anything else. Professional cook, professional Pullman car boy, really what's the difference, right? So he chased ideas. That's what took us west. He was an idealist; liked to think of himself as an entrepreneur when he wasn't thinking of himself as cook."

"And so he rode out into the Wild Wild West. That's where Wallie's from. No wonder the two of you connected."

Langston regretted saying it a moment later, because Louise's face darkened a little with the light, and she looked away.

"Aw, but I'm just going on about nothing." He lit a Lucky. "So where'd you go to school? Hampton?"

"Oh Lord, no. I went to Berkeley. All white. Ha! Just the opposite of Hampton."

"Tell me about it. I did time at Columbia. What'd you study?"

"Go figure. Economics." She smiled surreptitiously. "See my dad, he had it all wrong. He was chasing riches. I was chasing wealth. I wanted to know how money really works, you know? Get one up even on old Booker T. But then I heard Du Bois speak at Berkeley one day, and that was life changing for me."

"That Du Bois," flatly. "So why didn't you come as my guest to his wedding?"

Their eyes fluttered another meeting.

"I couldn't do that, silly." There was a tease in her voice. "Du Bois would've terrified me anyway. Are you kidding?"

They laughed again, and Langston considered how wonderfully easy Louise was to talk to. "Well, Miss Economics. At least don't turn down my offer to hire you as a typist. Betcha Booker T. would fully agree with me."

"Well, I'll think it over."

II

Who is Louise Thompson? Zora wondered. Louise Thompson Thurman? Zora laughed. She was reading a letter from New York, a letter from Langston. He'd finished a second draft of his novel; included was the first chapter; what did she think? Zora scanned the Gulf where Florida fell off in the distance receding, and the Bahamas far off against the august glare of the Atlantic on a September morning. Zora thought New York sounded like it was falling apart, is what she thought.

All lore has in its narrative remnants of an ancient theater, and initiated actors reveal their roles. Storytellers, of course, are especially special. This year in the south had changed her. What before were jigsaw islands of ideas in her head were becoming the land of thought. Along the Indian River in Florida she'd found some land she wanted to buy – even could buy – if she could get Madame Walker (*Not* Mrs. Mason!) to help. There maybe she and Lank and Wallie and Bruce and them could set up their own little group. Maybe Zora could get back to the communal Toomer work her soul so sorely missed from those early days in Harlem. She wasn't half finished with her study, there was so much more to learn; and think of a Negro artist town in the south! The city council had even agreed they could run a railroad line through it. Perhaps Zora's place in this sticky cosmic spiderweb was as the organizer of a Quasi-Gurdjieffian art colony. A Hurstonian version. Of course, Langston wasn't so much into all that, but he'd come around. Zora smiled slyly in the wind, flecks of waves against her face and lips. She'd conjure him to Obeah.

Which is what they called Conjure over in the Bahamas: Obeah. One night in Miami, dancing a shimmy with a swarthy, hunky gentleman in a strange jook, a wild rhythmic music suddenly launched into a cellular assault on the senses. Zora felt like the music had her hypnotized; hanging, jangling, jumping jack rhythms in trumpets and tambourines and instruments she didn't rightly know what they were. It was Bahamian music, and dancing to it made Zora remember the stories Langston told her of Havana. Click your heels three times, and here she was aboard ship, Langston's letter and litery in her hand, and for the first time in – oh months – a song, silly in her heart.

The Bahamian Islands were dense and lush in a mauve and orange twilight, thick fingers of shoals covered with shrubbery reaching out for the little boat as it pulled into port. Out in the town small white houses peered from beneath labyrinth rows of palm trees that cut alternate paths through the streets. It was a lusty, sweaty summer day, and brown bodies plodded along half dressed. A couple men called out vigorously as Zora passed by, and that made her smile and add an extra wiggle to her hips. She stopped in a hotel, booked a room for the night then had a drink downstairs. The drink led to long conversations with a couple people floating in and out, and then one drink turned to plurals, so she found herself by evening reclining on the porch beneath the stars, drinking Cuban rum and smiling to listen to the men who'd fallen in love with her serenade

Oh the Maise, Oh the Maise, Oh the Maise set me crazy
Oh the Maise, Oh the Maise, Oh the Maise set me crazy
Put Bellamina on the dock, and
Paint Bellamina bottom black!

A running, clapping rhythm accompanied, like a jook full of drunk and lovesick poets. Days open up, and suddenly you find the world has opened itself to you, without your even asking. Zora spent the night sleeping like she was back home again, for the first time ever in her life. When she got up the next morning, the sun flirting through the blinds a shy, blushing rose, a fly buzzing past her nose, she blinked and then sneezed, and sat up, feeling like, "well that's that. I've just exorcised the last of the old me from the new me for good."

And so the spell was cast. Zora blent into the island and its life as a new entity. She walked down to the market and met some of the musicians who'd played for her the night before.

"We play junkanoo," they told her. "Listen."

So she listened to them play a junkyard band arrangement of various percussion, strings and woodwinds, or so they were to all appearances, as they couldn't be identified as any actual known musical instruments; approximations, as it were. They played for a while, and attracted a small crowd. After the crowd reached a certain size, one of the drums dislodged itself from the band somehow, and rolled over on its belly, becoming, in a turn, a money collection pot. Zora laughed and laughed.

"Come see us play tonight at the Kilimanjaro," they told her after they'd finished a set. "You will hear and see music and dancing with more spirit than the spirit in your whole country."

The Kilimanjaro club turned out to be little more than another small old house, surrounded by leaning palms and a makeshift garden pathway of various yellow, purple and dark green flowers and herbs. Everywhere around the garden, bamboo torches cast large leaping shadows against the shaking black bodies dressed in vibrant African colors, and the whole tangle threw a shadowplay against the side of the house. Dances were a structured chaos, and the dancers sang, some wailed along with the music in rhythmic jerks, through the complex passages of music and trees and shadows, a kaleidoscope of color and contrast.

Zora wandered in and among the dancers and musicians, dancing with the men who approached her, and even approached some of the men herself. She made her way into the building, and twisted way up a spiral staircase. At the top of the stairs, a group of women were sharing a bottle in a dark, oblong room. They motioned to Zora, so she entered, and took a sip from the bottle. It was sweet like licorice, and strong enough to make you dizzy from the vapors. The rest of the room was empty except for grotesques and mythological pastiches painted on the walls, lit by two large torches. The women told Zora about the Lusca:

"She creates whirlpools around the island to drown the unworthy and uninitiated."

"Uninitiated?"

The women exchanged glances. "It is very long to explain."

"I have no quarrel with time."

"You know Atlantis?"

Zora smiled, but she didn't say anything.

"Lusca protects the secrets of Atlantis, they say. The knowledge of Ancient Atlantis is passed down generation to generation, but only to those initiated." The girl passed the bottle to Zora. "Lusca has no patience or sympathy or mercy for the uninitiated."

"Neither do I."

It was the right thing to say. The girl's name was Kali. She was a young lady, early twenties, dark and sexy and sly and frail. She stayed with her mother, she said, but they had some extra room, if Zora needed a place. "It will save you some money, no? And I want to hear more about your American Obeah."

"You mean Hoodoo."

"Yes, Hoodoo. And then this Beelzebub."

They'd been discussing abstruse spirituality all night, and they kept at it after the others left. They passed the bottle and got right deep into things, and finally, with the new day lighter and lighter burnished hues of blue, they walked arm in arm down the road, drinking and singing and talking like they'd been born the best of friends.

Which is how Zora found herself a place to stay, a new best friend, and a guide for the island. Mid September turned to late September, and a warm humid wind brought with it the cooler Atlantic autumn gusts. Zora and Kali spent the days all the same way, walking and talking and drinking and singing and occasionally joining in dancing. Kali took her to the markets, showed her the best places around the shore to catch fish, taught her to make cornmeal Johnnycakes, life was delicious. They exchanged folk tales, compared them, because their folk tales were often suspiciously similar. B'rer rabbit, Anansi the spider, even Moses, all made appearances in both.

For Zora the stories were a revelation. They were ancient as the earth and rivers, connected, oral, and most importantly, they felt true. They were real like something stumbling just beneath her consciousness. Zora and Kali walked across the island, stumbling into discoveries without understanding them.

One morning, low on the main road near the sea a large parade rambled downhill. Everyone was carrying an instrument and playing a part in a cacophonous wail of *His Eyes is on the Sparrow.*

"What's going on?"

"It's a jazz funeral."

"I thought that was only in New Orleans. Let's go mingle with them."

So they did just that. Kali had a pocket flute with her, and suddenly a big brown man was smiling at Zora and offering her a small drum.

"Gimbay," he said.

"How'd d'you do, Gimbay? Obliged. I'm Zora."

"Zora!" Kali giggled in delight. "Gimbay is the name of the drum, not the man!"

Zora learned the junkanoo dance right there and then. How's that for initiated? She banged the drum to a rhythm guided by her subconscious. The junkanoo was a warrior's dance, and apparently wildly appropriate for the occasion, and especially for the music. It was also exhausting, so much so, Zora thought she might have to roll on over and join the guest of honor by the time it was all done with.

She and Kali and Mr. Gimbay ended up alone by the ocean, with the wind bringing back refreshing energy, like each fresh sip of rum.

Once the fella's rum was plum done and gone good and proper, somehow Zora and Kali found themselves fellaless once more, and they laughed and laughed about it, and sang loud songs, and lay in the sand like a couple corpses. Zora looked up at the wide great sky, and screamed, "I'm never going back, and you can't make me."

Well, you know, you should never go to tempting the gods like that.

With all the fun she'd been having, Zora had neglected to read the chapter Langston sent her. This thought was triggered one afternoon by a group of Seminoles she saw shuffling along like a migration of birds. All that day the air had seemed still, and she hardly saw any of the snakes and rabbits she was so accustomed to. These stillnesses had periodic moments of descending over the island, and lately there had been rumors of a storm, but the eerie feeling in the air that particular afternoon, not to mention the spectacle of the Seminoles – the one who looked like an expressionless Langston Hughes in particular – well, they informed her that something was certainly wrong, and suddenly all she could think about was Langston, like some kind of trick of recollection was being played on her. So when she got back to Kali's, she went to her room, took out Langston's manuscript and looked at the cover page:

SO MOVES THE SWIFT WORLD

The novel opened with a storm, and came accompanied with its own orchestra: as soon as she read, "great drops of rain began to fall heavily," the heavens opened up and a thick gray shadow carpeted the ceiling. The whole house shook with a tremor, and there was a crash of thunder lit up by a stark shriek of lightning lancing an apocalyptic firmament.

From downstairs Zora heard Kali shriek, so she threw the manuscript aside, and bounded down the stairs. The whole first floor was in disarray. The wind had forced opened the door, and was roaring through it like a shotgun. Rain pelted in heavy and fast and a thin film was spreading across the floor. Kali and her mother were already scurrying about for an exit strategy. Zora caught Kali's eyes in a flash, and saw them drained of everything but terror.

"Zora!" whispered Kali. "We have to get out of here!"

Outside the rain made muddy canals of the roads. The trees, elegant in the balm, now stretched like tortured victims of witchdoctors against the roar, limbs hurling violently from their trunks with great agonized peals of laughter. The wind was an otherworldly element. Zora's hat flew off right away, and her suddenly soaked clothing strangled her tilting body. The three women locked arms, and trudged shivering against the monsoon.

Each moment that passed gave the wind greater strength, and took their strength away. The water flooded up to their ankles now, and was rising steadily faster than they could walk. Other groups of people pressed against the pelting rain around them. When the paneling on an old house wrenched free, hurtled through the air, and struck a man dead not far in front of them, Zora would've screamed if she could've. The man's body seemed to float right past, bearing a spreading red halo. His hair was a wet, red and black woolly shocking mess, and his face was twisted up in horror, his eyes still wide open as he passed, a pale yellow-brown brother, and for a moment he looked to Zora like Uncle Monday of the south, crossed over.

III

When Israel was in Egypt Land
Let my people go,

Oppress'd so hard they could not stand
Let my people go.
Go down, Moses,
Way down in Egypt Land,
Tell old Pharaoh
Let my people go!

"Langston, I'm going to tell you something," Godmother putting her hand over Langston's and making momentary quietus of the spirituals he kept hearing like a stuck victrola. He looked at her; her eyes were light and watery, her face gaunt, thin. He tried to look her in those peaked eyes, but it was too uncomfortable. Outside Manhattan spun past in a blur of orange streetlights. He wondered if she was going to tell him she was dying.

"I've been extremely ill as of late," Godmother swallowed a breath. "I haven't told anyone about it. Not you. Not Zora. Not even the magnificent Hall Johnson."

Whose new show they had just seen downtown. It had been spectacular, full of moving performances that only moved Langston more toward the theater. Once this book was done, boy was he ever ready to get started. Hall Johnson's arrangements were otherworldly in their spooky, haunting southern beauty. The south, sweetly rotten like an overripe fruit, like a dying old godmother. What would happen to all that money?

"I had a few bad months where I didn't know." Godmother continued. "Naturally Cornelia served as amanuensis for our communications. I am free and open with her, but you aren't. My letters might have been more forthright had I been able to anoint them with the force of my own hand. As it was, some of my messages I coded for you. Of course, you already know that."

"Of course. And Dr. Locke. Did he know?"

"Alain knew." A little curtly.

"Oh."

They rode on in silence for a while. As the limousine sailed north past the edge of Central Park, then up Seventh Avenue, Langston looked up where Harlem sat twinkling like a mythic city.

"I've found a room for you outside of New York. It's in a town in New Jersey. Your novel still needs a lot of work, and it won't get finished if you're in Harlem."

"Godmother!" Langston blurted, stopped himself, flustered about a moment in a whorl of fingers and shoulders, frowns and shrugs. He settled into his seat. "Listen Godmother, let's not – what I mean is, well gee. This is a lot all at once. You haven't even told me how you're doing now."

Godmother folded her hands and looked out the window. "Only a fool hopes to live forever, and never blend with the essence of Mother

Gaia. I simply hope to live long enough to see you produce the book the world needs from you." The car pulled up alongside the Y. "Good night, Langston. I believe we've arrived at your room. It will not be your room for much longer."

She wasn't kidding. Only a week later, he found himself in a long eerily silent ride with Godmother through the brand new Holland Tunnel, a long descent through crawling caterpillars of lights that felt like a shuttle straight to Hell, and then out into quaint New Jersey towns that all looked curiously just like each other, into a quiet, grassy tree lined town with lakes and parks everywhere you looked. He was to live with an elderly black couple, the Van Peebles. They lived on 514 Downer Street – no joke, Downer Street – and when he walked into their overly quaint, museum-like living room, Abraham Lincoln frowned at him from one wall and Jesus from the other.

Still, it really was lovely. Outside there was a small garden with yellow chrysanthemums, clusters of chamomile, fuchsia, dandelions and even a row of peach blossoms. Across the street a modestly lovely lopsided church leaned luxuriously into the landscape. Godmother touched Langston's arm, pointed.

"This church, Langston, is why I chose this place for you. The energy and spirit of Negro churches is amazing, and infectious. Zora took me to one in Harlem, where the preacher sermonized the ancient parable of the valley of the stones." She squeezed his hand affectionately. "But this church is the church where Paul Robeson's father preached. Those mighty words sang to Paul's soul, and sprang from his lips like they will your pen."

Inside, upstairs, Langston decided his room would do after all. It was large; probably quadruple the size of that old dorm room back at Lincoln. There were three sunny windows facing southwest over the Robeson church, across to a regal old row of chestnut trees. The room was unfurnished, and for a while, Langston just stood in the middle of it, smoking Luckys with the sun pouring in. He turned and turned, showering in the sunlight, as he considered just how he wanted to design the place.

He spent the next week moving things in. Godmother let him order anything he wanted: oak bookcases, a mahogany writing desk, the works. Whenever he wasn't busy with the move, he was with Louise. They would get together every day they could for lunch and drinks, a walk through Central Park.

"My life's falling apart," Louise brooded through a smile one afternoon. "Oh, but I don't know. Everyone goes through these things." She was quiet for a long while, then said, "My mother's dying Langston."

Langston thought about sick old Godmother, and wondered if folks died in threes. "Gee. I'm sorry to hear that Louise."

"It's stomach cancer. She's done nothing but slave away for white folks all her life, you know? Washing floors, being a maid, more or less a life lived as a professional mammy. It makes me miserable and angry at the same time, the life she's had to live."

"I know how you feel. You know, I told you how my mother always wanted to be on the stage, but never got the chance. I think it broke her heart."

Louise sighed impatiently. "And I told you every girl in Harlem wants to be a stage girl, supposing she's light enough for it." Then she laughed. "I'm sorry Lank, just between this and Wallie, I'm something of a bitch, huh? I couldn't get the divorce, you know, because I had to come back here for Mom. It's practically impossible to get divorced in New York, and besides, there's no more money for it anyway."

"Oh man."

"Yeah. You really need a solid reason here, like infidelity, and I don't have one, except -," She checked herself. "Or rather – I don't – there's this one bathroom incident I heard about. Anyway, I don't want to talk about that; it's too upsetting. The point being, I went to Reno to get the divorce, paid the court, but had to come back anyway, thus forfeiting money and divorce."

"So you're separated."

"What a word, right?"

They were walking Seventh Avenue of a late August afternoon. It was a cool, bright day, autumnal even, and crowds surged up and down the blocks. The cars prattled by, children played on the curbs, and in the air, the smell of rich southern food and likker.

"Let's stop somewhere for a drink," suggested Louise.

They ended up in a speakeasy just off 133rd Street. It was empty and cool inside, thick with the smell of day old cigarette smoke and fresh gin. A pool of sunlight dashed through the window of the steel door leading out.

"So watchoo gonna do now?" Langston asked her over a gin and ginger. "Why not take me up on my offer? Let Godmother pay you to be my typist. She's quite flush, so I understand."

Louise smiled. "Maybe." She drank, considered something. "Langston," after a while. "Do you ever worry that we're too insulated? Our whole movement, I mean."

Langston screwed up his brow, shrugged and frowned. "Probably."

"And how are we making a renaissance anyway, when there's never been a Negro art in the first place? Just African art, and that's not the same thing, is it? It seems to me it's all just a big fad and a fake, and it only involves just a lucky handful of us. And that hurts the work, I think. All of the work, from the civil rights work to the art work. And that's why all our New Negro novels all come out so decadent and deranged."

Langston looked Louise over curiously. "Well. Where's all this coming from?"

"I've been thinking about it a lot, is all. I did type up Wallie's book, you know." She took a drink. "And Wallie's book is good. I mean it really, is -," She paused.

"But?"

Louise glanced a deflated smile off him. "But." She took another quick drink. "Let me ask you Langston, what do you know about this Gurdjieff business?"

Langston frowned. "What, Toomer's spirituality group? Well. It's all fine and good, I guess, and might even work out if we lived in a better world."

"Well. You know Wallie. He struggles with it. He still takes it seriously, I mean. He says he's doomed, though. That he has too many buffers. For whatever that means."

"It's all a lot of hokum," said Langston. "But Wallie – and Jean was like this, too – he's looking for something to make him feel complete, transcendent and all hell. What Negro doesn't want to transcend all this insane race nonsense? But after a certain point transcendence seems to me to be downright blindness." Langston shrugged, but he was more irritated than he'd realized. "It's just more European metaphysical balderdash, and an escape from the harsh realities of life."

"Well and see," Louise pointedly. "That's just what I mean. I think we're prone to losing touch by virtue of being this isolated little group."

"The Niggerati." Langston considered how his work had been slipping lately, and worriedly wondered if maybe she was onto something. Were they not being in the world enough? He arched an eyebrow. "So are we just an insular little group of middle class Negro neurotics passing as writers?"

They laughed for a while in a blue shroud of cigarette smoke.

"But it's like you say about the girls and the stage," Langston decided. "Everyone in Harlem wants to be a writer. Everyone's writing a book. We're just the best at it." He winked at her. "After all, if it wasn't our clique, it would just be some other neurotic clique of Negroes."

Which made them laugh all over again. They finished their drinks, and then back out into the collapsing day.

"You want to catch a picture at the Renaissance?" Langston suggested. "While we're on the topic of such."

"Sure. You know Wallie's been working with Hollywood. He might even write a movie one of these days."

"That would be something. I bet he does it. He's managed to do everything else, right down to a Broadway show."

"Speaking of. Have you seen *Gold Diggers of Broadway* yet? The Times makes it sound like a lot of fun."

"No. No. I know. And everyone's talking about it."

They walked toward the theater just a couple blocks over.

"Color! Sound! Broadway shows as movies! What's the world coming to, eh?" Langston said. He looped his arm with Louise's. They crossed the street, right past Pocket Billiards, to where Renaissance Casino sat a regal red brick building, the marquee blinking gold and blue in the twilight.

An hour and a half later deposited them into a Harlem evening. They were both chuckling a little – a little at the movie, a little at themselves for liking the movie.

"Well. It was fun." Langston ventured.

"Very Broadway. It really was just like a Broadway show on a screen."

"I am the spirit of the ages, and the progress of civilization!"

"Oh dear. So is *Gold Diggers of Broadway* the future of American art?"

Langston considered this. "If so, it could've used some jazz."

"Tip toe through the tulips!"

"Some of us like to dance!"

"Say, let's go listen to some jazz someplace, now you mention it; get a drink. I need to get those show tunes out of my system."

"With you there, Louise, my darling."

The next week Langston arranged for Louise to meet with Godmother, and simple as that, she became his official typist. For all her skepticism, when Louise met Godmother, she was in awe of her. She even wrote a poem about her, and when she showed it to Langston, he arched an eyebrow, smiled and said, "Well! Wonders never cease!"

Things weren't looking so bad for Langston himself. He officially joined the editorial staff of *The New Masses,* an event he excitedly reported back to Louise.

"Looks like I'm officially going Red, I am, Louise. What will the old lady think of that!"

"Congratulations, Langston!"

Langston wondered how Wallie could have ever had reason to argue with her, except of course Wallie was really just arguing with himself. Langston hated to admit it, but Bruce was right: Wallie had done everything in his power to destroy this woman, consciously or otherwise. It was to Louise's credit that he failed.

One Thursday morning in late October Louise showed up to Westfield in a flush. She hurried out of Godmother's sedan without so much as glancing back at the driver, or even bothering to close the door on her way out of the vehicle. She hurried through the garden, into the house, up the stairs, and burst into Langston's room. Langston was in bed with a cup of coffee. He smiled pleasantly.

"Well, good morning Louise. And aren't we a little early today?"

Louise unfolded the copy of the New York Times under her arm and passed it to him. The headline she was pointing to read:

PRICES OF STOCKS CRASH
IN HEAVY LIQUIDATION;
TOTAL DROP OF BILLIONS

Langston frowned at it, then shrugged and smiled. He looked at Louise, and said, "Aw well. I'm sure the bankers will have it fixed by Halloween. Boo!" – and then regretted it, because Louise was looking at him confounded with anger. She was Miss Economics, after all.

"This is really serious, huh?"

"You have no idea."

CHAPTER SEVEN

This had happened before: coming around the curve of a hill in the road, passing over the railroad tracks, past the stationhouse, out into the town square, who should be standing there but Zora Neale Hurston herself.

He stopped, and she squinted. They regarded each other in the wonderful late April sunshine.

"Zora Neale! Fancy running into you here."

"No kidding. I'm having all sorts of spooky déjà vu myself right now, matter of fact."

Langston winked. "So long as Uncle Monday don't show up this time. Say, let's go for a stroll."

And just like that, like they'd never once for a moment parted ways, Langston and Zora promenaded down Main Street, a conspicuous couple of cosmopolitan Negroes, strutting through white old Westfield.

"Well, and we're not in the south this time," Zora observed. She lit a Pall Mall flamboyantly. "Which makes all the difference of course. The north's nowhere near as spellbound as the south."

"Yeah?" Following Zora's lead, Langston lit a Lucky. "Tell me all about it. You've picked up some color down there, you know."

"You too. Oddly enough. You look darker, Langston. Harlem or maybe it's Lincoln, but whatever it is, it must be rubbing off on you or something."

Laughing, inspecting his bare brown arms, "You don't say? Well, it's not that maybe. I just spent a couple months down in Cuba. Your tales of high adventure in the Bahamas inspired me."

"Oh, that was really something. Only the storm was terrible. I don't think – and well, I'm almost certain I was responsible for it, too. You see, I was down there challenging God."

"Always a bad idea."

They had no particular direction or destination, so almost by synchronicity they walked off toward the park. Westfield was a wonderful park town; every other block bloomed into a new broadcast of trees and lakes. Walking along the perfect circling curve of a stream, Zora talked about the work she'd collected.

"You've already seen a bunch of the good stuff. And then the scientific stuff I've mostly sent to Boas. Now I need time to clear my head and figure out how I want it all arranged. I really want to write a folklore book like nothing that's ever been written before: part folk novel itself, but still a solid work of anthropology, and also a book of pure folklore fun. Someone has to do it. Otherwise, a hundred years from now, and no one will even remember stories like these anymore."

"Not even half that, the way the world's looking nowadays."

"Which is why Godmother sent me out here anyway. To put all my notes together into a book." Zora gave Langston a curiously sly look. "She said you'd be a nearby neighbor."

"I didn't think you'd get out to Westfield this soon."

"Just got in this morning. I'm still unfurnished. What do you think of the Robeson church?"

They laughed and laughed.

"So she really sent you out here to do your book, too, huh? Put us out here together."

"She says New York's too much distraction for me."

"She says that about me, too," Langston mused. "What she doesn't get is that it's us that distract each other, not Harlem. That poor befuddled old thing has got it all wrong, once again. But us being out here's meant to be anyway, so there's nothing she could do about it. I've been thinking about our blues opera."

"Ha! Me too! Godmother said she doesn't want us working on that anymore."

"I know. Still, this gives us the perfect opportunity to write it all the same. Godmother's edict against it be damned."

"Surely. Speaking of, how's your book?"

"Days away from release. I changed the title."

"No more *So Moves This Swift World*?"

"Awful, huh? Well, hell. Titles are tough. Just ask Carlo. Anyway, it should be coming out in July. I'm looking forward to it. I have one positive review already coming from Wallie."

"You never know with Wallie, you know. So what you working on now?"

Langston picked up a pebble from the trail, skipped it across the lake. "Nothing for now, I s'pose."

"Oh, she's not gonna like that."

"She don't gotta know. Besides, we have our opera to write."

"So where do we start?"

"Well, and here it is, Zora," Langston threw down his cigarette and fished out another. "Since Godmother doesn't want us to do our opera together, I figured I'd tell her I'm doing it myself. That's why I was in Cuba. I was there looking for a composer to collaborate with. After you wrote me about all that Bahamian dance, it's like I say. I got inspired."

Zora squinted at him. "So you're doing it without me? What are you saying, Lank?"

"No." Langston lit his cigarette, stopped and turned to face her. "No. We'll do something together, but I had to tell Godmother I'm working, and so she thinks I'm working on the opera."

"Hm!" Zora continued to walk. "And who is your composer? And how do I get any credit for the work?"

"Aw, Zora," keeping her increased pace. "I couldn't find a composer down there. The opera's just a red herring for Godmother, and besides, not even Scott Joplin could pull one off. Opera's so European anyway. Why don't we two write a folk comedy – a play instead of an opera – together? I've been thinking it over. Theresa Helpern, a lady from the Dramatists Guild put the buzz in my brain, and it's not gone since. She said there haven't been any good Negro comedies for the stage. Everything's *The Emperor Jones*, or *Porgy*, or *Harlem*. Why don't we write one? We can use one of your stories."

Zora stopped again, peered peevishly at Langston. "Do you know," she said, "that around the Bahamian Island Andros, a half shark, half octopus guards Atlantis, and sucks uninitiated sailors into the big sea?"

Langston glanced at her, hopelessly confused. "Well, gee." Smiling. "Is that our Negro comedy?"

"Maybe it is. Maybe it is." She swiveled with a giggle, and kept on walking.

"You know, Lank," Zora one afternoon over gin and ice cream like old times back at Niggerati Manor, "I think we could use the story I always tell about the Methodists and the Baptists for this play of ours." They were listening to spirituals in the glow of the springtime firmament, Paul Robeson bellowing out the window above his papa's church.

"Which one is that again?"

"The turkey and the mule. The one I always tell about Dave Carter and Jim Weston where they both shoot at the same turkey, and they both of them claims the kill. So the Baptists and Methodists hold court."

"It could work. Go on and tell it again."

"Right now?"

"Yeah, now. Of course now. No time like the present."

"You just get a kick outta hearing me say it."

"Well, that's the truth." Langston lit a cigarette, turned off the victrola and grabbed a pen and pad. "But let's be serious about it, though. You tell the story, and I'll take notes."

"And I'm self conscious about this whole story, too. You know I tried and tried to write this thing before, but Locke never liked it."

"That humorless Dr. Locke."

"Well, Waldo Frank's the one suggested to me it should be a play in the first place. You remember him, don't you? Him and Jean were real close." Zora lit a Pall Mall. "I'm thinking maybe he was onto something."

Langston looked at Zora with ecstatic impatience. He blinked. "Um… Will you just go ahead and tell the story, then?"

They got started. Langston took notes. Gin and ice cream all through the afternoon hours, while Zora frowned and listened to Langston deconstruct the thing, reminding her of the Saturday Nighters in Washington all over again.

"We need a Wow moment," Langston lighting a Lucky and looking over his notes. "What we have right here is a two act play. It should be three. Act One's crisis is the dispute between Jim and Dave. In Act Two the crisis revolves around the trial, right? We got the Baptists and the Methodists, and the dispute between Dave and Jim symbolizes the larger dispute between the two sects. But then we just get a verdict like a punch line, and no Wow moment."

"Wow, Langston. Really? A Wow moment?"

"Wallie was telling me about this. With *Harlem,* you know. I mean, he wasn't so bully about the Wow moment in *Harlem,* all things considered – the producers more or less made him write one in, but the producers do have a point. An audience wants something to make the end satisfying, and the punch line of the verdict isn't enough. We need a third act, sure."

Zora frowned and drank. "So what do you suggest?"

"I don't know." Langston smoked thoughtfully. "I guess I'll need to think about it."

Zora stubbed out her cigarette and hopped to her feet. She put her hands out. "Here. Stand up."

Langston took her hands, stood. "What now?"

"Let's act it out."

"Huh?"

"Let's act out the first acts, and see if that inspires us. I reckon it just might."

"Gee, Zora. You're loony as the moon."

"No. I'm Dave Carter. You can be Jim Weston."

"But Dave wins."

"Yeah, that's right."

"So I gotta get run outta town?"

"Yeah, but all that's off stage."

"Let's put it on stage. Where I whoop you with a mule bone too. Put them both on stage. It's good drama. Matter of fact, Jim on the way out could be Act Three."

"Your Wow moment?"

"Well, and why not?"

"I fail to see the Wow in a brother wandering the train tracks out of town all alone."

"Dave could come after him."

"Oh, I don't think Dave would do that."

"No? Maybe not." Langston pondered this. "Well, let's act it out, and see what we get." He spread his hands in the air, stretching wide his fingers. "Curtain rises. What do we see?"

"So tell me about Cuba," Zora said a little later in the afternoon, the sun running angles of lines westward down the wall. "You said you couldn't find a composer to work with there. So what did you do?"

"Turned into something of a vacation." Langston refreshed his gin and ice cream with gin and ice cream. "Meeting with poets and writers more than musicians. They do have a lot to work with. *El Son Cubano!* It's like a Cuban jazz. Or blues. It works by the same call and response."

"Hm. Bahamian music is complete chaos blues."

"I wonder if we compared all the musics by peoples with African origins just what we'd discover common between them."

"A story."

"No kidding."

"I mean it clear as I say it, though. I think there's a story to be found there. You'd find it through musical suggestions, I suppose. Associations, who knows? You'd find the spirit of music. Like the origin of music. And since I'm with Boas that we probably all come from Africa originally anyway, then all musics by all peoples have African origins."

Langston considered this. "You know, Zora. I think you're getting too deep for me with all your anthropology talk. But I like that. That thought, I mean. That we all came from Africa."

"And we need to get back to it."

"Oh."

Zora winked. "If you could see your face right now. No, I haven't gone Garvey on you. I mean metaphorically, silly. Back to the wisdom of the ages and all that. Folks talk about the primitive and the ancient like they're one and the same, but there's nothing primitive about some of the lost ancient wisdom's what I say."

Langston looked at Zora and admired her leaning back lazy on one arm, light bronze and gold in the late afternoon plum slice of sun. Her hat flopped over her knee, a quizzing smile on her plump lips, as she looked down towards the straw brim, "play needs a frail," Langston said with a shrug.

"Come again."

"We ought to drop the turkey and have Dave and Jim fight over a frail instead." Langston grinned, drank some gin. "More Wow factor."

"You're hopeless."

"It might just work, though. It gives us a third act, too. Dave and Jim can make up, and they both drop the gal."

"Sounds like the Bruce Nugent adaptation."

Langston laughed. "Not like that, of course. Suppose Jim gets run out of town, and Daisy runs into him as she's going off to meet up with Dave."

"That's that Daisy."

"Well, and then here comes Dave, off to meet up with Daisy, and he runs into Jim and Daisy together. Which naturally he takes the wrong way. Voila."

"A third act."

"A third act."

Zora laughed, and lit a Pall Mall. "We could have some real fun with the woo-the-woman wordplay."

"So? You like it?"

"It's a good idea. I'm glad I thought it up."

They would need a stenographer of course. They would act the thing out, and keep what worked and drop what didn't. That way, the entire spirit of the thing would maintain a living sense of spontancity. The obvious choice for stenographer was Louise. By the time they'd finished talking themselves through it, the sun had slipped southwest past the last window, glowing the room autumn amber on a spring twilight, and they were so excited and exhausted, they swore each other to secrecy then promptly feel asleep, collapsed reclining into each other on Langston's loveseat.

The next morning they took the train into the city to kidnap Louise. It had been a hard, bitter fall for Manhattan. Harlem in particular. Winter was worse. Come spring all the downtown literati and Harlem Niggerati went around with long, lean faces, repeating *April is the cruelest month*. Homeless bodies in filthy stinking blankets sprouted up around Harlem like weeds wilting through the concrete. Arriving in Harlem, neither Langston nor Zora had ever remembered things looking so bad.

"It's worse by the week," Louise explained. The three of them walked up Seventh Avenue where storefront by storefront, old standbys had suddenly vanished, piles of blankets and bodies in their place. "Capitalism's finished, if you ask me." She swallowed a thought, then gulped out, "I think maybe it failed, and this is it. You know?"

Langston and Zora looked at each other and didn't know what to read in each other's eyes. Langston looked away and wondered fearfully what this desolation would really mean in a larger sociological way. His sociology classes at Lincoln hadn't prepared him for anything like this. Was this the beginning of a global Communist revolution? And if so, where did he stand in things? A feint in the gorgeous afternoon, the buildings, blue sky, wisps of clouds, supposing his association with Godmother was ultimately irreconcilable with his vision, and the future of that vision? After all, Godmother hated it when Negroes got political. Yet, it seemed like there was nothing more important for Negroes to be right now, than political.

Yeah, this could turn into something of a problem.

Zora kept looking at Langston, to where he got uncomfortable with it, and she followed his eyes as they floated down and away from hers. Later on she would import more meaning into this moment than she did right then. Instead, she took both Langston and Louise's hands, and she squeezed them. "Well, so long as there's bootleg gin, Harlem will stay Capitalist."

Everyone laughed. "You suggesting a speak?" said Langston.

"That I think, my two Jersey gentry, is what a great day in Harlem calls for." And Louise strutted voluptuously ahead, letting go of Zora's hand, aimed straight towards Lenox.

But after three glasses of whisky Louise was in tears. "It just makes me hate this so called Great Migration of Negroes. It's a trap, the whole thing, herding Negroes up to these northern cities to live cramped up in slums. They trick people with our own propaganda. Come to New York! Be a New Negro! A twentieth century slave instead of a nineteenth century one! A machine is better than a mule! Be a machine and not a man! Oh, it's atrocious. You know the south better than anyone, Zora. What do you think? Don't you think it's all just a lot of hokum, this paradise of northern cities?"

Langston didn't mean to smile, so he suppressed it. Zora started to speak, and then thought about the plantation in South Carolina she'd wanted to buy – about the life she and Langston and Wallie and Aaron and Bruce and sure, even Louise, could all be living over there as compared to up here, and all she did was sigh.

"Louise. I think we need to get you out to Westfield forthwith is what I think."

Zora had a big old stack of papers to go through over at her place, while movers shuffled through the house with chairs and tables and sofas and a desk. She had a whole small two-floor house by herself. "Godmother says I have more work to do than you, and besides, women need their privacy," she told Langston as he jealously toured the premises. "But we're neighbors anyway, and mi casa es tuyo."

"We want to hire you as a stenographer is what this all comes down to," Zora explained to Louise. "It will give you some income while you look for something regular in the city. And we really do need your help."

"Well, maybe. I can't figure Mrs. Mason out. She's been giving me a hard time right from the start. All because I don't send her weekly thank you letters. She's an employer, right? Who sends an employer weekly thank you notes?" Louise frowned, then smiled. "But she loves you, Zora. You're all she talks about." She laughed. "You're her pure child savage of the south."

"Ra! Ra!"

"Well, and but here's the thing though, Louise," Langston lit a Lucky. "Zora's work is a complete red herring."

Louise looked at Zora and Zora winked at her. "Not a complete red herring."

"We're writing – wait. We have to swear you to secrecy."

"Blood rituals and all," said Zora.

"What are you two up to anyway?" Louise looked curiously from Langston to Zora.

Out across Downer Street, and down to North Scott Plains, the three strolled arm in arm in arm through the politely quizzing white middle class town. Spring was bringing gifts every day, Brookside Park was a wash of sun and shadows beneath stately sycamores. Back and forth, Zora and Langston wrassled out the plot of the play. They were writing it, making it up as much on the spot as they were explaining it to Louise.

"Act Three starts with Davey leaving town," said Langston.

"Why are you starting with act three?"

"Oh, well, that's a long story," said Zora. "See it all starts one day on Joe Clarke's front porch. Folks telling lies, right?"

"Tall tales," explained Langston.

"Okay."

"And in come Davey and Jim. One's a singer, the other's a dancer."

"And one's a Baptist and the other's a Methodist," Zora added.

"Which one's which one's which?"

"Well, that's not important."

"Of course it's important," Zora cut across a very confused Louise. "The whole town's split over the sects. But Dave and Jim start out cool. They do a bunch of songs together in the first act. Then comes a real chippie."

"That's Daisy."

"Daisy Taylor. The town vamp."

"Aw, Zora, you're too hard on her."

"She's my character. What would you call her?"

"Misunderstood?"

"Ha!"

"Do Dave and Jim go on like an old married couple like the two of you?" asked Louise.

"What are you on about?" said Langston.

"But sure, they get on like grapes until Daisy shows up."

"Dave and Jim both want to walk her home of course."

"And wham!"

"Jim lams Dave upside the head with Brazzle's dead old mule's old hind bone."

"So Dave being Baptist, and Jim being Methodist, the Baptists and the Methodists hold court. See old Joe Clarke is a Baptist himself, and Pastor Simms is a Methodist, and he's scheming on Joe Clarke's mayorial spot. So the whole thing is politics."

Louise had been listening, bewildered a bit, but smiling. Now she sort of floated to a stop along the long lane of sycamore trees. "This thing could really work, you know? If you do it right. The Negro church, folk stories, the personal turned political, all in a comedy, and not another pathological Negro tragedy. I really think you two are onto something."

"Think so, huh?" Langston winked at Zora, and she winked back politely. "So whaddya say? You be our secret stenographer for our secret play, and have Godmother pay you for it without her even realizing it?"

"I'm on board. Sure, why not?" Louise shook Langston's hand, then Zora's. "We got ourselves a team."

Zora didn't know about the whole "team" thing, real familiar attitude for a damn glorified stenographer, you ask her, but she didn't have much time to think about it. The next day, a Wednesday, she received this telegram from Mrs. Mason:

I WILL BE EXPECTING YOU FRIDAY 3 PM
BRING MANUSCRIPTS AND NOTEBOOKS

Which meant, of course, she had about two days to accomplish Hercules' twelve tasks.

It rained hard that Friday morning. Zora and Langston had a quiet cup of coffee as they smoked cigarettes in the frayed light.

"How ready are you?" Langston asked her. Zora shrugged and smiled and said, "More ready than I was before I went collecting. She's a tough old bag, Godmother, but she's no black woman alone in the deep south."

The car arrived, and Zora rode down to Manhattan thinking without thinking, forgetting what she thought as soon as she thought it. She brought notebooks full of folklore, songs and myths, and she didn't even look at them on the way. Walking into the throne room again after all that time, and seating herself on a stool beneath Godmother's throne didn't even feel humiliating. She found herself feeling sorry for the old lady. Zora already felt more powerful than her. Mrs. Mason lived in a stage, because she couldn't bear to do otherwise.

"You're feeling better," Zora said. "I feel quite well, myself."

"Very good, Zora," appraising her for a moment. "Well, look at you! Why did you bring all that useless stationary? I want you to tell me everything." She smiled broadly. "Go on. I'm impatient, my lovely child."

So Zora launched into the long and tall of the tale. From the jooks to having a knife pulled on her to learning Hoodoo at the crossroads to the storm in the Bahamas, and she kept old Mrs. Mason entertained through the afternoon into the early evening. Despite what Zora had said earlier, Mrs. Mason seemed a touch peaked when she arrived, but by the time they'd been through an afternoon brunch, and a light evening supper with some extremely potent Peruvian wine, the old dame looked a sight more lively.

"Let's go to the theatre, Zora. What on Broadway should we see?"

The question was a set up, of course. The obvious choice was *Green Pastures.*

On the way to the theatre, they detoured uptown to pick up Alain, who was in town for the weekend, and wanted to see it himself. He'd been waiting for the opportunity to go with Godmother.

The three of them rode down Broadway in a suddenly sullen silence. Dr. Locke's presence. In an awful and hyperselfconscious moment, Zora wondered if she was afraid of Tomming in front of Godmother with another jig about. All three of them stuffed awkwardly in that car on their way to watch the son of a slave, Richard Harrison, play De Lawd in *Green Pastures.*

But wait it gets worse.

Right as they walked into the theatre, Locke turned to Zora and said, out of the blue, "Langston mentioned you two want to hire Louise as a stenographer for your folklore project and his opera. You do realize Louise is something of a *persona non grata* with us right now?"

"Oh."

And with those words they entered the auditorium, Zora burning up with anger at Alain Locke and Charlotte Mason and Langston Hughes, too. Why the hell did he talk to Locke without telling her about it?

So it took a while for her to get into the show. But then she fell into it, and found herself enjoying it. It reminded her of Jean, and then she wasn't angry at Langston at all. She thought about the meetings at Dorothy Peterson's and the meetings uptown, the meetings at Carl's place, Charles Johnson's apartment in Brooklyn, and Eddie Wasserman's downtown. The Moses stories in *Green Pastures* made her think of Sparta Georgia, and the dizzy magic of the night there with Langston. No, she wasn't mad at Langston at all.

Leaving the theater, riding to Park Avenue, the three of them fell silent again, but this time, for Zora it was a spellbound silence, almost as if she were alone in her room watching the stars make patterns and chasing allegories in them.

"Alain's right, Zora," Mrs. Mason said after a while. "Louise is on my last nerve, and she has nothing of the artist in her. She was born the wrong color, and under the wrong star. But Alain and I have discussed this at length. I'm happy with what you've collected, Zora. I am very happy with it. I think you will write a masterpiece. So if you think Louise will be of assistance to you, then she shall be of assistance to you."

It was a helluva way to put things, but whatever worked.

II

"See see rider, see what you done done,
See see rider, see what you done done,
You made me love you,
Now your fella's come.

I'm going away, baby,
I won't be back til fall.
Gonna go away baby,
And won't be back til fall
Lord knows, Lord willing,
I won't be back at all.

Zora!"

"What on earth are you doing?"

"Singing? What else? Well and good afternoon. You're awful familiar, you don't knock? This calls for gin."

"If you insist, Lank, but we've work to do. An outline to draft. There will be time enough tonight to drink in Harlem when we celebrate. I've settled things with Louise and Godmother."

"Yeah, how'd it go?"

"She seems pleased. For now."

"How's her health? She wasn't doing too well for a while there."

"She's –," Zora smiled faintly. "Recovering."

"Oh. Well, I'm glad to hear things went well. I was actually working, myself."

"I can see that."

"Well, hell. It needed a little litery first. But I was thinking about the third act. Since we're writing that first, it seems."

"Sure. What's up?"

"Well, we got Jim walking the tracks leaving town, right? And running on her way to meet Dave, here comes Daisy, looking this way and that like a cautious doe. And then not far behind comes Dave, off to meet Daisy. And that's how we get them all together. But at first it's just Jim walking the tracks. He's hopping mad, only what does he say? He could have a great little soliloquy right there, but everything I've come up with sounds either corny or off the cob."

Zora lit a Pall Mall. "You really are lost without me, aren't you, honey?"

"Aw, don't you ever forget it?"

"I don't fergit nothing. Why, I'll kill some of you ole box-ankled niggers!" Zora flourished. "*Voila*! We have an opening line for our third act."

They were in a Harlem speak by dusk. Louise was with them, and so was Bruce. Saturday afternoon was turning into a fine spring Saturday night, and Harlem blared broadcasts of its beauty in the rumble of motorcars, the honking of horns, jazz roaring out of doorways, folks gathered in conversations at every street corner. Everyone was out in their righteous rags, the best they could afford, red suits, black suits, blue suits, suits suited to suggest hope in depression. Chilly's speak on West 127th, down a short flight of steps, had just the lightest clientele though, it still being early. Smoke thick air heavy with the likker made the four feel sleepy and energetic at the same time, unreal, like they were in a black and white moving picture.

Langston was still laughing over Zora's line, repeating it occasionally at inappropriate intervals, when a scatty looking cat, tall, dark, wiry, horn-rimmed glasses leaning down his long flat nose, came in looking this way then that, surveying the scene from beneath a bowler brim two sizes too big for him. Bruce nudged Langston.

"See there? It's Slim. Wallie's friend."

Langston cocked his hat low. "Whaddya know?"

"Who's Wallie's friend?"

Bruce, Langston and Zora exchanged glances.

"What am I not being told here?" Louise flushed; her eyes widened as she looked from Bruce to Langston to Zora. "Zora?"

"He's just some ole pickpocket."

"Why's he Wallie's friend?"

"Becaue Wallie was a-lookin' for one."

"Bruce!" Langston suppressed a smile.

"He was," Bruce insisted. "Wallie needed a friend with money, bad. This is before he went Hollywood, remember. And Slim always shows up with a cache of wallets. Wallie figured if Charles Johnson can bank off a numbers runner like Casper Holstein, he could bank off a Harlem pickpocket like Slim. Same difference, really."

"Slim?"

"Slim pickings," said Zora. "You know, a pickpocket."

"So what do people call him to his face?"

"Slim, naturally," said Bruce.

"Or Otto," said Zora.

"Shhh! He's coming this way." Langston winked at Louise, which – surprising all of them, Louise included – made her hiccough a giggle.

"Bruce! Lanky! Ladies!" Slim's voice was lazy, a round plum, a sound so ripe you could taste it. He pulled a chair up beside them at the bar. "There's a round on me in this." He lit a Bull Durham. "Zora! It's a pleasant surprise to see you again, You done went from low black to lam black. More like me. It looks you swell." He took Zora's hand and kissed it. Looking up, he caught Louise's half-alarmed, half-charmed glance, and smiled. "Now I don't believe *we've* had the honor -,"

"Louise," Louise dangled out her hand, wondering if it too, would be kissed. It perched limp in the air like a trembling bird.

Slim took it with a gentle squeeze. "Otto. A pleasure."

Louise peered at him. "I thought they called you Slim."

Slim laughed very loud, but very brief. "They do."

"Which do you prefer?"

"Otto," and he kissed her hand.

"He's just putting on dicty airs for the new lass," said Bruce. "Slim it is."

"Nothin' in a name but the namer." Slim glanced at Bruce, released Louise's hand and flagged the bartender.

"Harlem's kind of low down since the crash, huh?" Langston asked.

"It ain't high up."

A round of gin floated the bar.

"To Harlem!" said Slim.

"To Harlem!" all around, and all down.

"But there's this rent party up on Lenox tonight," Slim glanced across the coterie.

"You don't say," said Zora.

"Wise old Zora. Some things don't change, do they?" Slim puffed thoughtfully a moment. "Why not y'all come on through with me? It's a litery clique. Just like y'all are. Some dicties, some shines, some ofays, some ahead of they time, and some behind."

They laughed, and Slim ordered another round.

"Might be interesting," said Louise. "Who are they? Any of them published?"

Slim looked at Louise and smoked. "Well. How do you mean? There's all kinds of published."

"*The Crisis*?" Langston suggested. "Or *Opportunity*?"

"Aw, git on out with that. This ain't no *Crisis* party or *Opportunity* banquet."

"Sure, we'll check it out. It's not like Du Bois knows every talented Negro in Harlem."

"Wise old Zora," Slim lit Zora's cigarette for her. "Bartender! We need some more gin!"

The rent party was in a large loft above a flower shop on Lenox. Pipes and tubes ran along the walls and ceilings, peeking from behind crumbling brick. Blue and red lights groaned glowing blankets of smoke through the music, a funky, swinging, startling, scatting jazz played, apparently by an ever-revolving number of the loft's residents. Slim pointed toward the stage, and confirmed this. "They don't hire musicians. They play all the music themselves, and that way they make even more money on their rent parties."

A limping piano jangled along beneath a curiously stiff jazz verse; the actual words were drowned beneath a heavy bass hard beat. Ofays from the Village, flapper girls from downtown, shines, bootleggers, black eccentrics, number runners, shuffled shoulder to shoulder in hypnotic sexy thrusting dancing.

"Let's grab a drink," said Langston. "Slim, we're following your lead to the bar."

I gave my baby
All my blues for free,

I gave my baby
All my blues for free,

I let my baby
Get the best of me.

Slim got a round of gin and White Rock, and then took them around to meet the hosts. The first they met was a white guy in a gray zoot. He had a gray top hat, a bright red tie, and pince-nez sunglasses. He was carrying a cane.

"Pleased to meet you. I'm known as Ether."

"A poet?" asked Langston.

"Yeah. Well. Probably." Ether adjusted his sunglasses, and stepped off, tapping his cane testily as he went.

"What's with him?" asked Louise.

"They take some getting used to," Slim pushed onward through the crowd toward a dark black man in construction clothes. "Jerusalem, I'd like you to meet some old friends of mine."

Jerusalem turned and looked and smiled and laughed. "You actually *know* these niggas?" Jerusalem laughed even harder to hear himself ask it, leaving the four guests a little flummoxed and uncomfortable.

"No disrespect to y'all," said Jerusalem, "but we never get Harlem celebrity here."

"Who's celebrity?" said Bruce.

"Just another group of artists," Langston added. "Like yourselves, I reckon."

"Except we don't publish."

"You don't publish?"

"Why not?" asked Louise.

"Well," Jerusalem said, "art is art, or else it's propaganda. If you're going to buy into the whole thing, by which I mean if you're going to publish in *The Crisis* and *The Nation* and if you're lucky, ooh, *The Atlantic*, then you better give a second consideration to your leader Dr. Du Bois' position. Everything you do or write, like it or not, is gonna be used as some kind of propaganda. So what kind of propaganda do you want your propaganda to be? That's your question. Now, us on the other hand?" Jerusalem took a dramatic moment to light a cigar. "We're just really artists, you know? We're not propagandists, so we don't publish"

"Well!" Langston said quickly, "that's all fine and good, if you don't want to contribute anything to society. We need black poets out there as well as white ones. Besides, you didn't even mention the magazines that are really interesting right now: *The New Masses, The New Republic, The Messenger.*"

"Well I see you're all decided on who you're propagandizing for already. But I don't see who this we you're referring to is. *We've* had black poets as long as there've been black people. What *we* don't need is black poets publishing to try and prove something to white people. "

"Negroes are part of this society," Louise said hotly, "however disenfranchised. Like it or not. You can pretend you're above it all, or you can open your eyes to the reality of things. It's our responsibility to engage in the society, so we can change it for the better."

"You're just pushing a rock up a mountain," said Jerusalem. "Right down to the roots this thing we like to call an evolving, progressive society, well it just disenfranchises the black man, the world over."

"So you're a Garveyite then?" said Louise.

"Oh no, I'm no Garveyite. Back to Africa! Imagine that. I already told you what I am, and that's an artist who lives in Harlem, and that's that."

This conversation was going nowhere, so they moved on. Langston joked the momentary awkwardness away the best he could.

"Well, they're a kooky lot, but I like them all the same!"

Slim gave him an amused look. "Come on. There's more people for you to meet. They're not all as extreme as those last two."

"I'd hope not," said Louise.

Through a black and tan pack of dancers, and into a narrow hallway where a few groups of people were pressed together in circles, talking fast. Zora recognized one of the men immediately.

"Waldo!"

Waldo Frank, who'd been talking to a pasty, wiry, blonde-haired ofay with a cliff and crater of a face, turned in her direction. His eyes lit up. "Zora Hurston? What are you doing here? Don't tell me you've joined up with this oddball lot."

Langston moved to defend their oddball lot, then realized the fellow might be referring to the radicals, and deferred to Zora.

"What are you doing here? That's the question," Zora hugged Waldo. "What are you doing in Harlem? And here of all places? Have you talked to Jean?"

Something terribly sad flashed across Waldo's face.

"You know Jean Toomer?" This from the pasty ofay beside Waldo. "How do you all know Jean?"

"How does anyone not know Jean?" said Bruce.

Langston put out his hand. "We know Jean through literary circles. Langston. Langston Hughes."

"You're Langston Hughes? The Negro poet?" The man's eyes brightened. They suddenly came right to life. "Jean talked about you!"

"Oh."

The man laughed, shook Hughes' hand warmly, then slapped him on the shoulder. "My name's Hart Crane."

"Oh, I've seen your work in *Poetry*."

"That's right. I just published a book, as a matter a fact."

"I just sold my first novel."

"Cheers!" They laughed and toasted gin.

"So tell me about your book."

"Oh, it's just one poem. One long poem. An epic. Like *The Wasteland*. I mean, I don't want to compare it to *The Wasteland*. That's a masterpiece.

But I hope mine is something of a response to Eliot."

"Wow. That's ambitious."

Hart smiled feebly. "So what's your novel about?"

"Well, it's not sensational like some of the other Negro novels you hear about. It's just about a black kid growing up in Kansas."

"You from Kansas?"

"Well, Kansas and Cleveland."

"I'm from Cleveland!"

"No kidding. Whereabouts?"

While Langston and Hart got to talking about Cleveland, Waldo and Zora and Bruce chatted each other up about the old days in Washington, Georgia Douglas Johnson and the old crew from back then; Louise looked on both groups, feeling something like an amateur sociologist. Slim had disappeared.

'How do you know this crowd?" Zora asked Waldo.

"We met them years ago through the Ouspensky work."

"How's that coming?"

"I don't know about all that esotericism anymore," said Waldo. "Or even Jean, to tell you the truth. But that's not worth getting into here. It's a long story, and it's no fun for anyone. How about you? What have you been up to?"

"Well, you remember that story I wrote?" said Zora. "The one about the two guys who fight over a turkey and one hits the other with a mule bone?"

"Who could forget it?" said Waldo. "I still think it sounds like a perfect idea for a play."

"Well that's the what. I'm writing it as a play. Langston's helping."

"Get out of town! You serious?"

"We're taking it to Broadway, Waldo."

"Congratulations, old girl. I always knew you were the best of the lot of us. Introduce me to Langston Hughes, why dontcha?"

Langston and Hart were shaking hands enthusiastically. "We've agreed to buy each other's books," said Langston.

"I look forward to reading your novel this summer. I'm divorcing this wretched city, you understand. I've been going out to Patterson to get away from time to time, where a man can find some rest. Read. Write. Drink in peace! Ha ha!"

Langston laughed. "I'm on your side there. We're out in Westfield these days, doing much the same. Me and Zora, that is."

They formed a larger circle against the wall, and introduced each other in a chaotic kind of chatter.

"Let's go do some dancing," said Zora.

Around the corner, they crashed into the crush of crowds and cymbals and shaking and shimmying and the cool mellow call of a trombone. Saxophone bass melody, low blues bass guitar, and a lovely lam black lady in baggy old green and beige garb, sang,

It's a sad old world
So I'll tell you what I'll do:
It's a sad old world
When your daddy won't be true.
Gonna leave my cheatin' daddy,
And his money leaving too!

Hart broke into a wild, savage gin romp, stomping a clumsy mixture of Charleston, Black Bottom and Fox-Trot. The rhythm of bodies swallowed his eccentricities elegantly. Langston and Louise found themselves suddenly locked together in a brisk, close, sexy two-step swing. Louise shivered and smiled and Langston felt the tingle of likker and smoke in his nose trickle back through his spine. They flirted smiles, and danced obligingly. Zora had barely met foot to floor before a husky black man lifted his hat to her, and lifted her into his arms. Bruce giggled his way into a sly wiggle of a dance, his eyes on Hart in the mix, while Waldo flailed somewhat helplessly in the surge, and doing so, seemed to blend right in.

The music thumped from blues to jazz and back again. The girl sang and scatted, hummed or let the hum of her silence do the phrasing. Bruce, finally making his way over to Hart, let his hand slip down and brush Hart's. Hart glanced up, caught Bruce's eye, caught the meaning, and looked quickly away.

"Look, it's okay with me," said Bruce.

Hart flushed bright red like a sudden onset of sunburn. His mouth opened, closed.

Bruce gave his most disarming smile. "We can always tell each other, you know. Of course, you know."

Hart shook his head dizzily, blinked. "It's – it's not that." His red color seemed, impossibly, to be deepening. With a few flustered words, he excused himself and disappeared.

Bruce shrugged, and found himself turning to face Waldo.

"Don't take it personal. Hart's – he's not. It's not that he's racist." Waldo breathed a wall of gin. "He actually has a thing about black men; he has dreams about them, but they frighten him too much."

"Oh!" Bruce's smile broke up like crockery into a frightening giggle. "Well, Boo!" and he disappeared in the crowd the opposite direction. A moment later he was swarming into another group of dancers, while Hart thundered away at his savage rhythms, the whole thing swallowed up and forgotten in the swell of the night.

Across the floor, Langston ran into a rejection of his own. Coming back from the bar he saw a short copper penny brown girl that looked a lot like Laudee. Passing her in the hall, a sweep of the joy of nostalgia overwhelmed him, and he embraced her, probably spilling some of his gin in the process.

"Nigga, touch me again, and I *will* cutchoo!"

"Oh."

"You heard me. Now step the hell off."

Zora, catching sight of the drama on her own way to the bar, started to laugh.

"And who the hell is you?"

The vamp's belligerent tone took Zora off guard. "The Queen of Sheba to you bitch," Zora retorted, and received a long look up and down as preface to a reply.

"I don't see no *Queen of Sheba*. I do see a greasy old dish rag of a woman with a face like a possum, and a body like a park ape!"

"Oh, you want it like that? Because I'm surprised someone like you'd even play the Dozens, when you're uglier than the bitch of a hound and a bulldog, and stanky as a back room Georgia jook. So short your man gotta lay on his back to eat your bread, not that any man in his right head would want that rotten yeast, you box-ankled, bone-brained, liver-lipped, cow-faced heifer!"

The woman moved towards Zora quick, but Langston caught her quicker.

"Nigga!" She swung towards Langston, "I told you touch me again, and I will cutchoo."

Maybe she might've too, but Langston suddenly roared, louder than he realized, "Why, I'll kill some of you ole box-ankled niggers!"

And well, that scared her right off.

III

The opening of act three was settled right then and there. They spent the night in Harlem with Louise, and in the morning, the three of them rode back out to Westfield together.

"You really need the vacation, I can tell," said Zora.

"Oh." Louise wasn't sure what she meant. "I do need to be looking for work, though."

"You've got a job!" Langston said. "We'll send Godmother a telegram right now, and tell her you'll be staying with us this week. Bet you sevens and elevens she gives you a little something extra for your time."

Well, Langston would've been betting on a slow bleed. Sunday and

Monday passed, and they worked on the play without a word from Godmother. By Tuesday they were getting worried. When Wednesday rolled around and not a word from her, no telegram, no phone call, no letter, no nothing, Zora wondered out loud if the old lady had up and died on them.

"Maybe we should call her," said Langston.

"Give it a couple days. You know how she hates to be bothered when she doesn't want to be. Plus, she'll think we're waiting for her to die."

"Are we?"

Thursday and Friday passed with no word from her, and by late Saturday afternoon their worry had turned into consternation.

"That old hag had best be dead, lest I kill her first," said Zora.

"Should we even bother to do our weekly reports?" Langston wondered.

"I'll need a real job eventually," Louise insisted.

The week had been irresponsibly productive. The third act already had a draft. They drank lots of gin and acted the thing out with Louise typing and laughing right along. Now here they were, like three petulant children, sitting in Langston's room, each propped drinking against a different wall, Langston and Zora with notebooks open, receipts splayed out over the floor. Duke Ellington on the victrola maintained a cool mellow atmosphere in the mellow sun, waning in six o' clock shadows.

"It's true we've been taking up all your time," said Langston. "Which isn't exactly fair. How much did Godmother agree to give you anyway?"

"Enough to help, but not enough to live. She doesn't like me all that much, you know."

"Well of course we'll cut you in on the profits when it goes to Broadway."

"Langston," Zora looked up. "That would make her a partner. And this really has to be our play."

"How is it not our play?"

"Besides, Louise needs an immediate solution. Not some vague promise for something at a later date."

"Oh. I'm not worth making this much fuss over."

Langston lit a cigarette and watched the smoke curl in the slow orange diminuendo of the sun. "Well," he said, but left it at that.

"I can pay you five dollars a week out of my own funds for now," said Zora. "Which isn't much, but it's something."

"Oh, that's not necessary," said Louise sheepishly. "Just remember me when you're on Broadway."

A warm glow of rage passed over Zora's face with the slant of the sun.

"Louise, there'd be no precedent for us paying you then. And besides, that won't keep you from starving right now."

"She can be our business manager or some such," Langston suggested lazily, still watching the smoke settle.

Zora just laughed at that, with more venom than she'd realized in her spleen. "We ought to just come clean to the old witch. Why not let's call her and ask her about it? It makes as much sense as making Louise business manager. Plus, we ought to call at this point anyhow."

"But if Godmother's upset with us already, won't this just make it worse?"

"You test my patience sometimes, Langston. She has to learn about our *Broadway* play eventually anyway, doesn't she?"

Langston started to object, but realized he had no good objection to offer. "All right. Let's call her and get it over with."

The last of the sun swept somberly past the windows, and a sturdy shadow settled over the room.

"Who calls?"

"Maybe I should call," Louise suggested.

"No!" Langston and Zora declared simultaneously.

"Then who?"

"Throw bones for it?" suggested Zora.

"No, it should be me," said Langston.

"Oh, isn't he valiant?" Zora lit a Pall Mall.

Langston got up and crossed the room like a man walking a plank. He winked at the ladies from the phone.

For a moment every one in the room was nervous to death.

"Good evening, Cordelia! This is Langston. Is Godmother available?"

Zora and Louise looked at each other, then over at Langston.

"Of course," Langston said. "I understand. Yes. Just let her know that I called, then. Thanks. Bye-bye." He hung up the phone.

Zora and Louise stared at Langston, all shrugs and eyes. "Well?"

Langston frowned and lit a cigarette, clearly uncomfortable. "She wouldn't take my call."

Work on the play halted that weekend for damage control. Instead of drafting their play, they went through draft after draft of apologies to Godmother.

"What are we even apologizing for?" Louise complained. It was a question none of them could answer, and made writing an apology a daunting proposition.

"We're supposed to be able to receive her thoughts," Zora said ironically. "If we can't do it anymore, that's our fault. Not hers."

"Just like a woman to expect you to read her mind," Langston muttered.

"Why you gotta take it there?"

"Aw, I didn't mean it like that, Zora."

"Why don't we just apologize for the play, and that way we admit to writing it at the same time?"

"We could do that."

"We should do that."

"Then that's what we'll do."

Langston wrote the letter, and Louise typed it. It took the three of them the whole weekend to figure out how to word it, and then the weekend melted into the weekdays in weird sleepy Westfield, awkward.

One afternoon, May maturing into a blossom of spring, Langston sat sipping gin and thinking things through. He thought about Harlem after the crash, about how the crash had made him more dependent on Godmother, and when he thought about that, his stomach flipped. After all, things seemed to just get more and more out of sorts between them. Unless you surrendered yourself entirely to her like Dr. Locke, you were never more than a Black Icarus, waiting for the plunge. He drank and listened to Gershwin's *Rhythm in Blues*, and thought about Dr. Locke, and how that's why Locke would never be an artist himself. As the sun flooded the windows with afternoon's peculiarly comforting glow, and the likker flooded his bloodstream with gin's peculiarly comforting glow, he wondered if the reason he was stalled lately had to do with Godmother. After all, it had to, didn't it? Everything in his life was conspiring to radicalize him as a person and a poet, from Lincoln to Cuba to his position with *The New Masses* to Harlem after the crash, and Godmother kept calling for more darky blues verse.

To hell with that old hag, said the gin.

He found himself out in the tremendousness of a pitch perfect spring day. He walked the block to Zora's and let himself in. Zora and Louise were in the kitchen drinking tea and talking over the newspaper.

"Ladies."

"Lank. Drinking already I see."

Flourishing. "The day calls for it." He took a seat.

He hadn't been there but discussing the various things he'd been thinking about no more than an hour when Zora gave Louise the queerest look, turned towards Langston and said, "Don't you have a house just two doors down of your own to go to?"

That hurt him to his heart, it did. But he knew when he wasn't wanted around. Back out into a cruelly lovely spring day, Langston didn't go back to his own room two doors down, but walked his way over to the park. He walked around the lake and thought about – just a few weeks ago – walking the lake with Zora and Louise. He thought about Louise in her halo of sunshine back with Wallie, and he thought about Wallie out in Long Island, and suddenly he was laughing. Who knew why? Maybe the crash would be good for him. Maybe he could leave his whole life behind, like Zora disappearing against a southern horizon.

He woke up the next morning with Zora at the typewriter, click-clacking away.

"Morning, Mr. Conkbuster."

Langston propped himself up in bed.

"There's coffee here for you. Might be cold, though."

"What you writing? The play?"

"Folklore. We got a letter from Godmother this morning, you know."

"How could I know? You read it?"

"Nope. I was waiting for you."

"Well, let's get at it. Where's that coffee?"

Over two pots of coffee and innumerable cigarettes they read the letter and discussed the fine points:

(1) Northern Negroes could not be trusted. They were no longer to work on the folk play in any capacity whatsoever.

(2) The "wretchedly overpaid Negress striver" would be paid for the time she had served that week, and would continue on at the same rate, so long as work on the folk play was terminated immediately and she henceforth worked solely on Zora's manuscript.

(3) Langston was required to submit proof that he was actively working on some project of his own.

"So what you gonna do now, Mr. Lay-Back-And-Live-High-On-The-Hog-A-Spell? She's expecting some tangible work from you."

"Yeah. Well. You too, you know."

"My work's cut out for me."

"Well, I don't know, Zora. A writer doesn't always feel like writing. You know that. Sometimes a fella's just gotta live life. Besides, I write best when I'm blue, and I'm not that."

"That's beginning to sound like an excuse, Langston. If you're not an empowered person, then maybe you should be *that*."

"Damn, Zora. I'm scandalized. No call for talk like that at all. I'm having some gin. You in?"

So the weeks passed by in pleasant insubordination. Act One wrote itself, what with Langston and Zora living the play out loud in their living spaces, and Louise laughing away at the typewriter. They didn't exactly ignore Godmother's letter, they simply took it under advisement. After all, she seemed willing to forgive them, and so long as the checks kept on coming in, well hey. But sometimes Langston would take long walks out to the park, and worry about that line about Northern Negroes. She'd never said anything like that before. Had something changed with her? There was no way to know. Should he try and get the low down from Alain?

The walks to the park warmed Langston to Locke somewhat, the more he thought about him. After all, the brother wasn't so bad; he remembered walking out to the woods in Lincoln with Locke to show him the draft of his sociology report on the state of the school's administration. Locke's input had been priceless; Locke knew everything about how black institutions worked, he'd been able to anticipate Lincoln's response. He also knew how Godmother thought, better than Langston or Zora or Louise did. Locke would know something about all this, sure.

A trip to Howard, then.

Without consulting Godmother first, he used funds from her monthly stipend to buy a ticket to Washington one morning on his walk to the park. He wouldn't tell her about it until right before he left for Penn Station. That way she wouldn't be able to object. It would be a done deal. And he wouldn't back down.

But object she did, all the same. She sat in that throne of hers and frowned. "You are to tear up the ticket. Under no circumstances are you allowed to travel to Washington."

Here it was. An argument that could go nowhere but circles. He felt almost as rebellious and suicidal as Nat Turner, just standing up from the stool without the proper permission.

"The ticket is already paid for. It's something I have to do, Godmother, as a man." He put on his hat. "We are always saying that the Great Man takes the reins of his own destiny. That's what I'm doing now."

Something sounded eerily final about the way he said it, and then the eeriness deepened with the silence. For a very long and awkward moment, neither spoke or moved, Langston standing, hat in hand, Godmother seated on her throne. Then, turning, his fingers suddenly clasping and unclasping involuntarily, Langston stumbled out the door, colliding with the stool on his way.

Back on Park Avenue, he walked briskly westward, feeling removed and detached from a perfect spring morning. He needed money, and he needed a friend, and he needed faith in ofay-kind. So he called Carlo.

"Carlo, are you in? Can I stop by?"

"Sure, Lank. What's the what?"

"We'll talk when I get there."

It was still early, and the afternoon was just gaining the day. Carlo was already drinking gin and writing when Langston arrived.

"Am I interrupting? I know how it is when you're on a roll."

Carlo laughed. "No, Langston. Not in the least. Let's put on some Stravinsky. I'm glad to see you, actually. You're my person from Porlock."

"You're writing Kubla Khan?"

Rites of Spring, gin and pipes, they each took a seat in Carlo's smoking room. Langston dazed up at the bookshelf's blur of titles.

"I think it's over. I don't think there's anything more to say," said Carlo, following Langston's gaze over the bookshelf. "I'm almost finished with this novel, and when it's finished I'm finished. Writing novels, that is. Going to parties and all that jazz. This book's my swan song for the whole lifestyle. I started it just after the crash, but no one will understand it, because it's too soon. A book about parties, called *Parties* that everyone will read as a celebration of such. It won't be until the effects of the crash are really felt that people will understand how sad the novel is."

"You get got bad by it?"

"Not really. But everyone else did. I mean, you're young, Langston. You'll weather it out, colored and all. But some of these other poor bastards, us middle-agers."

They smoked quietly, and Langston felt he understood something of Carlo's awkwardness at having money when no one else did.

"I'm done, Langston. I'm really done with writing."

"For good?"

"Well, I'm still supposed to write my increasingly more irrelevant memoirs. I'll never finish them. *Parties* says everything that needs to be said, but Alfred wants something after this novel. He's desperate. Nothing's selling anymore."

"Mr. Knopf?" Langston smiled uncomfortably. "He say whether Negro books will still sell?"

Carlo shifted. "Who knows? Honestly though, Langston, as a white man, and because I talk to white folks in the comfort and privacy of their own living rooms – well, I doubt it will ever be quite like it's been."

"Oh. Well. I guess it had to end sometime."

"It's not like it's over for you, though. You're still young, like I said. And besides, you're a natural poet. Or well, you were for a while. You might be finished as a poet. But you did write a fine novel. Me, though? I don't think I was much more than a poetaster of a novelist. I don't need to write books anymore. I don't think I'm helping."

"Damn, Carlo. I'm catching you in one helluva soul-searching moment here." Langston smiled, sipped some gin. "And I thought I was blue."

"Well. What is going on with you anyway?"

"I don't know, Carlo. It might be all over with for me, too. I think I just broke with my patron."

"You think?"

"It wasn't good."

"Just now?"

"Yeah. Just now."

"Oh. Well hell, Langston. You'll repair it."

"I don't know that I want to."

At first they were quiet for a while, and then they laughed a long time.

"So if that's what it is, what do you do?"

"Well, once I'm all settled up with her, I'll have maybe a little over two hundred dollars. I can stay in Westfield maybe another month or two. After that? I really don't know. Harlem's a nightmare right now."

"I can loan you a couple hundred to tide you over. But that won't solve your larger problems."

"The poverty might be good for me, all things considered." Langston felt like he was just trying to convince himself. "Maybe it'll bring the poetry back out of me."

"That it might. But it's a hard row to tow, and I'm glad it's you and not me that's gotta do it."

They laughed again, but there was a sting in the laughter for Langston.

He made Penn Station with a little time to spare, so he floated through the bookstore to pass the last few minutes. He found a copy of Hart Crane's book, *The Bridge,* so he bought it, tucked it into his bag, and boarded the train, his stomach in unbearable agony, and his mind in an acute state of disorder.

He tried to distract himself with Crane's book on the ride. As the train shuttled through Newark and Philly, through stockyards outside Delaware, Langston traversed Hart's strange American phantasmagoria over Brooklyn Bridge, and back into history – Indian history, Negro history a section called *The River* recalled Langston's own soul going deep like the rivers, evoking Whitman and wide landscapes out in the Midwest, evoking American voices parading in and amongst the lines like incantations – and though Langston couldn't say he really understood a word of what he read, the poem's optimistic journey through myth and history and the spirit cheered him up. Zora claimed he did no work on his spirit. He begged to differ. He arrived in Washington feeling transcendent and even a little lightheaded, if not altogether at ease, and definitely still distracted.

Dr. Locke was keen to Langston's discomfort right away.

"You don't look well, Langston. Godmother told me I should be expecting you. I wondered what state I'd find you in. Please, have a seat."

He sat down, and glanced around. Neither one said anything for a little while.

Finally Langston cleared his throat, sat upright and leaned forward.

"Say, Alain. Why haven't you done much creative writing yourself?" Langston wasn't sure what made him start off with this question. He thought maybe it might cut the tension, but it just made things worse.

Locke studied Langston for a moment. "I'm afraid I don't have the gift for it. My temperament has always been more academic." Locke pressed the tips of his fingers together. "But I suspect you're not here just to ask me that."

"Godmother really didn't want me to come," Langston croaked it like a confession.

"You don't say."

"Can I tell you something Bessie Smith told me once?"

Locke smiled politely; that thin pressed-lip smile of his.

"She said we can't trust white patronage."

"And what do you think?"

"I don't know anymore. Godmother seems like a white mistress sometimes, like someone out of slavery days. Doesn't she?" He smiled to disarm the harshness of the verdict. "Not that I don't love her, and not that I'm not grateful for all she's done. Just that. I don't know, Alain. Carlo I can talk to like a friend, so that's different. I think. But it's difficult with Godmother."

"Well, Mr. Van Vechten," Locke said carefully, "is something of a faddist, isn't he? Just an aging white hepcat, at the end of the day. Hardly as serious minded as Godmother. And while he does have money, Godmother's fortune pauperizes him."

"So is that all it's about, then? The money?" Langston fidgeted uneasily. "Listen, Alain, because I've been thinking things through. Maybe I need to make a clean break with Godmother's money. I think the money may be perverting the friendship. I don't want to think that."

"The money may be the friendship, Langston. You are aware of the state of the country's economy?"

"I know it will be tough, and I can't believe the money's the only basis for our relationship. Can you believe that? How could you believe that?" Langston puffed vigorously on his cigarette. "Besides, other folks manage without Godmother's money, so why shouldn't I be able to? Some artists don't even feel the need to publish at all, and they seem pretty free and happy. Not that I want to go that route." Langston stubbed out his Lucky. "I do have a degree. Maybe I can put my degree to work, huh? I don't know. But I also don't feel like I can grow into the poet I need to grow into with her always over my shoulder. You just said it yourself. Look at the state of the economy in this country. What poet can afford to ignore that? What Negro poet can ignore what we see every day in Harlem? But Godmother hates when I put politics into my poetry. She thinks it's not Negro enough or something. But Douglass was political, and Booker T.

was political and Du Bois is political, and what kind of poet takes money to keep silent about the state of his country?"

"You realize none of the men you mentioned ever was a poet. Those are all race men."

"Du Bois could be a poet."

"But he's not a poet. Which is precisely my point."

"So you agree with Godmother? A poet shouldn't be political?"

"I think," Locke leaned forward and looked Langston in the eye. "I think that you've been flirting with this new Communism fad for a while, and the stock market crash has accelerated that. Don't turn into a faddist like Van Vechten, Langston. If you want to explore Communism in your poetry, you should. But you shouldn't publish everything you produce. Like you said, some writers don't publish at all. You asked me why I don't write fiction or poetry. Well, Langston, I do. I simply don't publish that stuff.

"Of course, the ultimate decision as to what you do is yours. You've already made a few decisions. Just remember, every decision we make necessarily excludes others."

Langston left Locke feeling no clearer about anything. You might even say he felt more muddleheaded. He couldn't even remember why he'd gone in the first place. On the train back to Manhattan, he felt too distracted to read, too distracted to sleep, too distracted to live, and his stomach felt like it was doing somersaults in his belly. In a desperate moment, he decided to write a letter to Godmother. He would make a clean break of things. Godmother had clearly talked to Locke and prepped him for Langston's visit. There was nothing to do but strike out on his own.

Lawd, folks sho can be deceitful,
Lawd, folks sho will put you down,
They gave my Daisy to Dave Carter,
And they run me out of town.

Each draft of his letter to Godmother pled for her friendship and an end to their financial relationship. Locke was wrong. Hadn't he and Godmother moved beyond money? Locke was right. Probably they never could. Langston didn't know if his final draft sounded brave or just pathetic. He posted it as soon as he got to Manhattan without even reading it over.

IV

He didn't go straight home, but called Louise instead, and went uptown to her apartment in Harlem for a late night drink.

On the way over, he realized he was nervous about breaking the news to Zora. He'd always been her lifeline to the old lady. What would she think now? Would she think he was being selfish? Would she understand? He laughed himself sick – There is Confusion.

At least Louise was happy to see him. She hadn't been able to sleep. Her apartment was cool and comfortable and cozy in a dim red hush of candles and low light. They lounged side by side on the couch, lightly passing words.

"So what was keeping you up, anyway?"

"Oh, I don't know," Louise insisted. "Besides, you look a sight worse than I do."

"Do I?" Langston was suddenly self-conscious, considering the events of the day. He'd felt sick to his stomach, out of sorts and all sorts of awkward all day long, and he must've looked it at Carlo's, on the train, with Alain, here with Louise. What would he look like tomorrow when he had to face Zora?

"I have something to tell you."

Louise blinked. "What is it, Langston?"

He was quiet a moment, mesmerized by the fleck of the flames from maroon candles. "I'm leaving – I've left – I've split with – well," he swallowed hard, and chased it with gin. "Well, you know who."

"Mrs. Mason?" Louise almost whispered it.

"Yeah. I wrote her a letter."

"Well, gee, Langston. That's not what I expected." She leaned back, regarding him with a smile. "Wow. I'm really proud of you."

That took Langston by surprise. "Come again?"

"I'm proud of you."

"But I'll starve to death!"

The plaintive way he growled it made them both laugh for a while.

"You're gonna be just fine. Somehow, I'm certain of it. You're free now, Langston. As an artist and as a man."

"Yeah, that's something, huh?" Langston leaned on back himself, folding his arms behind his head like Mister Charlie watching over the plantation. "Figure I'll just go to roaming for a spell." He broke the pose, leaned back in. "Aw, I don't know. Hell if I know what to do in this crash."

"So now you're like the rest of us."

Their faces were very close now; the way Langston undid his position cast them quite intimate.

"Can I ask you something, Louise?"

"Yes, Langston."

"Are you a spiritual person?"

"What?" Louise giggled. "What do you mean?"

"Like Wallie."

"Oh." With a sigh. "Not like that."

"Like the spirituality in Toomer's *Cane*."

Louise paused for a breath. "Now see but that's something different."

"Is it?"

"*Cane's* not just spiritual. It's Negro, too. Which makes it political."

"True enough. But what about it makes it Negro? Just that it's from the south and from the soil? What about Waldo Frank's book, *Holiday*? Is that Negro, too? They say Frank traveled the south passing for black when he wrote it. Hell if I know. I just read Hart Crane's poem – his book he just published. *The Bridge*. He knew Jean pretty well down in the Village. He even writes like him, from the soil and such. But he's an ofay."

"I'd like to read it."

"I have it. Here. With me."

"Well go get it. Let's read it out loud."

"Now?"

"Now."

"It's long. It's like *The Wasteland*. The whole book is the poem. It's an epic."

Louise arched a skeptical eyebrow. "It's like *The Wasteland?*"

Langston winked. "Only longer. And better."

"So go get it, then. I'll get more gin. We can take turns reading it out loud."

Speaking of bridges, how was Langston supposed to get home? He woke up on the couch next to sleeping Louise, the candles burned down to knots of weeping wax, and daylight a fracture through the curtains. Now that he didn't have Godmother's blessings, how was he supposed to get home? He felt stranded in Harlem – a funny feeling. He could always pay for a car out of pocket, all the way to Westfield, but that was a bad idea. Between what he had, what he could expect from Godmother, and Carlo's two hundred, that was maybe a little more than four hundred bucks for the rest of his life.

He got up, went to the kitchen, made coffee, smoked Luckys, gritted his teeth and called Zora.

"Sure doll," she said. "I'll come rescue you. What's going on anyway? You sound feverish or something. You curse out the Wicked Witch of the West or what? Anyway, hold tight. You and me and L. can have lunch in Harlem."

Louise felt like sleeping in; she woke with a hangover creeping up on her. "Too much gin," she groaned. And she slumped limp against the couch. "You two go on ahead without me. Oh, Langston. Thank you!"

"For what?" Langston asked, but Louise didn't answer.

On the ride back to Westfield, Langston unburdened himself to Zora. He talked about everything – the last meeting with Godmother in that awful penthouse, going to see Carlo agitated, with Stravinsky howling in the background and Langston half out of his mind, the weird and awkward meeting with Alain. He tried to laugh his way though it, but kept getting pent up and pensive. It distracted him even though he was talking about it.

Zora didn't say a lot. As they got out of the vehicle at Westfield though, she paused, laid her hand to hip, and cocked her head so that her hat slid down crooked over her forehead. She lit a Pall Mall. "So what's all this mean for our play?"

"Well, I don't know. I guess we should just try to finish the second act, and once it's done, figure things out from there."

May turned to June that week, and the seasons changed octaves, the warm broad lingering summer sun resonating lazy oboe blues days. The work on the second act went along just as ploddingly. Even the few days Louise came up felt inactive and uninspired compared to how things had been. Langston almost felt like he was dreaming his life.

One morning lost in a blur of others just like it, he sat down to his typewriter, only to find it had already been loaded up:

```
I'm going away, baby,
I won't be back til fall.
Gonna go away baby,
And I won't be back til fall.
Lord knows, Lord willing,
I won't be back at all.

Love you honey,
Zora
```

CHAPTER EIGHT

"Let me tell you some things I've learned about the theater, because I've learned some things. First things first: forget about Broadway. But you should know this already, man. You've seen *Green Pastures*, you saw *Porgy*. And I can't believe Wallace Thurman's *Harlem* was really Wallace Thurman's Harlem. No, no, no. That was all Broadway's Harlem. And maybe Thurman's co-writer's Harlem – but not Thurman's. What's his name?"

"Rapp. William Rapp."

"Right. Rapp. But Langston. Let me tell you something about all that. That's not art. Broadway. That's product. That's Capitalism. Now art, that's something different. Art is about the work, and nothing but the work. And when you're talking theater, you're talking about something living, breathing, changing and adapting. Like a great chef can prepare the same dish a hundred times, and each time it's different. Now Broadway, see that's factory theater. Like sandwiches from a diner, it's always the same tepid, mediocre product, night after night. Year after year. People say Gene's great. You know, O'Neill. But he's just another American hustler. He's no artist.

"Just take a look around you. Our backdrop here changes with the seasons, and so do our productions and so do our actors and so do our ideas. Theater isn't New York City, Langston. Theater's local, regional, temperamental and unpredictable. But I'm not telling you something you don't already know. Then here you come talking about this play of yours, *Mule Bone*, a folk play, and you're talking to me about Broadway, and you know what I'm thinking? I'm thinking what could be more ridiculous or forced or artificial than that? A bad sandwich, my man. That's what you'll end up with. A bad sandwich and everything crass and commercial and exploitative shoved between your and Zora's original idea. Why, this fall, we're doing an all-Negro season right here at Hedgerows. And your play is perfect for our repertoire. Why not do it with us instead? I mean, you still need a second act, but what you have already is promising. Why let Broadway ruin your work like it did Thurman's?"

"Zora's writing Act Two now."

"So let her write it, and why not join us here in the fall? You're a free man, right? Don't let New York trick you into its peculiar mental slavery. Come here and make theater the way it's supposed to be made."

"Maybe you're right."

"Maybe I'm right, he says. When am I ever wrong? Listen, come on back in August. We'll probably be doing something by O'Neill. Maybe you can even play Emperor Brutus Jones."

It felt good to laugh. Langston had spent a few dull, dreadful days in that room in Westfield alone and more than a little confused, waiting for letters, waiting for telegrams. He felt sick to his stomach and sick to his spirit, and not even spirited enough for walks to the park, sunk in gin spirits, orange blossoms all day long.

So he caught a bus out to Lincoln, walked around campus with sighs rising from his soul, reminiscing and in a sentimental mood. An old professor had recommended coming out to see Jasper Deeter, here outside Media, and even gave him a lift. So here he was. Getting a professional opinion on *Mule Bone*. Hopefully Zora was at work on it in her own way. He frowned.

"Didn't you just say O'Neill is no artist?"

"Oh no. He's not. O'Neill's a genius."

They laughed again. "Well, I'll think it over. Send me notes on *Mule Bone*."

"There's not much to send. Your play is as beautiful and natural as a spring day. In any case, I'm not the right person to make notes on it."

The Hedgerows was a tempting distraction. It was a barnyard sized wooden white theater built by Deeter and a group of the players. A walkway of hedgerows connected the theater with a wild town of sparse woods and wood houses. It was a wonderful escape from the loneliness of Westfield, but Langston spent the whole time he was there anxious to get back home. He wanted to know if there'd been a response from Godmother. He'd heard nothing from her.

There was no letter from Godmother when he got back to Westfield, of course. Not that day nor the next nor the next after that. Summer sank in heavy and lumbering. Day in day out blinked on and off in long hot, sweating days of waiting, drinking, the aftertaste of gin to every evening's sheen, and not even considering the prospect of writing.

And then one morning, like the call of the executioner, a letter arrived.

"What's to be done about Langston Hughes?"

Godmother removed her glasses, and looked from Alain to Zora. "You know him better than anyone. What do you suggest, Zora?"

The three of them were on Godmother's balcony overlooking Manhattan. Zora, decked out in a blue dress, and a sharp black hat, was focusing on the red calla lilies on the table in front of her. She was remembering the first time she met Mrs. Mason, and remembering Bruce's story, and thinking how a friendship can be as fickle as a love affair.

"Langston's all washed up." Zora smoked carefully, looked from Mason to Locke. "That's why he ran down to Washington to see you, Alain. He's gone spineless and soft, and it's probably because of Lincoln."

Locke clasped his fingers together, pressed his face to his hands. "He did write his thesis on how Lincoln breeds self-loathing and insecurity in the Negro student body. One presumes he was not immune to the malady, simply clever enough to call the diagnosis."

"Well, it's a tragedy," Mrs. Mason said. "But it seems like you two are right. There are flashes of brilliance in his novel, but frankly, I expected better from him. And you should have seen it at first!"

"Now he's not writing at all," said Zora.

"And what he does write! Did you see his poem on the Waldorf Astoria?" Godmother grimaced.

"He's been reading Hart Crane lately," said Locke.

"Well he's not writing at all anymore. In fact, that play we told you about? That's my play. It's my story. It's the one about the turkey and the mule bone."

"Of course!" Mrs. Mason's eyes lit up. "The Baptists versus the Methodists. That's the play you two were working on? Why, Langston has nothing to do with that story, Zora. He could only ruin it."

"Well, he's been trying to steal it from me. Him and Louise."

"I beg your pardon."

"It's like we told you in the letter. She's been typing it for us, all this time out in Westfield. I act it out while she types and Langston drinks gin."

Zora lit a Pall Mall, frowned and glowered over the city. She narrowed her eyes into hard angry shadows beneath the brow of her bonnet. "Only now he and Louise are conspiring to take it for their own."

"This is very serious," Alain said after a while. "Godmother and I will have to discuss the matter further."

"With all due respect. I'd like to stay and discuss it with you," Zora paused to smoke. "It does involve me, after all. And I think I've earned the right to the inner circle."

"Zora, now, do you think-?"

"No," Mrs. Mason leaned forward. "Zora's right. She's earned it. She stays. We speak freely."

Outside on Park Avenue Zora put on a pair of Foster Grants and considered the things she'd said. Particularly the things she'd said about Langston. Biting her lip, lighting a Pall Mall, she decided she didn't regret it. Not a word of it. She'd meant it all. Life is hard, Lank. It's serious shit, and you'll either learn that or you'll learn the reason why. It was time for Langston to grow up.

Skyscrapers turned to tenements going uptown towards Harlem. There were faces in every building. Cold austere faces in the skyscrapers of Midtown crumbled westward into Harlem's ever more shocking slums, grumpy broken down, wide red-brown brick buildings with faces like broken-down Negroes.

Shanty-town, and a shimmy down into a speak. There's one on every corner. In she goes, Zora, drinking and talking about everything that matters to anyone who will listen. And when Zora talks, niggas lissen up:

"Hell, half the stuff my old pal Langston writes he lifted anyhow. He never even saw the south, 'til what I showed it to him."

"Go on with yourself. I heard he's from Alabamy."

"Ha! Dat's your mammy! He's from Chicago if he's from anywhere. Had me drive him around on tour down in Georgia once he'd safely published his second book of southern blues poetry. He'd lift the coins off a dead man's eyes. He tried to steal my folk play, him and his girlfriend, and pawn it off like they'd coined it themselves."

"See, now I know you're lying," a bookish brother across the bar called out. "Because word around Harlem is he's fruitier than an Orange Blossom. He ain't got no girlfriend."

"He swings both ways. E'rrybody knows that." Zora flicked her cigarette, puffed it up with two cheeks full of smoke, and gushed it out like a dragon. "But that Louise Thompson. If I see her around town, I'm gonna mop the floor with her."

So spoke Zora, and so she continued to speak, all over Harlem, speak to café to club. Morning came hard and heavy, the hangover of a lucid dream. West 66th Street again, like she'd never left; morning a hard brown shivering suggestion of light through the tiny windows. Since leaving Langston, Zora had been living in this apartment again, and she was lost in a mausoleum of her own memories. This downtown apartment was where Harlem had happened for her, and now Harlem was no more; why had she come back to the city at all?

Well, Westfield was just a nightmare of a town. All its beauty was fabricated, nothing like the wild wonderful living south, or the islands, or even the city, what with in Westfield all the people dull and settled and suburban and northern. Even the houses out there were too dull for faces. And Langston had started getting like that himself in the end. Him and Louise together. Zora didn't even know what she was doing out there anymore but attending to his needs all while writing him and Louise a play.

She wasn't really angry with Louise was she? She didn't know. She did know that she resented having to go pick up Langston from her apartment that last time, and she could spot a talentless opportunist a mile away. Louise was that if she was anything. A bona fide gold-digger of Broadway.

Zora got up and made coffee. She shook herself in the kitchen, shook herself awake and realized, amazingly, she actually felt quite lovely, despite how much she'd drank.

Out walking the city over to Central Park, she considered the play. Mrs. Mason was right. Langston would just ruin the thing. This new, dull, domesticated Langston anyway. Best to rewrite it herself and just drop discussing it with him. He wasn't long for the old lady's graces anyway. What would he do then? Die of a nervous stomachache? Oooh, when Zora got through with him he'd be bellyaching all the way back to Beluthahatchie, a thought which made her laugh. Hell, if she be witch, then witch she be. Enter the Black Lady Macbeth.

Days collapsed in this fashion. Lunches with Mrs. Mason and afternoons walking the city and evenings dancing in Harlem. Mrs. Mason was sending her back south, didn't want her in New York, but understood why she couldn't go back to Westfield, or some equally lifeless northern town. Zora really wished she could stay on in New York like she'd been doing, or settle somewhere in Florida or something without having to bother about the old lady at all, but the old lady would have to be dead and buried in her mean old grave for that to come to pass.

One evening alone in West 66th with the ghosts of Herbert and Langston and silly on gin and White Rock, Mamie Smith on the victrola, Zora even considered trying to conjure her. She laughed and laughed, shaking in the light of her kitchen lamp, shadows leaping lengthwise where the shelves winked back with herbs and spices and liquids and powders. Loas are fickle and tricky though, you know, and go figure, she'd probably just end up conjuring the old woman dead, and conjuring herself right out of the will in the process. And that wouldn't do at all.

When the gin ran thin, Zora threw on her coat, and headed out. She stopped a taxi-cap on Central Park West.

"Take to me to the Savoy!"

Oh boy, the Savoy! A block long and wide, it sat second floor of a large building on the corner of 140th and Lenox. Inside there were marble steps leading up to the second floor, which was one enormous room with two jazz bands, each on a separate spring operated stage across the room from the other. When one band finished a set, the other would swing into something new, segueing off the other band's vibe. Spacious as it was, it was busy, packed with people, black and tan. The walls were all mirrors and windows and made the room expand and expand with an infinite number of rhythmic apparitions beneath smoky blue and pale white lights.

It's a big topic
(Blow your horn!)
It's the big topic,
(Blow your horn!)
What's the big topic?
(Blow your horn!)

Mrs. Carolina Tropics
Go blow your horn,
Mrs. Carolina Tropics
Better blow that horn!

A couple fellas had asked Zora to dance, and a couple of the couple she allowed the honor; but stepping out of a dance, as the lights dimmed over one stage and lit over another, who should Zora see stumbling out of a dance with a high yaller brother, but little Louise Thompson, through the looking glass. Zora turned and saw, sure enough, the source of the image who, like she sensed the presence, looked up and caught Zora's glare.

Louise tripped over her stumble, and the fella with her had to steady her. She leaned in close and whispered something to him. His eyes fluttered briefly to Zora, then quickly away. By the time he dared a second glance, Zora had vanished into the crowd.

Clearly Louise had heard Zora's talk around town. That was the first thing. Second, if Louise had heard about Zora's talk, then Langston probably knew something was up as well. Then the door had been closed. There was no going back to how it was. The thought was a comfort and a heartbreak. She had never had a friend quite like Langston before, and now she'd just handed him over to Louise. Nonsense. She hadn't done any such thing. He'd already gone of his own accord. Across the room then, doubling back, eyes on Louise, feet with the stomp of the blues, Zora maneuvered her way over to and behind the unsuspecting couple like the spirit of a vengeful squaw.

The blues had a heavy jazz swing, and a stomp that was growing more agitated and erratic. It worked its way up to climax as Zora clipped between a couple cliques close behind Louise and her paramour, so she was standing staring at their backs. With a thunder of drums the music rolled to a stop.

The lights dimmed on the near stage and lit up on the far. Zora pulled her shoulders back, drew her chest up, and hissed a sound like the shriek of an arrow through the air right next to Louise's ear in the brief spell of silence. Louise hollered and started, stumbling forward, reaching for her companion, as the band began to challenge geometry with sound.

The man turned and seeing Zora, stepped back, taken aback. Louise turned around quickly along with him, and she stood gaping and staring. Zora looked at her trembling lips and her terrified eyes. She took her by the shoulders, held her shivering in her hands for a moment, then kissed her on the lips, warm and hard and lovely.

"Zora!" Louise stuttered. "This – this is my date. Reuben."

"Why, but where's Langston?" Zora said coyly, and Reuben went from high yaller to Indian red.

Louise flustered between Zora and Reuben. "Don't pay her any mind with that Langston talk," Louise fumbled. "She's such a troublemaker, aren't you Zora?" Louise smiled helplessly, stupidly.

But Zora didn't wait around to reply. She turned on her heel with the clip of the piano, and disappeared back into the surge of the crowd.

The Savoy had been a bad idea anyway. Fancy running into Louise here with a new fella! Well, and what would Langston say to that? Zora headed for the door, but somehow ended up at the bar.

The bar ended up introducing her to a fella of her own. A big brown brother with eyes like Egyptian sunsets. "Say, why don't you buy a lady a drink?"

And a terrible Tuesday morning to follow. Here's a novel beginning to a New Negro novel, Du Bois: dark princess Zora wakes up in strange man's bed, hung over, a hand hanging over the side, reaching for her purse for Pall Malls. Zora sat up, looked around. The fella was still sleeping, and so what?

Out of bed, then. Quickly dressed and quietly out the door into the streets of Harlem.

A good morning to be in Harlem, too. June's slumbering summer rhythm was finally setting in. Folks going about their Tuesday morning business. Zora adjusted her hat, her sunglasses, her dress, and lit another cigarette for the walk to the subway.

She hadn't had but time to get home, shower and make coffee before Mrs. Mason called.

"Good morning, Godmother."

"Zora. I have something to talk to you about."

"What's the what?"

"It's not good."

"Oh." Zora swallowed a smile, even if they were over the phone. You can still hear that kind of thing.

"It's Langston."

171

Zora frowned. "Hm!"

"I received a letter from him this morning. I want to read it to you."

"I'm all ears."

Godmother read the letter. It was a long and pathetic *cri de couer*, appealing to Godmother's pity, her kindness, some nonsense about new contacts at the Hedgerows; all in all it made Zora distinctly uncomfortable, and afterwards, she wished she hadn't heard it after all.

"Well that's just. I don't know. Disappointing. I've never heard him sound so sad."

"It's precisely as Dr. Locke suggested. Lincoln has ruined him. He's neither Negro nor white now. He's a man without a culture. He's not even a man." Godmother sighed. "I'm finished with Langston, Zora, and that breaks my heart. But I've wasted enough time and resources on him, and I don't have forever to wait for him to shape up into something. Especially when he seems to be regressing instead of progressing. I'll see no more of him and that is that."

The line went dead just as Zora thought maybe she should object to such finality, but then there it was. Langston was finished. A fine mess.

Zora needed sun.

II

Days of Sundays dragged by. Damn, but if he hadn't put everything he had into that last letter and what back? A telegram saying nothing at all, don't call me, I'll call you. Theater. No audience. No money. No love. No more stability for Langston Hughes, that's what it really meant. And just when the whole world's gone broke and crazy. Ma Rainey and gin didn't even help. Sulfur pills helped the gin go easy on his stomach, and the ice cream chaser chased the stomach burn of the sulfur pills.

Well hell, no news was good news, cuz when news came it was always bad news. Dr. Locke's letter was like that. A bitchy, catty affair, announcing all the fun he and Zora had had with Godmother the week before, and here's to hoping you're well too, what with no money in a broke city in a broke country. Locke had submitted Langston's name for the Harmon award, though, in connection with *Not Without Laughter*. Maybe he'd win, and it would bring some extra money.

Langston brushed the damn thing off. It was his own fault, after all. He'd broken with Godmother himself, and Locke was just reacting to that. You couldn't expect any different from Alain. But could Zora have turned on him too?

This was a cheering thought, because it was so absurd. Of course not. Langston laughed for the rest of that afternoon and evening, and drank gin, feeling mighty fine. Well, Zora and I will work our way out of this in the end. And history will judge Locke accordingly.

He tried to call Zora every now and then, but she must not have bothered to reconnect her phone, because the old number was out of service. With Locke's snippy letters, and Godmother's loopy Godlike silence roaring through his days, he started to go a little loopy himself, alone in Westfield with no other voices than theirs. Dayginned days, lazing out the window with no shirt on, the sun and the wonderful Westfield wind howling through the houses, rolling through the lindens. He would howl right back at that wind, he screamed and hollered the blues.

Well, I'm lowdown baby,
I got the got no laughter blues,
Well, I'm lowdown honey,
I got them got not laughter blues,
I ain't had no laughter
Since I been after you.

Without meaning to he found himself working again. As the days passed he started jotting down poems and fragments of poems, and that hadn't happened for a while. Long poems about love and death, short poems about revolution, blues poetry and worker songs. He tried blending styles, got stuck in it, and penciled bitter racialist verse in the margins of old anthologies, slept on it all, and then got started over again come the morning.

Now the gin was going down easier than ever, and the writing was coming up easy as well. Something inside him wanted to present itself, but he wasn't sure what. He wanted to write something sprawling and important, like *The Bridge*, but he didn't want to do anything quite as impenetrable as all that. His thoughts started instead to revolve around the theater. While Zora was away, maybe he would work on a play all his own. Many of his poems had stories in them already. *Cross,* for example. An interesting triumphant (if still tragic) mulatto play could come of something like that. That's what he'd do. He'd turn *Cross* into a play.

As soon as he was decided on it, though, he was distracted. Weeks had passed and nothing from Godmother. A note to say she'd received a copy of his now published novel he sent her, and the rest – was silence? Whenever he took any time to ponder upon it at length, he felt sick to his stomach. He didn't even know where in the world Zora might be, and she was quickly becoming his last link to that world of Godmother and Locke, money and power.

The Fourth of July came and went and Langston tried to be ironic about it. At first he thought to go on into Manhattan and maybe party things up, but just thinking about Manhattan made him feel as sad as a shipwrecked sailor, and so he stayed out in Westfield. He drank gin and listened to Bessie and Son House and Charlie Patton and figured he was free at last, and that was to be celebrated, even if freedom could sometimes be terrifying and lonely. As the sun went down over Westfield, and the gin settled down over Langston's spleen, he finally walked out and down by the park where fireworks were being set off over the lake. It was his first July Fourth by himself in a very long time, longer than he could remember, and this odd isolation here in Westfield made his loneliness suddenly feel wonderfully, romantically sad, so that the rest of the weekend he felt sad and happy about that sadness, and able to write verse with it, and came to think of it as a gift, made better with large quantities of gin.

The Monday after the holiday brought a heavy hangover and a letter under the door.

Godmother!

Only it wasn't. It was Mrs. Spingarn, and she had rushed home from California to be back on the East Coast for the Fourth. She'd made it just in time, time enough even to dash Langston a quick letter of how-do? Well, she was a sweetheart for it. She was, after all, the lady who'd paid his first year Lincoln tuition; the lady whose husband, Joel, was Chairman of the Board of the NAACP. If she wasn't quite Godmother, then she was a Salvador Dali converse mirror reproduction – or would it be the other way around?

Harlem was looking worse than ever these days. Even downtown looked depressed. Folks were saying bankers were jumping out of windows. Funny. Negroes knew how to love life without money.

Langston distracted himself with travel. He visited Joel and Amy Spingarn in Armenia, New York, where Joel told him that, looked at through the specter of New Criticism, Langston's poetry was moving more inward lately, and adopting older forms. New Criticism made him feel old hat, so he went out to the Hedgerows again, to check out the fall season of Negro theater; the Negro theater season turned out to be a casualty of the crash; they'd be doing a season of Eugene O'Neil instead. By the time he resettled in Westfield, he felt like there was nowhere worth being in the world. One evening Louise called him in tears.

"Oh, I'm ruined, Langston. Have you talked to Zora?"

"Just a postcard from her a few weeks back. Why? What's up?"

Louise started crying again.

"Now there's no reason for that. Tell me what's going on?" But Langston could feel his own heart rate accelerate. "You're worrying me."

"It's Mrs. Mason. She just dismissed me."

"Dismissed you?"

"Just like that. She says she's through with niggers. She even used that word. She says that we just take advantage, and now that the market's collapsed, it goes double."

"What about Zora? What about Locke?"

"I don't know. I don't know anything about what's going on." Louise's voice convulsed like a gasp. "Langston, she just dismissed me. Like a dog. Like one time when I was there, and one of her servants dropped a tea cup, she just snapped her fingers, just like that, dismissed. Be gone. How can people behave like that towards other people?"

"Well, I'm sure that means me too."

"When are you coming to the city? I need to see you."

When he visited Louise, all he could do was try to make her laugh. It sounded like she'd been without laughter for a little while.

"How ya been holding up anyhow?"

"I'm better now. I was real shook up at first, but now that I've had time to think it over, I've decided it's for the best. I feel like I've learned from it."

"Yeah? What's that?"

"I don't know. I don't know how to process it yet, but I can feel that it's there. Some learned life experience."

"I still wonder about Zora. I haven't heard a word from her since she went back south. I'm sure Locke's doing just fine, though."

"Zora went south all right, but now she's back in New York. That's why I asked you about her. I haven't seen her since the summer, and she was acting weird back then. But I heard she was at Small's last weekend. I figured you'd know all about it, if anyone knew anything about it."

"No kidding. I'd think I would too. But I don't."

Langston tried calling Zora the next day, but her number was still disconnected, so he threw on his hat and jacket and walked all the way down Broadway to the West 60's to see if she was really there or not. Autumn in New York, Harlem to Midtown, Langston swept along with the leaves, shuffling thoughts. Why hadn't Zora told him she was home? What was going on with Godmother? Was she really through with Negroes? And when would he, Langston Hughes, finally be tired, finally be sick and tired of being sick and tired of these white folks?

Zora answered the door and to see him there, her eyes widened like a rippling lake. She giggled an otherworldly giggle, something near a shriek. "Langston Hughes! What in the world are you doing here?"

"Is it a bad time?"

Zora shivered, glanced left, then right. She shook her head. "No." Then hesitated. "No." Hesitated again, and smiled. "Your timing is perfect, as always. Come right in."

Langston wandered into Zora's tiny space, thick with a sweet but stringent blue incense, so heavy with smoke his eyes watered up right away; dusty books and manuscripts; pages scattering desks, chairs and floors.

"Just been awfully busy lately, as you can see," Zora gestured helplessly around the room. "And you? How are you?"

"I'm good Zora. Listen. Are you sure you're all right?"

"Never better but for being busy is all." Zora lit a Pall Mall; reclined against the hallway wall.

"I guess that means no work on *Mule Bone*?"

Zora's smile frowned.

"I've been meaning to discuss that with you Langston. I changed it some, the play, I did, coming to work on the second act. So that it's not so much your play anymore at all. After all. I put the turkey back in for one thing-."

"But the girl-!"

"Oh the hell with Daisy! You *would* like that strumpet. I played her out years ago anyway, Langston. But just to say things have changed up somewhat. But look, now listen. I have some errands to run. I was on my way out when you just showed up. So make yourself at home. I'm not sure how long I'll be."

With no more than that, Zora lunged forward, stabbed her Pall Mall crushed smoking in the ashtray, and was out the door with hat and coat.

Langston sat in the quiet thick smoke of her apartment alone, wondering what just happened. He focused on the walls, the windows, the soul of the room, and tried, through its familiarity to channel the peculiar mind of Zora Neale Hurston, and what was going on with her.

November afternoon, chilly and colorful, Zora straightened her coat and hat together proper for a lady – which is to say, she straightened the coat and crooked the hat. Imagine Langston just showing up like that. What to tell him? Well to hell with him. Well, no, she didn't mean that, not really. To hell with Louise, but Langston was all right. Besides he looked awful. Like he might drop dead any minute. Gotta pity him a little. How had he found out she was back in town? He couldn't have talked to Godmother or Alain. They only agreed to let her come back home so long as she spent most of her time in New Jersey with her brother, and apparently Godmother was wise in this. That was one place Langston would never find her.

She walked uptown, all the way up Broadway to 128th Street, while day dwindled gray against gray, fall in Manhattan. A quick drink at Skinny Mike's speak, and she was warmed up for the long walk back home. She would tell Langston the truth. She was quite decided on the matter. Didn't he have his Haitian opera anyway? So he had that and she had *Mule Bone* and that was an end to things.

She stormed the stairs, burst into her apartment, lit a Pall Mall and said, "Now Langston." But of course by that time he was gone, probably long gone. Had she expected anything else?

The mind gets muddy sometimes, swampy like quicksand, and thoughts that seemed safe are just lies, illusions that swallow you up as soon as you venture them a pass. Langston was a thought like that with Zora. He irked her and then he charmed her and then annoyed her all over again, and she lost track of her motivations.

The next day she called him right bright early in the morning. "Let's meet this Saturday," she said. "My place."

She looked forward to it. Thought about reconciliations, and Langston understanding *Mule Bone* was hers now, and Langston understanding Louise had to go away. But when Saturday arrived Zora was nowhere to be found. Or rather she was to be found dancing at the Savoy (oh boy!), and so she should've anticipated Langston's furious phone call the next morning.

"Bruce says he saw you at the Savoy last night? You know how long I waited for you? What were you thinking?"

"Langston listen. I'm sorry. I just forgot."

"Do you still wanna do this thing?"

She could have killed it right then and there. She could have told him everything, just like she'd intended to do. She hesitated. She didn't even lie to him. She said: "I'll call you. We'll reschedule." And then hung up very quickly, but carefully.

Only she did lie to him, guess you could say, since she never called to reschedule.

A week passed and he might have called a couple times, but Zora had decided to stop answering the phone, just to get away from the magnetic effects of telegraphic wires for a while, why not? She let the phone ring when it wanted to ring, and she put on the victrola when she wanted to hear Blind Willie Johnson sing,

Who's that writin'?
John the Revelator.
Who's the writin'?
John the Revelator.
Wrote the Book of the Seven Seals.

Things would have to come to an uncomfortable confrontation eventually of course, and Zora would have to protect her writing one way or the next. Leave Lank to steal it quicker'n a fox snatching dinner from a henhouse. And she'd need to protect it with as objective a mediator as she could find.

So instead of calling Langston that week, or the next, Zora hired a stenographer instead, and she had a copy of *Mule Bone* typed up. Her own version of the play. It wasn't quite finished, but it was hers at least. And just as soon as she had three good copies, she mailed one off to the Library of Congress, one to dear old Carlo, and she kept the last, God bless, for herself.

Days passed, he wondered whatever happened to her. Days turned to weeks and autumn turned to winter. He kept busy in the meantime. There were speaking arrangements for extra cash. He was even getting good at them. But still, despite the distractions, nothing from Zora. He called and he called, and she never picked up and she never called him. He even tried going over there again unexpected. No luck. He sent her telegrams, electric signals across the city, and still, nothing. What did she mean she had changed up the play? What was going on with her? Should he be worried about her? Was she hysterical? He was used to an eccentric Zora, but this was out of hand. He lectured for extra cash, but he was lecturing out of a peculiar perplexity about people, while pretending to understand them.

Thanksgiving crawled up and collapsed on him like a dying friend. He spent it alone, not a word from Zora, not a word from Godmother, not even a word from Alain. His mother wrote him. She was back in Cleveland again; she'd made up with his stepfather. Why not come on home for Christmas?

Langston cried and cried all day long Thanksgiving Day and felt just about as low and lonely and blue as can be. He tried to think to make a Thanksgiving dinner, late in the day, afternoon waning evening, Blind Willie Johnson telling him,

Well Moses to Moses,
Watching the flock,
Saw the bush where they had to stop.
God told Moses:
Pull off your shoes,
Out of the flock, well, you I chose.

Who's that writing?

But he couldn't think to think what he'd even like to have for Thanksgiving dinner. Out into the cold street, over to Lenox to get some groceries. Turning the corner, there was Moses, coming up out of a bleak looking speak across the street. He blinked to get a better look at the man, and would be damned if it wasn't the same man who appeared to him and Zora that night, Uncle Monday, and had been appearing ever since.

He crossed the street in pursuit. It was just a short half block to the subway, and that's where Monday was headed. Langston, Devil may care, dashed out his Lucky and dashed down the subway steps after the apparition. He followed a shadow down the stairs and around the corner, then into the station. The air was suddenly rank with the rush of urine blowing in with garbage and the lights of the train. Monday was nowhere to be seen.

It was Monday for sure, and it had to be, but the air was putrid, and Langston started not feeling so well. Just as soon as he got home, the heaviness of fatigue hit him, and he went lightheaded and disoriented right away. He'd forgotten to pick up food for Thanksgiving dinner, so he drank gin all night and tried to write a poem about being thankful instead.

III

A funny thing happened to Zora as she was turning the corner of 129th and Lenox one blustery December afternoon. She was coming out of a deli with a cup of coffee when she thought she caught old Uncle Monday turning the corner. She hurried around to catch up with him, curiosity you could say, and doing so found nothing but another windy Harlem street, regular non-Monday folk moseying about their business. Only when she turned toward the direction of the subway, there he was again, large and black and blinking. But it wasn't Uncle Monday after all. It was Brother Martin.

Everyone in Harlem knew Brother Martin, the Barefoot Prophet. He was ancient and wizened and black, like an old oak tree, gray hair shocking his large head unruly, bushy, gnarled and knotted like his bare feet, which stuck out from beneath the oversized slacks of a worn black Brooks Brothers suit. He held up his hand.

"Whar's that boy you always with?"

"Pardon?"

"You heard. The poet." Brother Martin peered down at her impatiently.

"You mean Langston?"

"That's him."

"Oh." Zora hesitated. "Langston."

"Tell him I have a story and he needs to hear it."

"Oh."

"Tell him this, and you tell him just the way you hear me tell it now. You hear me?"

"Oh." Zora nodded.

"Accidents are a blur of noise, and Gospels are the grace of God," Brother Martin frowned. "Accidents are acts of faith, too. A blur of noise is a whirling wheel, and the accident is you."

Zora frowned. "Oh."

Then past the crazy old prophet and his nonsense. She walked down into the subway and considered Brother Martin. The old man was either way ahead of the times or way behind them. That made her laugh, thinking about his life, the way he'd watched the world change like Kudjo Lewis had watched his world change, and if America freed its slaves from the psychosis of slavery, it had done so only to enslave them again with a peculiarly alienating black madness, mired in poverty and disenfranchisement. There was something about poverty that smelled of death, and it often left *my people! my people!* psychotic living dead; black zombies, sure.

IV

"Langston Hughes! It's wonderful to have you home here in Cleveland. Are you staying long?"

This particularly painful question was posed by Mrs. Rowena Jeliffe, a middle-aged white woman who led the theater troupe The Gilpin Players. The Gilpin Players were the most (some would say the only) successful all black theater company in the country, though most of their paltry six performances a year were basically white plays performed by black actors.

Wisps of snow were blinking in and out of a cerulean winter morning in mid January, and Langston watched them wandering, wondering, just what was he gonna do now? When just this past Saturday a letter from Godmother had announced that she was cutting him off for good. And no check. He'd been counting on that check, and now he had to count that out. Sunny Florida called, but cold old Cleveland held him captive.

"Maybe a little while," he said to the snow, sipped his coffee and shrugged. "Mom's glad to have me around, and it's good to get away from New York's nuttiness from time to time." He sipped his coffee again, and found himself unconvincing. "Besides, I have a play to finish."

"You could finish it here, with us. We need some good black playwrights on board."

"Maybe that's what I'll do then. You know Jasper Deeter of the Hedgerows? He says local theater's better than Broadway, anyway."

"A wise man that Jasper Deeter."

"I also saw an article about The Gilpin Players in *The Crisis* last summer. It's part what brought me back home." Not convincing at all. "Cleveland's changed, huh?"

"It sure has."

"I like it, though. More black folk. I worry sometimes too. I guess with the market crash and Negroes still moving north in droves to these segregated northern cities. Harlem's been brutal lately."

"Oh, I can imagine. Some of the neighborhoods here in Cleveland aren't exactly royalty. But I try to be optimistic. I think we're just in the growing pains of the industrial revolution. Technology's outstripping our economic theories. We'll catch up in time." Mrs. Jeliffe smiled brightly, and Langston couldn't help but think she looked just like Mary Pickford's Pollyanna. "The Negro especially has a natural talent for theater, and from there the screen. Culturally, I think if the Negro harnesses his potential right, he can sweep the field in America."

Langston smiled awkwardly. "Oh, well, that is optimistic. But maybe you're wrong. What if Negroes aren't naturally theatrical?"

"Oh, but there's something there, all right. Maybe it's passed down from African culture, but it hasn't disappeared. I've watched white children play and black children play, and -," Mrs. Jeliffe chuckled and matched Langston's ironic smile. "Well, if I can't convince you, I have just the thing. I'm waiting on this play – it's a black folk comedy, and I hear it's the bells. That no white person could have written it, and no white person could convincingly carry off the roles in it. It's as real and natural and American and hilarious and beautiful and Negro as it gets."

"No kidding. I'm jealous already. What is it? Who wrote it?"

"It's a play called *Mule Bone*, and it's by a rising young writer named Zora Neale Hurston."

All the rest of the day Langston's stomach bellowed and moaned. The cold Cleveland air and the harsh smoke of his Luckys burned his throat raw; a glass of gin back home just gave him a headache. He spent the afternoon and evening in bed, listening to his mother and stepfather bicker in the background like a blues beat steady on a bass. He slept poorly the whole night long.

The next morning he called Zora and listened to her phone ring and ring and ring. He still felt awful, but he soldiered up and went and sent her a wire. He came home and tried to write her a letter, but when he tried to write, he got hot and dizzy and had to lie down. If he recollected right, his mother came in and fussed over him some, tried to get him to eat something. Breathing became sucking shards of glass, and he sweated the sheets through.

By evening he felt better. Good enough to read Arna's new novel, *God Sends Sunday*. Reading about Little Augie and his helpless, restless, self-destructive wandering made Langston feel even better, like he had a friend. He was about fifty pages deep when he was interrupted by a knock.

"Langston?"

"Yeah mom, come in."

She cracked the door, peered around the corner with that sly trickster brown wink of a face of hers. "Phone for you. Sounds like theater folk."

It was Rowena. "The play arrived this morning," she said. "*Mule Bone.* You should come out and take a look at it. Identify the body, you could say."

"I'm on my way," said Langston. "Have you read it?"

"Oh, I've read it."

"How is it?"

"Grand. Sloppy, but grand."

"Sloppy Jaloppi! Then it ain't mine. See you in a bit."

It was *Mule Bone* all reet, and it was a mess. The first act had bloated into nonsense and incoherence. The turkey was back for one thing, confounding as all git-out to Langston. One of the men on the porch, Hambo, leers at Daisy. Dave and Jim leer at Daisy; and then Hambo goes off on some kind of incantation of the octaves. Had Zora gone off her gourd? There were two third acts. One was the very copy they'd made a carbon of back in Westfield, same coffee stain on it and everything. Another was strange and similar to the first, just with more nonsense and turkey talk, and finally there was a mess of a second act. The thing was put together like a three headed hydra.

"Well, it's our play," Langston told Rowena. "But Zora sure made a monster of it."

"It's got potential, Langston. A lot. Get in touch with her. We'll put it on downtown, at the Karamu, or even the Ohio. If the Plain Dealer writes a good review of it, you might even get a shot at taking it to Broadway. The Theater Guild already turned it down, but they'll give it a second look if we can get it into shape and get it produced and reviewed."

"How exactly did you get this anyway?"

"Well, The Samuel French agency sent it from the Theater Guild. They said it had potential, even if they couldn't use it themselves. I'm not sure where they got it from."

"Most strange. I guess Zora sent it to them. I wonder what in the world is going on with her."

Langston tried Zora again that night without luck. Friday night in Manhattan, well, what were the chances? He tried to go to bed early himself, but stayed up late nursing the gin in his tin with ginger ale and Luckys. What to make of the new *Mule Bone?* Had Zora gone completely nuts, was she taking theater for reality and acting out the play in real life? Langston laughed. Maybe that was it. The thought intrigued him. He spilled some gin in his glass with a chuckle and a cheers. "Why, I'll kill some of you ol' box-ankled niggas. Gimme back my turkey or I'm like to lam you with a Mule Bone!" He'd call Carlo in the morning. Carlo would know what to do.

Carlo laughed up a storm when Langston told him. "Zora sent me that play back in November! I sent it off to a friend at the Theater Guild for an opinion only. He wasn't supposed to submit it. You're telling me it's in Cleveland now?"

"It's more serious than you're taking it, Carl. Zora's passing it off as hers. When we wrote it together. Besides, it's a mess."

"I can't explain what's going on with Zora, but it was understood the thing wasn't finished. I'm sure it's just a miscommunication between you two. I'll try to talk to her, though."

The rest of the afternoon Langston worked on getting *Mule Bone* into shape. First he went through and took out all the turkey references. Then he second guessed himself, thinking what would Zora think? So he ended up compiling two additional drafts in addition to the drafts already extant; one to compromise with Zora's turkey and one to suit himself.

A phone call in the evening got him away from his work. "It's some woman for you. Not Rowena, someone else" his mother said, and that got him right up. Zora, at last.

It was Louise. "I'm in town for a few, with the American Interracial Seminar," she said. "I finally managed to get myself a respectable, decent job. Getting the boot from Mrs. Mason turned out to be the best thing that could have happened to me. Anyway, what are you doing tonight? Come meet me downtown?"

"Sure, I'll introduce you to the Gilpin Players."

Langston called Rowena, and went out feeling better than he'd felt in a few days. The work on *Mule Bone* had done him some good. By the time he got to the restaurant, everyone was already seated, and he was feeling downright delightful. Louise looked lovelier and more confident than ever.

"Rowena was just telling me about *Mule Bone*," Louise said. "Has Zora gone crazy? Have you talked to her?"

"I can't reach her. I don't know. I really don't know what's going on with her."

"She was acting loopy back in New York too. She nearly scared me to death one night at the Savoy."

"Well, I talked to Carl Van Vechten about it, and he's the one that first got it from Zora. He then sent it off to a friend of his at the Guild, who submitted it without anyone's permission, it seems. Did Rowena tell you about the condition it's in? It's a mess. I've been trying to do something with it."

"We're hoping to get it in shape for the spring season," said Rowena. "Which means we have our work cut out for us if we want to make it." She hesitated. "Assuming we can get in touch with Zora, and she gives her permission to produce it."

"When's the season start?"

"Mid-February. We'd have to be ready to open on the 15th."

"Ouch," said Louise.

"You said it. Not even a month."

"Well, I'll call her again tomorrow."

"Just how much of it is hers, anyway?" Louise said with a petulant frown. "You did all the real work it seems to me. She just talked up a storm without any form."

Langston supplemented his ginger ale with a dash of gin. "Yeah."

"You're too nice, is what it is," one of the Players said. "I wouldn't take that from anyone. Sounds like she's stealing your work and accusing you of what she's doing."

"Well, I'm not that nice. It's just that Zora and I are old friends, and we worked on the thing together."

"She hasn't acted like much of a friend lately," said Louise.

"And you ought to be big enough to stand up to her," the Player said. "No Negro wants to be the one who takes it and stays in his place. Not in this day and age. Not even from another Negro."

"Especially not from another Negro," another of the Players chimed in.

Langston dashed more gin in his drink. "Well, I'm not just taking it. Gee, I said I would catch up with her, and I will. And when I do, I'll get some straight answers, or know the reason why."

But Sunday passed slowly. Beneath a gray sky and a ghost of a moon, day turned to a twilight of unanswered phone calls and pacing the floor, listening to records and listlessly dialing Zora's number, apparently just to listen to the ring of it.

As evening crystallized over the sky, and the moon spread into a semi-circular sliver of ice, Langston listened to the hypnotizing ring of the telephone of the receiver, only to be surprised suddenly by,

"Langston?"

"Zora? How'd you know it was me?"

"Who else? I just knew."

"Well -," exasperated. Where to begin? "Well, Zora. Look. We need to talk."

"So speak."

"I'm back in Cleveland."

"So I've heard."

"Godmother?"

"Who else, Langston?"

"Well, it could've been Locke-" Langston flailed for focus. "What's with *Mule Bone*?"

"What do you mean? What's with it?"

"Zora. I've had just about enough of this. Rowena Jeliffe of the Gilpin Players has our play out here in Cleveland. Under your name alone. And she wants to produce it."

"Who of the what wants huh?"

"Our play, Zora. *Mule Bone*. A theater company out here in Cleveland has it. They got it from the Theater Guild. The Guild got it from Carlo. And now the Gilpin Players want to produce it out here in Cleveland."

"In Cleveland?"

"Well, gee. You say it like that. What's wrong with Cleveland?"

"Impossible. That play should be on Broadway."

"What play do you even think you're talking about, Zora? There are two third acts here. And you've overstuffed the first two with that damn turkey."

"Langston, you and I are very different artists, and –"

"What is this all about, Zora? We were writing this play together, right?"

"Well, I can't agree to any version of my play being produced in Cleveland. It's just like you to try and get it produced out there in that rinky-dink hometown of yours."

"Zora, let's try to stay reasonable."

"I'm the only one that's being reasonable here. Why would I want *Mule Bone* performed in Cleveland, Langston? We kept it secret, because it's big. It's too big for Cleveland. It's never been done before, and it needs to be done, and we did it, and now it needs to be on Broadway."

"So now you admit it's ours?"

"Langston, you can't have it both ways. You just go off and write your Haiti play or your Cuba opera and what else – you take my material and put it in your novel, but when I want to keep something of my own for myself, suddenly that's a problem for you. I grew up on this story, Langston, not you. I knew the people in the play and the way they talked and thought and how they went about their ways. Not you. So, no. It's not your play. It's mine."

"Zora, now you know it's not like that. I thought we'd agreed this was a joint effort. Do you not want that anymore? I thought we'd both agreed, right? I never meant to take anything from you. So are we not collaborators anymore, and do we call the whole thing off?"

There was a long pause. "Well. It's complicated. I'm writing you a letter."

"Why not just tell me now?"

"Oh Langston," Zora sighed, paused with a purse of air over the line like she might speak. But instead she hung up.

The next afternoon Zora showed up at Carlo's apartment unexpected and in a panic.

"Carlo, I will probably kill myself," she swept like a tornado through his apartment. "It's not Langston's play to take." She strode into the living room and collapsed in a chair. Puccini playing on the stereo. *La Boheme,* what else? "And besides," she went on, "how can he steal my play and put it on all the way out in Cleveland? Cleveland of all places. The play is about my hometown, not his."

"Now, hold on – calm down a minute," an astonished Carl Van Vechten bumbled awkwardly. He eased himself into a chair facing her, and lit a pipe. "What's this about now? More *Mule Bone?* Oh, Zora. I can't get anymore involved in this spat of yours than I've been. I just got through telling Langston -,"

"And I couldn't agree more!" Zora launched from the seat and began to pace. "I never would've dragged you into it in the first place. Langston's so selfish sometimes. Just what did he tell you?"

"Only that the play arrived in Cleveland through Barrett Clark of the Theater Guild. Barrett sent it to the Gilpin Players. He didn't have my permission, mind you. I didn't even know he did it until this whole thing blew up a few days ago. I gave it to him just to see what he thought of it."

"Oh." Zora stopped pacing for a moment. She turned to Carl. "I thought Langston suggested the Guild send it out there. That he heard it was with the Guild through Theresa Helpern or something."

"No. No, see I see what happened already," said Carl. "That this whole disagreement arises out of a simple miscommunication. And you should work to patch things up right away. I told Langston the same thing. He said it started because you didn't like Louise as stenographer, and things just blew up from there. Lack of communication, and you were out of town."

Zora's temperature wavered and rose. Carlo was useless. He understood nothing. She turned around, but the edges of the room were red and dark, and everything was getting warm. She turned to face Carl, suddenly, helplessly aware that she was delirious, and she didn't know if it was from shock, shame, anger or fever. Next thing she knew she heard someone collapse.

Carl started from his seat, his hair a wild silver flop, fumbling at Zora's arms and chest. Zora shrieked, curled and shuddered. She seized on the floor, pounding her fists. "I don't hate Langston Hughes! I don't hate him!"

Just as suddenly, she clambered back to her feet, composed herself hastily and, with a quick crook of her hat, strode straight out the door, leaving Carlo in a bewildered whirl of smoke.

Out in the street the cool air felt good. Zora was still feverish. She hailed a cab home, dizzily wondering where her composure went. Let her be dead and gone. Lack of communication, it all started with Louise as stenographer, and things blew up from there. For such a quick wit, Carlo could be dull as the doldrums sometimes.

It wasn't Langston she hated, looking at the blur of buildings, faces like a funeral party; it was Louise, but not because she didn't like her as a stenographer. She wasn't sure exactly why she didn't like her, only Louise had somehow turned Langston into a stranger, and Langston was the only friend Zora had ever really had in the world. All her other loved ones had left her or changed, and here it was, happening again. And Louise was the Lusca.

The next morning Zora's fever had burned itself into energy. She received a letter from Langston, and she wrote him right back. She wrote Godmother next. Then, feeling powerful and vindictive, she sent a telegram to Cleveland refusing them permission to put on the play. It would go on in New York once it was in ready condition, or it would not go on at all. She was quite decided.

She took a walk around Central Park in the chilly winter afternoon and watched the skeletons of trees reach up like fingers in a cemetery of giants, condemning the heavens. Langston wasn't so bad after all. Just pathetic and childish and young. That had to be remembered. He was still very young, and it was wrong to smash him, no matter how much she'd love to right now. She shivered and sucked the frigid sky.

> *Ezekiel saw the wheel of time,*
> *Wheel whirling in the middle of a wheel,*
> *And each spoke spoke of human kind,*
> *Way in the middle of the air.*

She got back home just in time to catch a call from the Cleveland Plain Dealer. They wanted to do a big send up of *Mule Bone*, make a big deal of it; an interview in the paper and everything, along with a profile of her and Langston. Was she coming out to work on the play and give her permission to have it produced at the Ohio?

"Yes," said Zora. "Yes, I am."

She went at once and posted a telegram to Rowena. OKAY. Nothing else. She went home and drank coffee and smoked cigarettes and paced the floors and the walls and the ceilings and the windows, wondering, wondering, wondering what to do.

She had just turned forty years old, and no significant publishing credits to show. A black woman in the black man's movement, and patronized by a wealthy white woman who considered her nothing but a pickaninny. How could she turn down a write-up in the Plain Dealer, even if it did mean compromising *Mule Bone*? *Mule Bone* would have to be compromised. Besides, hadn't they originally agreed to do it together anyway? So she wasn't compromising anything, just going back to the original plan. But the thought of Langston back on her play made her stomach turn. Plus, he'd use this compromise as a power play on her, sure as you're born.

Back out into what was now a New York night, Zora hurried another telegram to Rowena, this time stating that acceptance was granted only on condition that she had complete creative control of the final draft. Satisfied, she went back home and cried for a couple hours for no reason at all. She spent the night trying to re-observe her recent erratic behavior, and determine the method or measure of it, but only found her thoughts were more subtle and clever than she. They dodged all queries with nonsense hieroglyphics, and turned the logic principle into a confounding Anansi's web.

When morning brought a call from Langston's lawyer, Arthur Spingarn, and a registered letter from Langston hinting at legal action, Zora kept her cool. She agreed to see Mr. Spingarn on Friday, and then lay down low because she suddenly felt very ill again.

As she squirmed and blinked and turned in bed, she thought things through, logical and sequential like in a game of chess. Langston had Carlo; Langston had Spingarn; Langston had Louise, but she was pretty much powerless. Not worth thinking about. Zora had Godmother; and Zora had Locke; and Locke could be used to turn Carlo and Spingarn against Langston. This line of thinking needed some exploring.

Thursday she felt no better. Matter of fact, she felt worse. She refused to see a doctor. If the bug meant to kill her, then it would kill her. Besides, she knew it was just nerves, and any Baptist can tell you the waters of purification burn. Zora sweated through a bright chilly afternoon and watched the day collapse in gray patterns of shadows. She kicked the sheets like a dying mule all night long, and Friday morning came creaking open like a coffin. Zora felt about as alive as a mummy. She shut the blinds, cancelled her meeting with Spingarn until the following afternoon, and whirled into bed.

Friday came through in awful pounding fragments of the same four corners. By evening she managed to fall into a sustained sleep.

Come Saturday morning, she woke bright with health and energy, more lively than Saturnalia.

She got up and walked the apartment, pulled the blinds and flooded the floors and walls with wan January sun. She stood in the kitchen smoking Pall Malls, drinking coffee, turning in place, Lord, but she had licked it all reet!

First thing she did after her morning coffee was call Dr. Locke.

"Have you talked to Godmother?" she asked him. "I'm going to

Cleveland to make amends with Langston. I have a meeting with his lawyer this afternoon. Are you caught up? This is a long story."

"Spare me a recapitulation. I'm already familiar with the details. The question is what we do from here. Your fondness for Langston clouds your judgment from time to time, Zora. And it adds to your natural hysteria. Langston is safe for now, but you must realize, ultimately he is doomed. Disabuse yourself of any other notions."

"Oh."

"Anyway, I'm sure you're more than capable of explaining your side of the story to Arthur Spingarn. I can corroborate anything you say. Would you like me to go and speak to him myself tomorrow?"

"Could you?"

"It would be my pleasure."

"What are you going to say?"

"Precisely what needs to be said. Don't concern yourself with that. Just call me once you've seen him and let me know how things went."

"I'm gonna go easy on Langston. Talk to you on the other side."

V

Everything had been going just lovely, a snowy Cleveland winter, rehearsals had started, Zora had come to her senses about things, and it even sounded like there was a possibility all wasn't lost between him and Godmother. So go figure a few days before his twenty-ninth birthday, what should he receive, but a chilly letter from Arthur Spingarn. Arthur had spoken with Dr. Alain Locke, and Dr. Locke had painted a most unflattering portrait of Langston Hughes.

Langston felt sick right away. Was everyone crooked? Involved in conspiracies and counter-conspiracies and secret societies and only he was left out?

The first thing he did was telegram Locke. Locke wired him right back: *Congratulations on the Harmon Award. Isn't that enough?*

What did it all mean? The more he thought about it, the worse he felt. Was Zora really even coming to Cleveland? It seemed like everyone in New York was back there conspiring against him, and here he was stuck out in the Midwest, sick and helpless.

His twenty-ninth birthday came in like the tolling of bells. A rolling headache and a tremolo of stomach pains kept him in bed all morning, and on into the afternoon. Rowena came by to see him in the evening, and when she looked at him she frowned. "Any paler, Langston, and you could pass." She fixed an awkward sort of smile. "But happy twenty-ninth anyway."

Langston was nearly too weak to laugh or even respond. He gasped a thank you.

"Everyone's worried," Rowena hurried on. "Who knows what's up with Zora, you know? And then with you sick, we think it's best all around if maybe we cancel the show. You should have time to rest and recover, and we should all stop giving ourselves an endless case of the nerves fussing with Zora. Anyway, it's decided."

Langston groaned.

"Well, maybe if Zora shows up," Rowena said empathetically. "Maybe we'll see if we can still shape things up in time."

The next morning Langston awoke to Rowena in the room, with Zora beside her.

Zora winked. "Well, and good morning! You don't look so swell."

"I'll let you two talk," Rowena said. She left, closing the door gently.

"You contagious?"

"I don't think so. It's mostly nerves. Well, that and my tonsils." Langston affected a smile, weakly. "I think my nerves affected my tonsils."

"Good." Zora sat next to Langston on the bed, stretched her legs out, kicked off her boots. "I don't think I'm contagious either." She lit a Pall Mall, gave Langston a look. "Just like old times, eh?"

"So what's all this been about, Zora? And what was with Alain visiting Arthur Spingarn? What did he say to him?"

Zora blew a series of small smoke rings. "I sent Locke of course. You have your soldiers and I have mine. And you know very well what this is about. It's about you and Louise. We were partners in this thing together, and you just dragged her on into the circle. I mean, who is she but a pretty high-yaller gal from California? A dime a dozen, Langston. She wasn't even there for the old days, for *Fire!* and Niggerati Manor." Zora puffed, paused, looked at Langston. "And you wanted to make her producer or something. I should be the one asking you what all this has been about. What happened to you, Langston?"

"You're blowing that whole thing out of proportion. Once we came clean about the play and Louise was paid by Godmother, all that old talk was off. And you know it."

"It didn't change the way I felt things between us had changed."

"Well why didn't you tell me any of this then?"

"I should've, could've, would've with anyone else but you, Langston. I coulda said aplenty. But we, well, we were too close, I guess, and I couldn't bring myself to say a thing. You know me, Lank. When I'm mad I use my words like weapons."

"Oh." Langston frowned. "Well, I would've been able to take it." He smiled uncertainly. "Let's call it bygones. This is our play, not Louise's." He extended his hand.

"Shake on it," Zora took his hand, warm in hers. They looked at each other, smiled slightly and hung on for a long time.

"We'll have to sign on it, of course," Langston said.

"Of course. So long as it's understood that the bulk of the play is mine. My name should even precede yours on the playbill. We'll have to sign on all these particulars too, of course."

"Zora! Don't be petty. I never claimed it was more mine than yours. On the contrary, I always said you could claim two-thirds of it." Langston puffed hard. "Still, I don't see how you can claim my part of it wasn't equally important, as dialogue in a play without structure isn't exactly a play. And I did lay down the structure."

Zora glowered. "Don't start with me, Langston." She stubbed out her cigarette. "Besides, the play I sent Carlo was an entirely new play with an entirely original structure."

"Oh, Zora. They were just the same."

"You'd think so, you would. My structure is circular, whereas yours is sensational. You and your damn Wow moment."

"Look. Let's not fight, huh? Let's just get back to work. Like old times."

Zora grinned sideways. "Like old times."

Time passed. They smoked, holding hands, side by side in bed watching the sun crawl pale along the windows, while Zora hummed

Oh the Maise, Oh the Maise, Oh the Maise set me crazy
Oh the Maise, Oh the Maise, Oh the Maise set me crazy
Put Bellamina on the dock, and
Paint Bellamina bottom black!

"Is Godmother really through with Negroes?" Langston asked after a while.

Zora looked at him bemused. "Where'd you hear that?"

Langston hesitated. "Locke."

"Locke doesn't qualify as Negro himself?"

They laughed for a while.

"We've really made a mess of things, huh? All of us, I mean," Zora said.

"Maybe looks that way maybe. Wallie would say so. Even Locke seems to have given up the hope. Carlo says he's quitting writing."

Zora mumbled something, low and quick. It hung around the corners of the room. "What about you? What are you gonna do after this?"

"I don't know. Since it looks like I probably am finished with Godmother, maybe just reconsider things. Travel some. Figure out how to make my living as a writer."

Zora regarded Langston for a while. She shrugged. "Never been done by a Negro before. Maybe you'll be the first."

"What about you?" Langston almost couldn't bring himself to ask the second part of his question. "You staying with Godmother?"

Zora didn't say anything. The clouds crossed the room and fractured the sun into patterns of shadows against the walls like a floating field of dandelion seeds. She leaned slowly over to Langston, put her lips right by his ear, squeezed his hand and whispered, "Bessie was right."

Zora wasn't back in her hotel room in downtown Cleveland but a quarter of an hour before Dr. Locke called. She'd been in a light, happy, quiet mood. A little unsettled by the sight of the theater company, a muddy, dumpy spot, not suitable for rehearsing a play of the size she thought *Mule Bone* should be, but that could be worked around. Overall things were going just swell, and she was settling in, looking for something to read, when the phone rang.

"So I trust things went well?"

Zora lit a Pall Mall. "Of course, Alain. Why are you calling me?" She didn't bother to conceal her irritation.

"Godmother's orders, Zora. Frankly, Godmother doesn't trust Langston, and neither do I. There are still too many unanswered questions with him. For example, Langston claims Louise is out of *Mule Bone* completely, does he not?"

"Of course she's out."

"Did he explain what she was doing in Cleveland last week? Why she was discussing *Mule Bone* with him and Rowena and the Gilpin Players?"

"She was what?"

"Oh. I see. He overlooked mentioning *that* altogether."

Zora could almost hear Locke grin. She sighed.

"That sneaky little Langston. Tell me something, Alain. Did you tell him Godmother was through with Negroes?"

"I told him no such thing. Nor is it true. Is that what he told you?"

"That's what he told me."

"Well, Zora. I think you know what to do."

Langston woke up with a headache and a fever, and Rowena Jeliffe hysterical on the telephone. Zora had just called her, she said – and she had never in her life heard such language! And from a woman!

If Langston smiled for a moment, he was still alarmed.

"Calm down and tell me what's going on."

"Oh, it's no use. We're all coming over to your place at five. Zora's on a warpath, she's really out for blood. So be prepared."

And that was it. Come five o' clock Zora stormed through in a whorl of red and black, with Rowena trailing timidly behind. Zora was flanked by a large black man, Mr. Banks, her driver apparently, and Rowena looked flustered, flushed red, a mess of hair and hasty dressing. So much for Pollyanna.

Zora sat down and waited for Rowena to do the same.

"Well , aint it just grand to have us all here together at last?"

"Sure, Zora. Sure, it's grand." Langston looked to Rowena, and Rowena looked back in blank bewilderment.

"Say, but where's Louise?" said Zora.

"Louise?" Langton looked quickly back at Rowena.

"Louise Thompson Thurman. Rumor runs round she's hereabouts somewhere."

"Louise isn't here, Zora," Rowena said firmly.

"Well, then I'll be, because I coulda sworn I almost seen her myself."

"What's all this about, Zora?"

"I'll tell you what it's about. It's about that old mud-sunk theater you want to hold my play in, Langston, well that's what it's about. That mucky pilch looks a lot like you do lately, Langston, and it's well you dwell on that image a minute because that gutter-jawed old thing is just like the way you are now: a shambling shadow; a wrecked mumbling ghost; a man no more!"

"Christ, Zora. Well, that's a terrible thing to say. I thought we'd patched things up, and if this is about Louise-,"

"Oh, terrible, is it? Well, do pardon me my dear if I spoke out of turn. Of course one good turn deserves another, so here it is straight gin: I despise you Langston. I despise the weak, wily worm you've turned into. It's good you're here in Cleveland, because you're finished in New York. It's best you know that, and know it final. You're finished with Godmother, and you're finished with Alain. You're finished with the Harlem Group, you're finished with everyone, because everyone sees you for the foolishness you are. You came to Harlem cleaned up nice, but after a while, those boxy old eyes came out dull and hard and dumb and squinting, hungry for a hustle, just like a Cleveland theater. Your boyish act turned boxish and ugly, and now here you are. Even your own body can't stand you. Sick to death with yourself."

The door opened, and Mr. Jeliffe walked in. He halted in the puzzling aura of the room, and looked from his wife to Langston.

"Russell!" Langston croaked as heartily as he could.

"Do come in," said Zora. "I was just getting down to the real specifics of specifyin' on Langston here. On how he has the wisdom of a St. Louis trollop hopping a freight train to Georgia, the courage of a confederate soldier alone in an African jungle, the discipline of a ginhead in a Beale Street jook, and about as much sense of justice as Henry Billings Brown. You know what, Langston? I'm really just sick of this. I'm sick of you. I don't know any more plain way to put it, and you said you could take it, so here it is:

"You want to be radical, but you've been a fake flake pancake poet for years now, and you're a fake flake pancake novelist for sure. Yeah, you had a talented stroll for a while, and when I read your poems down south, there was no one like you for the folks down there. But that was you a long time ago and all we've seen from you since is a novel that's half mine anyhow – only without the spirit I put into it – and then these poems you've been publishing in the *New Masses* and other Red journals; your propaganda papers of choice.

"You think your patron was trying to control you, but she was just calling your new poetry for the free school that it is. Your naïve radical verse is the hackneyed product of a dicty New York New Negro whose name could appear on a social register of Harlem. Now how downlow with the folks is that? Oh, I know, I know, Lawd, you don't want to do nothing but sing the blues all your life – but until you start putting yourself into your work and not the newest word percolating through Harlem, you're always going to come up false, fraudulent, phony, a huckster who capitalized on the blues to write his poetry, and wrote himself into a corner he couldn't write himself out of; the social-climbing socialist you are. You and that Louise Thompson Thurman, too."

"We should leave, Rowena," said Russell, passing his wife her coat.

"No need," Zora lit a Pall Mall. "There will be no production of *Mule Bone*. Not now or ever. It is written. This meeting is over." And with that she tipped her hat back on her head, swiveled about, and strode lustily out the door, like she hadn't a care in the world.

But back in the back of the car, all she could do was cry. Cleveland's mean old streets streaked by in a windy winterscape of mud and ice. She wiped away her tears, and they sprang right back. She took off her hat, forced a smile.

What's the matter with you, silly?

Love is a fire without insurance.

ABOUT THE AUTHOR

Whit Frazier has lived in Washington DC, Boston and New York. He ran Strawberry Press Magazine from 2003 to 2004, and is currently living in Stuttgart, Germany, while working on another novel.

JUL / 2018

96953419R00126

Made in the USA
Columbia, SC
08 June 2018